God, Guns, *and* Charter Schools

Author of *MacKenzie's Farewell*

God, Guns, *and* Charter Schools

William Allen Burley

GOD, GUNS, AND CHARTER SCHOOLS

iUniverse books may be ordered through booksellers or by contacting:

iUniverse
1663 Liberty Drive
Bloomington, IN 47403
www.iuniverse.com
1-800-Authors (1-800-288-4677)

ISBN: 978-1-5320-3636-1 (sc)
ISBN: 978-1-5320-3635-4 (e)

Library of Congress Control Number: 2017919328

Print information available on the last page.

iUniverse rev. date: 01/09/2018

For Bill, the artist

Prologue

★

Unholy Trinity
by
Robert MacKenzie

Past
Smith's exhortation, laissez faire,
Watt's invention, blackened air,
Malthusian numbers, human despair.

Present
Bountiful weapons, enemy to kill,
Biblical verses, gullible to shill,
Scholarly research, denials to fill.

Future
Past full of promise, so much to learn,
Present now with us, evidence to spurn,
Future's uncertain, wisdom to earn.

God

The First Folio

★

Contrition Prayer of Pippin the Prophet

You make me strong, they are weak!
You let me thrive, they will wither!
You let me live, they will die!
You are God of all apples. You are God of all fruit.
You are the seed of all knowledge.
When I stray, you cleanse my core.
Guide me through life's orchard, O Malum Malus.

So sayeth Jonathan the Servant in honor of Pippin,
Prophet of Malum Malus, God of all wisdom.

1

Mo

As you know, Tim, I'm not a busybody making up a story. No. I'm just old Mo, a guy pushing eighty, anxious to pass on what I witnessed take place here in Roxbridge, and what I see happening in America. It's hard to believe my tale about Roxbridge occurred years ago; seems like it was only yesterday. As I recall, you had just been appointed a principal in Danbury and moved into town. At the time, you may not have caught on to some of the local shenanigans.

Have I ever told you I have a brother and a sister? My brother's name is Lars, short for Larson. We're identical twins. Mo is for Morrison. My sister's name is Kerliss. She's eight years younger than Lars and me. Kerliss is an old family name on my mother's side. I don't know where Larson came from. We have no Swedish ancestors as far as I know.

As it turns out, my parents couldn't have picked a more descriptive name for my sister. Kerliss has a head of black ringlets that tumble in all directions. In her teenage years, no amount of relaxing goop or ironing could control her Shirley Temple mane.

When she was three, fawning adults began calling her Curly-Q. The name stuck while she was a child. But when she was in high school, she shortened it to Q.

Lars and I have always been close. Psychologists call it the Identical Twin Syndrome. A grade school teacher began calling us the teeth twins. Mo and Lars. Get it? Molars?

Before I unload about Roxbridge, I need to get off my chest my concern about the growing national crisis. Perhaps Roxbridge can avoid succumbing to the same pernicious trends presently threatening the United States. Time will tell.

Tim, in my opinion America is seriously fractured. The fracturing process has been underway for a long time, certainly since 2017. In fact, America never has been a whole, healthy nation, and any belief that we are one nation under God, with liberty and justice for all, is a myth.

The narrative of a great America is nonsense. Our country was never great. It was stolen from the original indigenous inhabitants. It was plundered by robber barons. It was built on the backs of millions of slaves.

Today, the lack of greatness continues and intensifies. Racism and xenophobia are rampant. The educated are vilified. The rich get richer, the poor get poorer. Right-leaning theocratic shamans ignore their holy books directing them to help the sick and infirm. Lying has become the new truth. Free speech can now be dangerous and costly. The same hatreds and regional prides that spawned the Civil War are again on the march.

Sadly, the Grand Old Party has degraded into a coalition of self-serving narrow-minded men and women. This was the party of The Great Emancipator, Abraham Lincoln. Our 16th President welcomed the traitorous South back into the Union with malice toward none. He understood the power of a free, united citizenry. And he was willing to risk everything, including war, to keep America one nation. He forgave our enemies, and for a time national healing occurred.

Compare that with what happened in 2017. Our nation was led by a vile, vindictive man interested only in his personal legacy and glory. He isolated the United States from the world community and made us the laughing stock of nations. And he showed no interest nor capacity to bind us together. He was neither a forgiver nor a healer. Rather, he was an ignorant bully and tyrant. He earned his title: The Narcissistic Divider.

America was never great, is not great now, and will never be great in the future. Corporate and personal greed, oligarchical entitlement, and disdain for the less powerful are all colluding to make America second-rate. Moreover, it appears we will continue degrading the environment until our nation and the planet are burned-out hollow shells. The process is underway and, I predict, will sadly come to a tragic conclusion by the end of the 21st Century. I apologize if I've offended you, Tim, but that's what I believe.

Phew! I'm sorry! I got sidetracked by America's decline and a past president's rapaciousness. Instead, let's consider the Roxbridge saga. I may get some parts or facts of the story mixed up, out of sequence, but I think you'll be able to fit them together when I'm done. Aging! That's what happens with getting old. Everything you ever learned is somewhere in your head, you just need to find the right file. I don't hold to the notion a person's hard drive becomes overloaded.

Becka was real good helping me sort things out. She kept me on the straight and narrow, so to speak. Since she's gone, I gotta pace myself keeping things organized. Alzheimers? My doc told me no, simply old age. Fortunately, I still remember where the bathroom is. It's an important detail to know. My bladder's shrunk to the size of a walnut.

The guy sleeping over there is Ruggles. He was Becka's pooch. He's my responsibility now. The thing I love about him is his predictability. If I tell him he's a good boy, he grins, wags his tail, and squints at me with adoring eyes. If I tell him he's a bad boy, he grins, wags his tail, and squints at me with adoring eyes. His response depends entirely on the tone of my voice. If I yell while telling him he's a good boy, his ears fall, and he slinks away. If I yell while telling him he's a bad boy, his ears fall, and he slinks away. I'd show you, but I'd rather let him sleep. At night he's my foot warmer. It's his job. In return, I reward him with treats. He's a very compatible housemate.

Tim, do you remember the MacKenzies? They didn't live in Roxbridge very long, maybe three or four years before moving west. Maryann originally owned the house as part of a divorce settlement. Rob didn't move in until a year or two later. Sometimes people called Maryann, Wee Annie. Physically she was a slight woman. Spiritually she was a dynamo.

I was told they met in New York City and hit it off immediately. They were married nine months later. I went to the wedding. It took place on New Year's Eve. Can you believe it? He wore a kilt!

So did Annie's son, Jake, although he was only nine years old at the time. It was a funny sight, but quite charming. The church was jam packed.

They were lucky to have wed at all. Three weeks before the ceremony, MacKenzie was detained at JFK on suspicion of promoting domestic terrorism. Sounds silly now thinking about it. The propane tank bombs those wild Larkin kids set off on Granite Hill were blamed on MacKenzie. Dozens of M-80's were strung together in each cylinder. Boom! You could hear the blast all over this end of town. It didn't help that Mac had just returned from the Middle East, or that he had been a demolitions expert in the army. Fortunately, it all got straightened out quickly, so the wedding wasn't postponed. If he had been implicated, there wouldn't have been a wedding--at least one outside prison walls.

A note about Jake. A year after he moved to Roxbridge with Annie and her marriage to Rob, his father died in an auto accident on the Long Island Expressway. It happened in the winter. He was speeding east in his Porsche, hit a shadowed section of black ice, and crashed into a bridge abutment. Jake was disconsolate for a time, but Rob pulled him through. That man's an angel.

Speaking of Rob, did you know he played the bagpipes? Good, you did. It shouldn't come as a surprise, since he was born and raised in Scotland. He had a warm Scottish burr in his speech, especially when he said words with multiple r's. I often kidded him saying his burr sounded more like a purr. It captured Annie's heart, that's for sure. He was a fantastic piper! Man, his fingers could fly! He composed original pipe tunes, too. Very talented! I'll bet he's still at it. I was told piping is what brought him to America--something about getting a music scholarship to a college in North Carolina.

You've probably heard some of this, Tim, but do you realize he was also a published poet? That guy had an amazing breadth of talent! He cranked out three books. I have them upstairs in my bedroom bookcase. Becka loved his verse . . . memorized a few. Maybe someday we'll read that another book's been published. It wouldn't surprise me. The last one, his third, was titled, *The Hidden Door.*

Last week I trudged up to the tunnels on Granite Hill. I can still do it, only now much slower. The Conservation Trust bought the land a year after Connecticut named Millington as the nuclear waste repository. Land ownership issues in Roxbridge needed resolving before Granite Hill land could be sold. Annie sorted that out. Total price for Granite Hill was set at sixteen million dollars--an astounding sum! With the exception of Lem Cable's land, the Gronk Family Foundation bought and donated the whole hill to the Trust. They paid the full freight as a way to get their tentacles into Roxbridge. At least, that's what I think. But here's the irony. After holding out for so long, Lem Cable came around and donated his acreage. The old coot won five million dollars in Connecticut's Scratch and Sniff Lottery. He bragged he finally had enough money to replace any body part, if he wanted. When he smelled the money, he ditched his pitchfork, sold his two Belgians, Big and Bigger, and moved to Phoenix. We haven't heard from him since.

Annie handled the legal details of the sale of the property. It was her last act lawyering for her New York firm before she set up shop for herself here in town. A few months after that, she became town attorney when Tom Blair died. Her office was in rooms over the Crossroads Market.

She helped Roxbridge dodge the waste repository as attorney for the Conservation Trust. A year later she argued the Maligned Fruit case at the Connecticut Supreme Court. Unfortunately, she lost that one. The court ruled the church was legit. As a result, the town couldn't levy taxes on acreage they owned. Because of Trump era decisions, churches can now advocate like political action committees while keeping their federal tax-free status. Whatever happened to the Constitution's First Amendment separating church and state?

Those apple polishers looked like a cult to me. They still do, but the court didn't see it that way. They argued the difference between a cult--which often looks like a spiritual Ponzi scheme compared with mainstream churches traditionally accepted as normal--is only a difference by degree. They found a person can believe whatever nonsense they want to believe, and there are no limits defining a church. To me, it's perfect fodder for hoodwinking people over and over again. Their decision sounded like they thought every faith-based religion was cultish in one form or another, and citizens are constitutionally protected to behave like fools. When I think about it, the argument is a scathing indictment against all religions. Next thing you know, courts will say it's okay to shout Fire! in crowded theaters.

Your son and Jake Canfeld knew each other, right? Holden must be happy he was accepted at UNC. I read it's a good school with a strong program in environmental studies. That's where Dr. Mac earned his Ph.D.

Jake will probably attend the University of Colorado. It's a good deal for their family. Rob's appointment to the faculty will save them a ton of money. It turns out, Annie's deceased husband, Zachary, was a deadbeat dad. He refused paying into Jake's college fund because Annie was threatening to move farther away than was stipulated in the divorce decree. Ironically, the distance clause originally was meant to keep Zachary nearby, not penalize Maryann. But all that's past history with Zachary long gone.

Annie wrote and told me that Jake was curious about the dangers of fracking. CU has a degree program in the extractive sciences underwritten by the Western Carbon and Mineral Alliance. Their involvement sounds a bit fishy to me. I hope Jacko stays focused on his high school studies and doesn't get side-tracked into rock climbing. Boulder's Front Range attracts climbers like honey attracts bears. He started that nonsense when he was a kid in camp in New Hampshire. After that, he climbed all over Connecticut's cliffs. In case you didn't know, Tim, there's a small crag in Woodbury.

I admit Roxbridge has had its share of characters, me included. I was a friend of Henry Turner. He lived on Square Road down at the intersection of Appletree Lane. Henry was part of the Greatest Generation, but not as a soldier. He worked as an aviation engineer living in Hawaii. He said he witnessed the attack on Pearl Harbor from a distant office. What he told me he saw firsthand about Zeros mowing down civilians was pretty shocking.

I worried about Henry's safety as he approached ninety. In his last years, he wandered up and down Square Road in a floral Hawaiian shirt and baggy shorts. At least drivers could see him. When I visited for our weekly chess match, Don Ho records were playing. He had a stack of old 78's. To this day, I can only take slide-guitar music for so long. Henry went to MacKenzie's wedding with me.

I'm getting sidetracked again, Tim. I was telling you about the MacKenzies. Let's see, where was I? I remember now. In 2017, the year Trump became President and America's decline accelerated, troublesome social changes made their way into Litchfield County and sadly into Roxbridge. That's what I remember. But before I begin boring you stiff with my story, may I get you something to drink, Tim? Tea? Beer? Water? Okay, you got it. A cold one. Is a bottle okay or do you want a glass?

2
The Mail

"The mail's here. I'll get it."

"Okay, Rob. I'll be down in a minute."

"What are you doing?"

"Changing the sheets. It's the weekend."

MacKenzie walked down the driveway and emptied the letter box. It was a beautiful early autumn day. He and Annie planned to go out later, either for a bike ride or a hike. Jake's soccer team was having Saturday afternoon practice, so a pedal to the high school definitely was in the cards. He shuffled through the mail, mostly uninterested in what had arrived.

By the time he returned to the kitchen, Annie had a kettle on to heat. It was time to drink before exercising. Tea with honey set them up for a few hours with adequate hydration.

"Any bills in the mail, love?" Annie carried honey and milk to the table. She arranged tea bags in their cups.

"Aye. One from CL&P. We better get to it, lass, or they'll be shutting off the lights." Rob chuckled, then he tied his tea bag string to the cup handle.

"And also our computer," she said. "I won't be able to pay online. What's the big piece, a catalogue from IKEA?"

"I don't know . . . let's see."

Rob pulled the brochure-like item from the pile and placed it on the table. It was a glossy four-color mailer of some sort. Its cover was photoshopped with a vividly provocative illustration. Printing expense had not been a concern when it was designed.

Pictured was a stylized orchard, trees aligned, perfectly straight. Hidden behind a tree on the left side of the orchard was the image of what appeared to be a naked woman, coiled around the tree, looking right. Similarly concealed on the right was a man gazing left, apparently interested in the woman. Rob did a double-take. *I see nudes,* he thought, *but a red apple is hanging from a limb, exactly in the middle of the picture. Is that their focus? Is the orchard supposed to be the Garden of Eden?*

Above the trees, suspended in an endless clear sky, was the proclamation *Praise be to Pippin!* written in fluffy cloud script, as if it had been penned by God--or more likely an airplane skywriter. Below, printed in yellow ink, the organization's name and leader overlaid the orchard's image. Rob read the cover text aloud for Annie's benefit:

Praise be to Pippen!
CHURCH OF THE MALIGNED FRUIT
Rev. Harmon Mayham, B.Div., WEC

Maryann began laughing. "What in hell's bells is the Church of the Maligned Fruit?" she asked. "Who's Harmon Mayham, another Billy Sunday? And Pippin? Sounds like a Broadway show's coming to Litchfield County." The kettle's whistle signaled it was time to scald the tea bags and let them steep.

"I don't know, lassie," Rob chuckled. "I'll read the rest to you." The title was followed by a prayer. It was attributed to Jonathan the Servant, whoever he was. Between sentences, Rob carefully sipped his steaming brew.

Prayer of Core Values

"I am the seed of the fruit. They who forswear the worm will eat of my flesh for millennia. They who reject my fruit will rot to the center of their cores. Take a bite of my Big Apple, and the Prophets of Doom will be driven away." --Jonathan the Servant

Rob knew Maryann had a short laugh fuse. She tried controlling a mouthful of tea, but it exploded into the kitchen with the force of a car wash. Her eyes teared, her nose dripped. She gasped for air as if trying to stay conscious. If she had been Jake drinking milk, a half pint would have snorted out her nose. The tea was damned hot, but the nonsense Rob recited was hellishly funny.

"What a mess! You're a waterfall," Rob said, laughing, holding her chin and blotting her lips. He handed her a wad of Kleenex. When tissues proved insufficient, he helped her find a dish towel, something more absorbent than paper to dry her face from her eruption. She tried calming herself, but laughter kept tumbling out. At last, after a series of deep breaths and a stab at self-control, Rob passed her the mailer so she could see it for herself.

"Yikes, it's . . . hic . . . sincere!" She coughed while giggling. "I thought it was an advertisement for . . . hic . . . *Mad Magazine*!

What kind of . . . hic . . . nonsense is this?" Her onslaught of hiccupping now competed with laughter.

"Let's see what it says inside," chuckled Rob. "There are more pages to enlighten us. Hey love, drink some water while holding a swizzle stick between your teeth. That helps me get rid of those damn things."

Rob caught the bug from Annie and began laughing himself in fits and spurts. She returned the mailer to him still hiccuping. He opened to the inside front cover and resumed reading.

The Story of Pippin From the Book of Geniuses

Circa 1937: It was a time when lost souls retreated to the truth of the Great Awakening, when miraculous angels and devout believers forswore Darwin, Singh, Marx, and Shelley. It was a time when science could be silenced; data and statistics forever locked away as blasphemous lies. It was a time when the hungry could sup on ignorance without tasting the bile of a rotting future.

Our beloved founder, John Chapman III, was awestruck by the Revelation of Pippin the Angel who appeared in an orchard in Appleton, Wisconsin, on what is now known as the *Fiesta de Doce Manzanas*. Brother Chapman feared the stern power of Pippin, but humbly inquired why Pippin had appeared on Earth and had chosen Chapman to announce a new beginning.

"I am the folly of the fruit!" Pippin thundered. "I have brought seeds of ignorance, branches of enmity, and roots of retrenchment. He who eats in my garden and lusts after my fruit shall sit with the serpent and grope for the core of Eve. I have scattered seeds to the two corners of the Earth and have hidden twelve petrified apple fortune-tarts filled with my words. Ye shall seek my tarts, reveal my truth, and spread my apple wisdom.

"Hear me, O John Chapman III. Wander the plains, climb the hills, swim the waters. Spread my seed over the barren land. Proclaim me thy Fruit of the Earth."

Here endeth the revealed truth of Pippin the Angel and Chapman the messenger as told anew by Jonathan the Servant.

"C'mon, Rob! This . . . hic . . . can't be real." Annie slapped her thigh. Sometimes pain worked getting rid of the hiccups. "This is bullshit! Two corners of the Earth? What the hell are they . . . hic . . . talking about?" Admittedly, the Pippin story was weird and funny to hear. But it had a dark side, too. Her laughing became tinged with a hint of annoyance. She drank, then set her tea cup down to keep from spilling it. A deeply held breath ended the hiccups.

"Oh, it's real for sure," he said chuckling, sensing he might be winding up for a laughing jag of his own. "I'm holding it in my hands."

"That's not what I mean, you goofball. Stop being so literal. You'll give me the hiccups again. I know the mailer's an animate object. I mean the church--or whatever it is. The pamphlet words are all blather." Her annoyance was evident. She dumped her cooling tea into the sink.

"I'm sorry I messed with you, my love. You're right. This mailer's about religion or another crazy philosophy. It's insane, but it's serious, too. I'll read more. There are four pages." He took a deep breath, shook his head in wonder, shrugged, and continued reading:

Chapman's Creed

I believe in Chapman III, our leader evident, creator of rapt confusion, confessor of lies well meant.

I believe in the fruit of the bud, the Waldorf Salad tree--man, woman, snake unbound, unchained at last, all three.

Her name's Eve, Adam's his, the asp's we're quite unsure; the beast's a snake, Adam's a rake, Eve's a holy whore.

We forgive the three miscreants, good days lie just ahead. We embrace the seed and the greed, ready to be led.

"It's all gobbledygook, Rob!" Annie insisted. "It's publicly professed insanity!" Despite her annoyance, Annie entered a new state of mirth, her laughing became big and bold, unlike the tee-hee of a lady.

Rob held up his hand. "But wait, there's more," he announced like a TV pitchman. "I'm not done reading." Rob pointed to the lower half of the page containing a set of foreworns and reveals.

Chapman's Five Revelations

- 'Tis revealed the serpent made by God was forsworn by God.
- 'Tis revealed the woman made by God was forsworn by the asp.
- 'Tis revealed the man made by God was forsworn by the woman.
- 'Tis revealed the fruit made by God was blessed by God.

- 'Tis revealed all who eat God's fruit will flourish in the holy sepulcher of wealth and good health.

Maryann and Rob collapsed into each other's arms, hugging tightly to keep from falling to the floor. They laughed uncontrollably, one person's joy fueling the other's glee. Shared laughter helped overcome doubt. In a few minutes they were composed.

"Rob! For Jake's sake, they're talking about Johnny Appleseed! That's who John Chapman is."

"Then this Chapman III must be a grandchild," Rob concluded.

"Is there an address for this group? Where are they located?"

Rob flipped the mailer to the back cover. "You're not gonna believe this, Annie. The address is on Appletree Lane here in Roxbridge."

"Wait a minute! Let me see that." Maryann snatched the mailer and studied the address. "Now I know who these yahoos are. A group filed forms with the tax assessor to remove their property from the tax rolls. They claimed to be a new religion and were exempt from contributing to the secular world."

Rob shook his head doubtfully. "If they're on Appletree Lane, they'll be happy the secular world plows their road in January. That's a steep hill. Are you part of this?"

"Not yet, and I hope I don't get involved," said Annie. "That's up to the selectmen. They can accept this group as a legitimate church or fight it. I'm not up to date on church-state issues. I've been involved with environmental law for too many years."

"Thank heavens you were, love. You're good at it. Your work kept the nuke dump outta here."

"Yep, but this stuff's a creed of a different breed." She giggled at her clever turn of phrase. "Cool of me to think up that one, huh, laddie? Seriously, if I'm involved, I'll have to bone up on what defines a religion, what's a sect, what's a cult."

"Does it make any difference?" Rob asked. "It seems to me that cults get as much respect from the courts as Methodists. Google the Branch Davidians and Jim Jones' Peoples Temple. See what you can find out. You were a teenager at the time of the Davidian event, but the Jones tragedy was much earlier--in '78, I think. I was ten when I heard about Guyana. Anyway, what you learn might come in handy, if you take on a church."

Maryann returned the mailer to Rob. He flipped to the last pages and continued reading. "This brochure is the gift that keeps on giving, Annie. Listen to what's on page three."

Pippin's Dance
Twelve Obligations According to Chapman III

1. Procreation: Thou shalt plant seeds and bear fruit.
2. Isolation: Thou shalt fear the unwashed fruit.
3. Prostration: Thou shalt lie prone and eat drops off the ground.
4. Proclamation: Thou shalt announce the bloom of the tree.
5. Intimidation: Thou shalt face the sun unafraid of the glare.
6. Notation: Thou shalt write to describe the maggot.
7. Substantiation: Thou shalt flaunt wealth as ye shall harvest.
8. Damnation: Thou shalt curse the decaying fruit.
9. Authentication: Thou shalt separate the wine from the sap.

10. Negation: Thou shalt decry all but the sweetest fruit.
11. Contribution: Thou shalt tithe to fill the bushel.
12. Education: Thou shalt seek the apple's wisdom.

**Share the Ambrosia of the Gala as ye
demand the taste of the Empire.**

Annie slumped in her chair. "I get it! The first letter of each obligation spells out *Pippin's Dance*. It's hilarious, but I'm worn out from laughing. I can't take anymore of this nonsense. This stuff's material for *Saturday Night Live* and the Church Lady." She breathed deeply to retain her composure.

"I don't want to put you in cardiac arrest, dear," said Rob, "but there's one more page."

"Okay, I'm sitting down," she said, resigned to more propaganda. Lay it on me."

Rob scratched his ear then began reading a list printed on page four. He said the mailer attributed the list to the twelfth chapter of the Book of Genius.

Apple Bee Attitudes

Honey to the clever, they shall win by stealth.
Honey to the strong, they shall own the wealth.
Honey to the virile men, they shall share their seed.
Honey to the pregnant girl, she shall bear their deed.
Honey to their newborn, a stain to overcome.
Honey to their bastard, his life has just begun.
Honey to their child, a misfit born to kill.
Honey to their psychopath, murder for the thrill.
Honey to the judge, death sentence his to make.

Honey to the bailiff, convicted his to take.
Honey to the hangman, he shall fit the rope.
Honey to the parents, they never give up hope.
Honey to the foolish, they listen to their glands.
Honey to the apples, peace in all our lands.

"How's that for a honey-do list?" laughed Rob. "Fourteen honey-do chores would take me more than one weekend to complete." He blotted away a new set of tears winding down his cheeks. "What the hell is the Book of Genius?" he asked. "Is it an old publication from MENSA?"

"I don't think so, dear. MENSA's about intelligence, not stupidity." Annie wiped away her own tears. "I'm so worn out from laughing, Rob, I'm not sure I'll be able to exercise this afternoon." "Aye, I know how you feel." He blew his nose. "Want this mailer for future reference?"

"I don't know. Yeah . . . well okay . . . that makes sense," she said. "I may get involved with them. Hey, I have an idea. Tomorrow, let's walk to Appletree Lane and see if we can sneak into their church. We know the location, and the service is listed for 10 a.m."

"Okay with me," agreed Rob. "I wonder if any of my students will be there?"

"Maybe, love. A disguise might be a good idea. Should we take guns for protection?" she asked, only half-kidding.

No matter what Rob's response might be, her question was moot. Unless bagpipes could be considered deadly, no weapons were kept in their house.

"I don't think guns are necessary," said Rob, "but an apple peeler might come in handy."

3
Mo

I'm not a religious man, Tim, never was, never will be. When my time comes, I'll die knowing I was just a regular guy, someone who tried doing his best. I worked hard being nice to others, and that wasn't always easy. I loved my wife. Sometimes I ache missing her. I'm glad to have Ruggles, but he doesn't make up for Becka. It's not even close.

My kids turned out to be responsible adults. I can't say anything better than that. And they did a good job with my grandchildren. Great grandkids are heading in the right direction, too. For us fortunate few, that's the natural course of events. Our history lives on through them. I admit, good genes help. As the old saying goes: we're born to die, so don't fight it. Accept the inevitable, my friend.

You've got plenty of miles left on your odometer, Tim, so make good use of them. Don't sit around waiting for something better to happen. Nothing's better than right now. I know the old argument--tomorrow will be a sunnier day. Maybe, but don't bet on it. Rain's always possible. Jeez! Listen to me spouting off like a philosopher. You'll figure it out, Tim. We all do.

Aah . . . yes! Let's get back to the MacKenzies. The high school was mighty lucky getting Rob as a teacher. When his one year assignment at WestConn ended, Connecticut public schools were eager to gobble him up. They were competing for a world-class environmental scientist with teaching experience--and at a modest union salary.

As it turned out, working in Roxbridge was perfect for him, at least for awhile. The high school opened the new science wing and began its program in environmental studies. The fit between the school and MacKenzie couldn't have been better.

I think it's telling, though, that none of the charter schools were interested in him. It was the first time science deniers gained traction in Litchfield County. I remember when stupidity made its appearance on national TV. During the 2016 Republican campaign, many of the candidates were asked by the press what they thought about climate change or global warming. The standard answer was, "I'm not a scientist." They may have known the answer or had opinions, but the worry of angering a large chunk of voters sewed their lips shut. Sadly, the more they acted ignorant, the more the anti-science factions were emboldened.

Damned shame! Look who we wound up with--the orange man! His extreme narcissism made him behave like a psychopath. After his legal appeals end, I'm hoping he winds up in Leavenworth. However, if he's not in a federal prison, his mental illness certainly makes him a candidate for an asylum. In my opinion, his executive orders attacking the environment and backing out of the Paris

Climate Accord were his highest crimes and misdemeanors, even more than threatening war with North Korea, his naval stand-off with China over the South China Sea, and his bromance with Putin. As far as armed conflict is concerned, he couldn't grasp the concept that Congress declares war and authorizes preemptive attacks--not the President. Especially not him!

It's taking time for the Justice Department to decide what to do with the Donald, now that he's been impeached and found guilty. Also, the Special Counsel nailed him for criminal money laundering that occurred before his presidency. Trump refused to accept culpability in exchange for resigning. Even though he's been forcibly removed from the White House since his impeachment, he continues to Tweet, as if he's still in charge. He's delusional. He's arrogant beyond imagination. He thinks he can beat the rap. Fortunately, a conservative Supreme Court ruled he couldn't pardon himself. But his appeals linger on.

He was dangerous to the United States and the world writ large. He was a real-life Hannibal Lecter. What a stain on America! Shame on us for electing him!

Maybe the new President can right our ship. After trouncing Pence, she seems to be able to bridge the philosophical gap separating the major parties. With her at the helm, the ship of state seems to be in good hands..

Sorry . . . I digressed again. Back to Roxbridge. The arrival of the apple pickers in Roxbridge intrigued both MacKenzies. Rob was curious about the pickers' positions on the environment. Annie became involved because of their so-called religion and how it affected the tax and civic structure of the town. Both were

God, Guns, and Charter Schools

flummoxed by the details of the cult. I think it's now safe to call it a cult. It seems to me to be even less than a sect. A faith that worships the apple? My God! What have we become?

On Sunday, cars streamed into town carrying the Disciples of Pippin. During the week parents ferried their children to the Johnny Appleseed Academy. I'll be the first to admit, to this day, mindlessness is widespread in this country.

The MacKenzies needed to find out for themselves what was happening on Appletree Lane. They needed to see with their own eyes, not fall prey to rumor. So, one Sunday in October they walked to church, not as potential supplicants but as practicing skeptics. One was an expert on the environment, the other an expert on the law

4

To Church

The MacKenzies headed out at 9 a.m. for the half-hour walk to the Church of the Maligned Fruit on Appletree Lane. From door to door, it was only a thirty minute stroll, but they allowed extra time to enjoy the October colors. Jake stayed home sleeping.

"I'm glad you left the mailer back at the house," Annie said. "As newcomers, we're gonna be conspicuous enough without carrying their advertisement." She lengthened her stride to keep pace with Rob.

"Aye. I didn't want to schlep the bloody thing. Besides, you ought to file it. It might come in handy one day." Rob took shorter steps. "Do you know who owned the property before the church moved in?"

"Yes," she said, "Bob Repeater. He died two years ago. His daughters sold out to the Gronks."

"When the girls sold it, did they know their dad's place would turn into a church?" Rob picked up two acorns. He compared them to ball bearings, finally tossing them to the squirrels.

"I'm unsure. Probably not. The area's zoned residential for

non-commercial use. I expect they thought the Gronks were planning a retreat or something like that--maybe a meditation center. So, buying the Appletree Lane property was legal, although a bit unusual."

"Aye, I get it. The sale was legit so long as no commerce transpired. When did the church appear?"

"Soon after the deal closed. Repeater's barn and airstrip morphed into a worship center and day school. No zoning laws were violated. The operation has every right to exist."

"Annie, I bet I know what happened when they declared themselves a church. None of the no commerce stuff mattered anymore. As a church they can do anything they want, any way, any time. Am I correct?"

"Yes you are, my brainy Scottish husband!"

He grinned and tapped his head.

Annie scanned the woods devouring the colors. She grinned broadly from ear to ear. Her reverie glowed brighter when, on occasion, she was able to make Rob laugh at himself. She continued. "We read the gibberish in the brochure, Rob. You're the versifier. I dare you to dream up a song for walking, something we can follow marching. Make it even sillier than the mailer."

"Right this minute?"

"Sure. Can you do it?"

"Do you have anything in mind? Is there a tune you like?"

"At Columbia after swim meets, the girls' team sang a cheer mocking the other Ivy League Schools. We used the familiar Hail! Hail! Hail! refrain that's often belted out after drinking too many beers. I don't think I can sing it, but I remember the words. It goes like this." Annie recited in a rhythmical monotone:

> Brown! Harvard! Yale! Sing Lion daughters.
> Give all three the French salute!
> Have Princeton meet its fate,
> Kick Cornell back upstate,
> Give Penn and Dartmouth both the royal boot!

"Brilliant! I love it!" chuckled Rob. "Did you dream it up?"

"No. It was the creation of a student from Bangladesh. She wanted a career on Broadway. Wha'd'ya think? Can you match it?"

"Give me a moment. I need a list of rhyming words to fit our walking pattern.

Hmm . . . let me see . . . ." He dropped Annie's hand.

She watched him air-write in his palm, as if he was making a word list on a Post-it note.

"I think I have it, love. I may stumble over the lyrics at first until I get them nailed, but I'll give it a try. You know the melody, so here goes. Ready?"

She laughed, "I guess so. I hope it's as good as your poetry, or your reputation may suffer."

"Suffer? This could end my career!"

He began singing in a strong baritone, the words belted out in a marching cadence.

> *I looked up in the sky and saw the title high,*
> *In the propaganda sent us in the mail.*
> *I opened and I read, the words we all should dread,*

God is great, God is good, the Holy Grail.

"That's good! Is there a chorus? Annie asked. She was humming along with the melody.

"Aye, there is. Here goes."

Hail! Hail! Hail! you perpetrators,
Spreading lies both day and night.
Foolish notions always breed, religion's dangerous creed.
Superstition trumps living in the light.

"I love it, Rob!" she giggled. "But it's so serious. Can't you dream up something sillier?"

"Aye. 'Tis a wee bit heavy, I admit." He thought for a few strides. "How about this? If we're heading to an apple cathedral, words about Satan's favorite fruit make sense."

You're the apple of my eye, it isn't just a stye,
Piñata on the corner of my lid.
I tried to blink it gone, as I burst into a song.
You're my Lady, Ann, the wife I like to kid.

From the start of the silly version, Annie was chuckling hard trying not to erupt into a full fledged Three Stooges belly laugh. Her abdomen was tender from the laugh-riot of the previous day. "Damn, Rob, that's good!" she sputtered. "I love *Apple of my eye, it isn't just a stye.* Any more to add, or have you run out of steam?"

"No, there's more," he said happily, joining her mirth. "Every verse needs a chorus and I have one silly enough to do the trick.

I'll sing it first, then we can put the whole tune together and sing it out loud. I'll help you remember the lyrics."

Rob sang the chorus, his voice booming out the *hails*, jarring bluejays off their perches, sending them screeching away in terror into the woods.

Hail! Hail! Hail! all Pippin eaters.
Honey Crisp and Northern Spy.
I look up in the tree, where Baldwins hang for free,
Prefer Granny Smith, Ambrosia apple pie!

Spitting out *ambrosia apple pie* proved difficult. Rob howled like a demented banshee on a caffeine high, all decorum erased by his newly discovered lunacy.

Annie also was in mirthful stitches. She tightly clutched Rob to keep from collapsing onto the road. She grabbed his Post-it hand joining them together. They marched down the center of the road toward the Church of the Maligned Fruit, a phalanx of two, singing at the top of their lungs. As if on cue, they pirouetted and marched backwards, loving their oneness and their shared willingness to behave like fools.

5

Church of the Maligned Fruit

A wagon train of pilgrims rolled up Appletree Lane. Area residents were easily identified by bumper stickers: Millbury, Home of the Goats; Proud Parents of a New Milford Honor Roll Student; Woodbury Kennel Club; Johnny Appleseed Academy. All were heading to the gated entrance and sacred soil of the Church of the Maligned Fruit.

The worship service was scheduled to begin at 10 a.m. The road was potholed and emaciated. As a result, The MacKenzies were forced to step aside as cars trundled by. They were surprised by the amount of passing traffic.

Walking into the compound, Rob pointed out signage warning drivers to stay on the pavement and proceed to assigned orchards. They turned out to be parking areas divided into quadrants on Bob Repeater's former runway. The airstrip no longer operated to accommodate Repeater's old Piper Tri-Pacer. Now it was used for parking Ford Explorers, Chevy pick-ups, and Honda Accords.

The MacKenzies followed a path to the Apple Barn, Repeater's dated arched hangar, hunkered low at the end of the runway. The building was a long half-cylinder structure. The shape identified it as a World War II Quonset Hut. Depthwise, the Apple Barn appeared as if it was half the length of a football field.

The front façade of the building was bright green-yellow, rimmed with an apple red border. It contrasted with the dull galvanized grey of the building's corrugated metal siding. Painted randomly around the double door entrance were six brown ovals. Rob said they looked like seeds. Sprouting from the roof above the front entrance was an apple stem replica. He guessed it was probably fabricated from *Cor-Ten* steel. Its shape added to the building's apple imagery. No symbols associated with mainstream religion were in sight--no crosses, no hexagonal stars, no crescent moons, no heavenly steeples the public might recognize.

Maryann whispered to Rob, "It looks like we're entering an apple sliced in half."

He glanced around to see if she had been overheard by others heading toward the entrance. "'Tis what 'tis," said Rob. He clasped her hand tightly and smiled. "I love that ridiculous expression. It's as silly as saying this place is a church. What fools we mortals be!"

"Shakespeare?" she asked. "*A Midsummer Night's Dream?*"

"Aye, that's right, love. Let's go in and see more absurdity. Pippin was a Shakespeare character, too."

A greeter welcomed them and asked if they were new.

They smiled. "Aye, we are," said Rob.

"We live in town," Maryann added.

The greeter pointed in the direction of the core of the church. He gave them each plastic shopping bags, an apple pin for their shirts, and a program listing the order of worship. Rob quickly noticed the bags originally were the property of an Apple Computer store.

Inside the arched building, grey metal folding chairs were arranged on two sides, leaving a center aisle. Side aisles flanked the chair set-up. A partition beyond the pulpit closed off an area at the far end. Rob guessed meeting rooms and classrooms were behind the wall.

As they made their way to seats, it became obvious to Rob where they were meant to sit. In the middle of the grey chairs, one row was painted apple red--seats obviously reserved for newcomers. Up to now, as far as he could tell, they were the only guests.

They proceeded to their seats and immediately were swarmed by the smiling faithful sitting in front and behind. Effusive welcomes were offered as well as ripe apples. Each welcomer gave them a Gala or Fuji, first kissing the fruit as it was passed on.

"What do I do with them?" asked Maryann to a lady behind her.

"Of course, you eat them, young lady. It's fine and dandy to wait until you get home. For now put them in your apple bag, but save one for the service. You're going to need it."

Maryann carefully dropped seven apples in her bag. Rob did the same with his fruit. Fourteen apples were ready to go home at the end of the service, enough for cobbler and a couple of pies.

"What am I going to need the last apple for?" Maryann asked the lady.

"It's part of the *Last Words*, honey, our benediction. You'll see."

Maryann's interest was piqued. "Does your church have Baptism? I don't know what you call it."

"Yes, dear. We call it *Robert's Wash*. We bob for apples."

She poked Rob in the arm. "I didn't know you were mixed up in this," she whispered. "Robert's Wash," she chuckled. "On top of all your other talents, you're a church ritual advisor."

"Och! Don't blame Robert's Wash on me. I wash my hands of any involvement."

They sat on their red chairs and looked at each other in amusement. Maryann lowered her voice. "Speaking of wash, Rob, we need to clean these apples before eating. They were kissed by alien mouths."

"Aye, that they were--from Pluto, maybe. Rub them on your sleeve, love. That ought to do the trick."

"What if they see me? They might get insulted."

"Don't worry, if anyone asks, tell them you're a world class apple polisher." Rob smiled at his joke, a grin now glued to his face. He instinctively knew more funny nonsense was about to begin.

"I don't want to whisper during the service, Rob. If something funny comes up, I'll slip you a note."

"I hope you have lots of paper, love. You may be writing a comedy screenplay."

They studied their programs. The cover's illustration was a reprise of the mailer, an orchard, a naked woman, a naked man, and an apple. It was titled: *ALL GLORY TO PIPPIN!* The day's program was laid out inside.

Good Morning All Lovers of Pippin
Rev. Harman Mayham

Welcoming Hymn:	*What a Friend We Have in Pippin*	Anon
Zither Music:	Ann and Nan McIntosh	The Zitherettes
Welcoming Words:	*Hello! Hello!*	Br. Malcolm Braeburn
Hymn:	*Pippin Loves Me*	Comp. W. Sapp
	First verse solo by Jona Gold Second verse solo by Ruby Frost Chorus sung by Orchard Choir	
First Reading:	*Share Your Faith*	*Genius 1:11*
Hymn:	*Faith in Lord Pippin*	Comp. W. Waldo
Second Reading:	*Pruning is the Key to Heaven*	*Arborian 7:11*
Pippins Points:	*The Great Malus Lie*	Rev. Mayham
Give More:	*Ten.Five Anthem*	Alice, the Organ Lady
Hymn:	*Apple Tree Hymn*	Comp. D. Roote
Last words:	*Good-bye, Come back*	Rev. Mayham

The back cover of the program featured a two column list of Core Donors, members of the Ten.Five Club. An email address for making on-line donations completed the page. With the McIntosh sisters rapidly zithering, Maryann passed a pencil and note to Rob.

"Looks like other Sunday bulletins I've seen. **rb**!"

He wrote: "Aye, format's traditional, crazy's in the words. Hold tight! What does **rb** mean?"

"**R**eport **B**ack."

They endured the welcome by Brother Braeburn, understanding words but making no sense of their context.

Rob wrote: "Braeburn is Scot name. Speaks like druid. I no comprehend. **rb.**"

"Is druid talk same as BS? **rb**?"

"Not to druid. **rb.**"

The next note was postponed during the hollerin' of *Pippin Loves Me.*

Pippin loves me, this I know. For John Chapman tells me so.
Pale pink buds soon will bloom. Nature's harvest born in June.
Yo, Pippin loves me! Yo, Pippin loves me!
Yo, Pippin loves me! John Chapman tells me so.

★

Autumn's promise soon will grow. Pippin's gifts, juice will flow.
Pippin's largesse, mine to pick. Eating apples none grow sick.
Yo, Pippin loves me! Yo, Pippin loves me!
Yo, Pippin loves me! John Chapman tells me so.

"Sounds like *Jesus Loves Me*? Right? **rb.**"

"Aye. Anna Warner music. **rb.**"

"How u know Warner? **rb.**"

"Me poet. Google help. **rb.**"

"Does Pippin really love me? **rb.**"

"Don't think Pippin knows you. But I do! ♡ **rb.**"

A lady sitting behind the MacKenzies leaned forward and quietly kidded Maryann. "I see you two passing notes back and forth. What lovebirds! How sweet!"

Maryann surreptitiously slipped a note to Rob. "Careful what u write. Periscope Polly watching. **rb**."

The first reading was from the Book of Genius. The sacred text exhorted the faithful to share with the less faithful even if it meant the less faithful might grow mightier than the faithful, at which point the faithful would be less faithful than the less faithful.

As the last *less faithful* drifted to the heavens, Alice, the Organ Lady, blasted out the easily recognizable melody of the chorus of the second hymn, *Faith in Lord Pippin*. The congregation pounced on the first verse and began hootin' and hollerin'.

Faith in Lord Pippin

Verse One
Faith is a folly, sweet ignorant bliss. To
follow a savior, we'd be remiss.
Tithe meager wages, forswear your own wealth.
Poverty's saintly, obeyance is health.
Chorus
Faith is a folly, ignorant bliss. Pippin's an angel, never dismiss.

Verse Two
You are less human, unable to think. You
have a choice, to swim or to sink.

Choosing the latter confirms your birth.
Choosing the former, burdens the Earth.
Chorus
Faith is a folly, ignorant bliss. Pippin's an angel, never dismiss.

Verse Three

Priests want your money, coffers to swell.
Ignoring their needs, you'll go to hell.
There's no salvation, priests teach every day.
Contribute, give, submit, and obey.
Chorus
Faith is a folly, ignorant bliss. Pippin's an angel, never dismiss.

Verse Four

Select from two choices, unfetter your mind. Bow to the tyrant,
dutifully blind.
Reject lesser prophets, rekindle your soul.
Relinquish free-will, Pippin's your goal.
Chorus
Faith is a folly, ignorant bliss. Pippin's an angel, never dismiss.

Rob quickly handed Maryann a new note. "This melody sung at Irish sporting events. Led to beer and brawls. **rb**."

"I learn hymn in comparative religion. Where u learn? **rb**."

"In Belfast, duckin' bottles. **rb**."

The second reading, *Pruning is the Key to Heaven*, prompted the faithful to shout out amens along with a loud cheer.

It was time for *Pippin's Points*, the sermon. Rev. Mayham lumbered to the center of the dais. No PA system broadcasted his words. None was needed.

Good morning, brethren and sisteren! What a beautiful day! It's the perfect day to take a bite of the apple--little, medium, or big! I prefer big! I command you to take a bite of the Big Apple! Only kidding! Not now! Wait for the Last Words!

"Can't stop watching Rev's Adam's Apple. Same ↕ as yoyo. Caught in throat? **rb**."

"3 X ha! ☺! Yoyo good description. Caught in throat? Maybe. **rb**."

"Every sentence exclamation point**! rb**."

"Not surprised. Enthusiastic**! rb**."

"Or nuts**! rb**."

We are at a crossroads in our country, my fruits! Everything's going to hell in an apple basket! Public schools are rotting! Free speech promotes smut! Weapons are decaying into powdery mildew! Whoring and drinking are spawning fire blight! Mini-cars are but mere flyspecks! Professional women are paid more than men! It's a symptom of white collar rot!

Maryann reacted indignantly. "He can go to hell! I worth what I earn! **rb**."

"U r worth lot 2 me. I ♡ you! ☺ **rb**."

I implore you, my fruits, with malice toward but a few! Together, let us march to the core of our faith and proclaim Pippin our spiritual seed! Herein sprouts the truth of Pippin!

"Bulldozed, hornswoggled, & bullied! Insane asylum here! **rb**." Maryann seethed.

"All churches same. Holy ghost accepted as best friend. Guard wallet. **Rb**."

Harvest baskets were passed along the rows as Alice, the Organ Lady, pounded out another recognizable tune with an apple theme. Checks and cash were deposited in the till. Rob saw the faithful peek in when the basket passed, as if they were surveying their handkerchiefs after a crusty nose blow. He wondered if they were comparing their contributions with what others had dropped in. They seemed to be asking: is there anything in the basket that shouldn't be there? Are there any c-notes? Up front, Rev. Mayham harvested the loot.

This is our gift to Pippin! I trust you have tithed ten point five! All 10.5 Faithful are Core-Givers and sit on the left hand of Pippin! Don't get off His hand until He begs, then give more! Don't bite His hand until He feeds you! Trust in Pippen, for He is the Elstar and the Gala of all! Join me in the final song of praise, the *Apple Tree Paean*! You know it's sung to the melody of that blasphemous old anthem, *Holy, Holy, Holy! Lord God Almighty!* Thanks be to Pippin we've moved on to a more devout tune!

White Transparent, Cortland. Apple trees of Portland,
Fruit we covet everyday, Health for thee and thine.

Mutsu, Ashmead Kernal, Discovery maternal.
Trees without Collar Rot, perfect deep-dish pie.

Holy, holy, moly! Canker, sooty, blotchy.
Prune the trees, feel the breeze, end all fire blight.
Holy, holy, moly! Fly speck, black rot, moldy.
Free trees of rust disease, we spray with all our might.

"See? Mind waste is precious, 3 X ha! **rb**."

"I laughing. ☺ Puns! Apple/day keeps doc away. **rb**."

"EZ 2 bed, EZ 2 rise, makes dude healthy, wealthy, wise. **rb**."

"Can top w/ apple names. Mel rose from bed, he very healthy. Went to gold rush, asked, kan-zi get wealthy? **rb**."

"Where U learn about apples? **rb**."

"Eating cobbler while Googling. **rb**."

"Heads up! Here comes Rev's benediction. **rb**."

Hallelujah, my brethren and sisteren fruits! Aren't we lucky! Another day embraced in the boughs of Pippin! It's time to go our separate ways! But before we do, I command you to take a bite of the Big Apple!

A synchronous *crunch* echoed in the Apple Barn. It was the sound of dozens of apples being consumed. The faithful attacked their apples in unison and with conviction. Maryann and Rob were caught off guard but quickly dug out fruit from their bags. Their weak, after-the-fact, duo-crunches caused annoyed heads to glare in their direction, as if they were being accused of a crime during the Inquisition.

"I think I may throw up," whispered Maryann.

Rob nodded. "Aye, I didn't see the big bite coming. I guess I wasn't hungry. I've had enough of this codswallop! Let's leave here and get back into sunlight."

6
Home Again

MacKenzie stepped out of the shower and closed the window. Even with it wide open and the fact that clouds of moisture had escaped into the October evening as he showered, the mirror over the sink was steamed. He briskly dried himself. Then he used the damp towel to clear the glass. He stretched forward to inspect the damage he had inflicted on his face. His custom was to shave in the shower. Tonight he had committed hairy-kari. His mustache was gone after living on his upper lip for seventeen years. He remembered the gestation sequence--peach fuzz in one week, tickling whiskers after three weeks, respectable stash in two months. Eventually, it matured into a yellow-ginger hedge of stiff hair. He rubbed his lip wondering if he would ever grow another.

The mirror again clouded over. He wiped away the new condensation. His upper lip was necrotically pale compared with the color of his face. Moreover, his face wasn't very tan to begin with. His fair Celtic skin required daily applications of SPF 50 sun block. He stared at the stranger in the mirror wondering how long it would take for him to become friends with the new lad. But he recognized the green eyes. They were his.

What the hell? He saw more grey hair intruders setting up shop on his temples. His rusty hair was beginning to be sprinkled with grains of cane sugar.

He finished drying and stepped on the scale. Twelve and a half stone, he calculated, instinctively converting one hundred seventy-five American pounds into Scotland's measure of weight. He wondered: Why was American poundage named the same as Scottish money, and Scottish weight was based on a lump of rock?

At forty-eight he was beginning to inventory himself regularly, noting signs of possible aging. *I wonder if I'm shrinking?* he thought. *I'll have Annie make my mark on the tall-Paul door trim. Am I still 6-3?* While brushing his teeth he stood ramrod straight, as if he had just won the Bronze Star.

He dressed for dinner the same as usual--flannel shirt, jeans, and Tevas. Then he descended to the kitchen gritting his teeth, preparing for the excoriation he was about to receive from Maryann. She had never seen him without a mustache. Would she recognize him or demand that a stranger get out of her house?

When he entered the kitchen she looked up from slicing tomatoes, then handed him a cup of tea. "Hello, sweetie. I'm planning to sauté shrimp with broccoli in sesame oil and garlic. Sound yummy? Oh, by the way . . . have a good shower?" After every shower, each asked the other if the experience was good. It was a silly game they played.

"Aye, shower was good. Shrimp sounds good. You look good. You're the apple of my eye."

"I've had sufficient apple puns to last the whole harvest season. Enough, already!"

"Aye. We survived today's wackiness." He hesitated. "Well? What do you think?"

She smirked. "About what? That we didn't upset the applecart?"

"You said no more apple puns. I declare truce!"

"Okay, truce." She wiped her hands on a towel, then engulfed him in an embrace, finally kissing him on the lips.

When they parted he asked, "Annie, isn't there anything unusual about me?"

She grabbed her chin as if pondering an important idea. "You're wearing a new shirt?"

"No, no, no! I've had this shirt for years. C'mon, I know you're pulling my leg. My face! My face!"

"You have a beautiful face! What more can I say?"

"You can say, 'Yikes! You shaved off your mustache!'"

"Oh, you're right! Yes, you did! By golly, I missed it!" She doubled over laughing, pleased with the straight face she had barely managed. It was amazing to ambush Rob with the type of silliness he liked to perpetrate on her.

"Good one, lassie," he grinned. You got me! How did you keep from laughing?"

"I was prepared. When you were in the shower, I went into the bathroom to get tweezers. I had a hair on my chin." She pointed to the spot. "You were shaving away in there, eyes closed, cutting it off. There was nothing I could do about it, except wait for the result and prepare my ambush."

"What do you think? Still love me?"

"The kiss was perfect, mustache or not. Your lip will darken with the sun. I'll get used to it." She took a step back as if evaluating a floor lamp. "Aye, Scotsman! I still love you. Hair or nae hair, you're a fair sonsie laddie, and you're all mine."

He touched his lip wondering when it would start sprouting. "I had to do it, love. Peanut butter kept getting stuck in my whiskers. I could never get it out. I even tried gum."

She laughed again. "My clueless Celt! You loosen stuck gum with peanut butter, not the other way around."

Rob thought for a moment. "Of course! The oils in the peanut butter soften the gum. My stash was so clogged up with Skippy, I didn't think it through."

Maryann, thinking like an economist, said, "Now you won't waste good food anymore."

Rob sipped his tea then remembered his height concern. "Before we eat, will you measure me? I've been taking an inventory of signs of my aging." He used his hand to illustrate his meaning.

"Okay. Get a pencil, the ruler, and the step stool."

Rob found the stool in the broom closet, then opened it next to the tall-Paul door moulding. The stool wasn't for him. Maryann used it to get high enough to make a level mark above his head. He located a pencil and ruler in the junk drawer.

At Maryann's command to get his shoulders back, he stood redwood straight against the door jamb. Maryann climbed up and used dead reckoning to keep her pencil level with the top of his head. She made a mark and used the ruler to measure its distance from the seventy-two inch mark. She saw Jake's mark at fifty-nine and hers at sixty-three.

"Seventy-five," she said critically evaluating her work. You haven't shrunk. You're still an Annie-and-a-foot taller than I am."

"While we're at it, your turn, peanut." He moved the step stool aside. She backed in. He flattened the ruler atop her head to get an accurate mark.

"Sixty-two and three quarters," he announced.

"Damn! I'm shrinking!" she snapped. "You were pushing down too hard on my head!"

He tried reassuring her. "Maybe the original sixty-three mark was inaccurate. Don't worry. When you're in heels, no one will know."

"But I'll know!" She scanned the kitchen counter. "Where did I put those calcium pills?" she asked.

As if on cue, Jake showed up for dinner. His knees and elbows were grass stained from tag football that had morphed into smash-mouth tackle.

"Hi, Mom! Hi, Rob! Hey, Rob, you cut off your stash! It looks weird! Oh, boy! Shrimp for dinner! Cool!"

"Looks like you were in quite a dust-up, Jacko. Did the other team coalesce into a well-lubricated juggernaut?"

"Huh? What are you talking about?"

"Did you win or lose?"

"We won! We killed 'em!"

Maryann broke into her boys' conversation. "After dinner, Jake, I want you to take a shower. Get the stink washed off. Tomorrow's school. Is your homework done?"

"No problem! For some reason I don't mind doing homework in Roxbridge. I like seeing Ms Baldridge smile when I hand it in."

"It's always a good thing to make a lady smile," affirmed Rob.

★

"All kidding aside, Rob, what did you make of the insanity we saw today?" After dinner they were enjoying second mugs of decaf. Jake was showering.

"'Tis crazy, isn't it? Yet, it's no different than other beliefs people hold. Anyone can get caught up in a swindle, if they're not careful. I hate to pick on the Church of the Latter Day Saints, but they're a perfect example."

"The Mormons?"

"Aye. If you don't know their story, I recommend reading *Under the Banner of Heaven*. It's the tale of a Mormon murder, but includes a good dose of Mormon history. I won't tell you the details. You're a smart woman, read it for yourself. Then we can discuss what happened, maybe over beers. Saints don't drink, at least not in public." He chuckled. "I love irony!" He put his mug in the dishwasher. "What we saw today is remarkably similar to how the Saints sprouted. It can happen any time, any place. People are gullible. They want to be hoodwinked. Superstition is more fun than reason."

"It's hard to believe the Mormons are as loony as the Pippinites," Maryann said. She shrugged, wrestling with scepticism. "Young Mormon men who come to the door are always scrubbed clean wearing shirts and ties. They want to talk. I'm always embarrassed to shoo them away."

"You shouldn't be reluctant to tell anyone at your door to take a hike, unless you're prepared to buy a vacuum cleaner or Bible. Look, they're simply doing their missionary work. I'm not sure they even care about signing you up. If they do, great. If they don't, at least they've fulfilled their mission obligation."

Maryann nodded her head as if recognizing the obvious. "Now that I think about it, there's an army of religions who canvass us during the year: Mormons, Jehovah's Witnesses, Acolytes of St. Francis, Temple Jor-el, Church of Scientology, Congregational Outreach, Seventh Day Adventists, Christian Scientists, Rosicrucians, the 42 Club, St. Peter-St. Paul Society, Sisters of Piety, Buddhists Sans Guns, Baptists for Righteousness, Christians for Cannabis. It's endless."

"Annie, I predict soon we'll have one more visitor: The Church of the Maligned Fruit."

7

Mo

From the get-go I was puzzled by the Church of the Maligned Fruit. On one hand, it was a cult. At least that's how it appeared to me. For Pete's sake, Tim! They were worshipping apples! What kind of nonsense is that? Then, I thought more about it. It dawned on me they were celebrating one of nature's greatest inventions. I admit, apples aren't overloaded with nutrients, but they're sweet, crunchy, and have countless culinary uses. Apple worship may be idiotic, but it's better than bowing to tobacco.

Nevertheless, I remain cautious of the cult. Often, there's a dark side to what some might consider normal. The neighbor who borrows your chain saw could be cutting up more than firewood. Do you know what I'm talking about, Tim? Remember the psychiatrist who butchered his wife into steaks, chops, and hamburger? Remember that nightmare? After that, I considered becoming a vegetarian.

Mayham is the cult's spiritual leader. I think you know that. He calls himself Reverend, but that's questionable. I learned he was a Burpee Seed salesman in Iowa before donning the robe.

And his academic degrees are hilarious. Apparently, D.Div. means Dowser/Diviner, and WEC stands for Whole Earth Catalogue. I'm surprised PRA hasn't been added to his list of credentials. What does that mean? It's obvious: Poor Richard's Almanac!

How are you doing with your beer, Tim? Another? No? I agree. One's enough this time of day. I have to be sober to do the cooking now that Becka's gone.

I think MacKenzie found himself in a predicament with the emergence of the Pippinites. A few Pippin students were in his classes at the high school. That's where the dark side of the cult became evident. Those kids may have venerated the apple, but they disavowed any other empirical science.

Is this happening in Danbury at your school, Tim? No? Okay, I understand--not so much because you have elementary kids. Just wait a few years until their young minds get brainwashed by the science deniers.

As I heard it, MacKenzie once presented a unit on climate change. The apple students argued with him. They thought apple power could overcome anything. How do you teach kids like that? Their minds are locked tight as a safe and the combination's been lost.

It didn't take long before Pippin parents showed up at the school and got their children excused from any science not solely focused on apple agriculture. When mainstream science units were being taught, their children went to the library to read about the dangers of spraying apple trees with daminozide. I'm sorry for using the chemical name. I mean Alar. Tim, you're correct--it's a growth regulator. The Pippin kids were becoming expert orchard managers, but knew little about anything else. Some knowledge of aquifers and soil chemistry might have been smart. The denial of logic and learning in favor of faith-based mythology is one of the reasons charter schools are springing up like poison mushrooms.

One night, waiting to fall asleep, I started thinking about the Jewish-Christian narrative. Boy, then I really woke! The Bible tells us that in Eden, God used a snake to convince Eve to eat an apple. Eve shared the apple with Adam. Think about it, Tim. Sharing is a generous thing to do. All at once, without a crystal ball, both became knowledgeable of evil temptations and descended into sin itself. Poor Eve! She was hungry and willing to share with a stranger. They had only been created for an hour or two, so Adam was still new to her. And the poor snake! He was merely helping them out, like telling a lost motorist how to get to the nearest Dunkin' Donuts.

I know! I know! It's all allegorical, Tim, nothing more than that. But meanwhile, scribes depicted Eve as a nude, a whore, and a slut. She came to represent all women as being naive, foolish, ignorant, and temptresses. But she also had good qualities-- saintliness, cleanliness, care-giving, and birthing. Will the real Eve please step forward? Or are all her qualities just a hodgepodge of smoke and mirrors? Take your pick.

Meanwhile, since Adam wasn't the apple snatcher the way Eve was and had donated a rib to make her, he was depicted as a righteous father-figure, an honorable man. But he was bonkers over Eve, the way men are today about women in short skirts. He contributed to the pair's fall from grace. The emergence of sin can't be placed all on Eve. Adam was equally to blame. I know it's a weird story, Tim, but millions believe it in one form or another.

All this time, the lovely apple has been consigned to the dustbin of history as a satanic icon. It's a product of the tree of knowledge that is also the tree of inquiry. Aren't we all tempted to inquire *why*? And to answer *why*, we're obligated to turn to the tree of knowledge for information. If we don't try to find the answers to our questions, we're no different than the apple worm, a creature just eating and reproducing.

Bonum est malum. That's Latin for good and evil. Malum is also the root for naming the apple genus, malus. I feel badly for lovely apples. To have their family forever labeled evil is a shame. Talk about a bad rap!

That's the way it's been for thousands of years, Tim. Without a shred of damning empirical evidence, despite being sweet and healthful, despite providing food and shade, and despite volunteering to be a target for William Tell's arrow, the apple has gracefully borne the brunt of religion's ignorance.

If that's not enough to exonerate the apple, I learned that China is the world's largest grower and consumer of apples. The Chinese word for apple is *ping*. *Ping* is also the Chinese word for peace. Makes you wonder.

8

Is God Real?

"Finally! I found you! You're like the will-o'-the-wisp when we split up. I think I see you in an aisle, then when I blink, you're gone. It usually happens near the pickles and relish."

Rob caught up to Maryann at the checkout lanes. He was searching for her after picking up a jar of peanut butter, a bag of carrots, and an economy pack of TP. He could never figure out why the tasks Annie assigned him were so randomly ordered. To deepen his annoyance, Big Y frequently rearranged products in aisles and shelves adding to his confusion.

"I was held up over by the yogurt," she explained.

Rob briefly imagined an armed woman in a babushka snatching Annie's chocolate Yoplait, then bolting for the door.

"Sometimes you disappear faster than fifty dollars at a tag sale," he said, the imaginary robber quickly erased from his thoughts.

"Very funny! I bumped into Trish Hammond. She asked us to dinner after Halloween. Jake's invited, too. Pete heard we went to the Apple Church and wants to get our impressions."

"Impression? Depression's more like it. Every time I think about the nonsense we saw on Appletree Lane, I know there's no hope for mankind. We're doomed!"

"Shhh! People are going to hear you."

"We need less hearing and more heeding."

"What's that supposed to mean?"

"Quit listening to the voices of superstition and start heeding advice about reason, especially at the Big Y." He laughed. "Ignore forty-two."

"Forty-two?"

"Aye, forty-two. It's from that book, *The Hitchhiker's Guide to the Galaxy*. Remember? It's an answer to the universal question: What's the meaning of life? Turns out the answer's forty-two. Here's my big poser. Is peanut butter the perfect food? My answer: Is the Earth a sphere? Nowadays, it seems as if apple veneration is the solution to everything, and apple worshipers are getting the upper hand." Rob weakly smiled as if his logic might not have been clearly laid out.

"I don't follow what you're saying, honey. How does forty-two fit in with hearing and heeding?"

"I'll show you when we get home, dear. I have it on the computer. Hearing and heeding are sine and cosine waves synchronously crossing both the X and Y axis at non-linear frequencies. You'll see. It's easy to understand."

★

Jake perched on the deck steps gazing across the back field as if searching for the source of a distant sound. The weakening sunlight cut through the crystalline air of the late October afternoon. A formation of migrating birds silently crossed the sky. Jake saw a deer emerge from the woods. In the blink of an eye it was gone.

Jake was scraping out seeds and pulp from a pumpkin, preparing it for Halloween. For him, it was all about the pumpkin this year. He decided to skip a costume. The door to the kitchen opened then banged closed. Maryann joined him on the step.

"How are you making out, sweetie? Do you need a spoon with a sharper edge?"

"No. This one's fine. Look at all the junk that's come out so far." He pointed to a pile of pumpkin innards mounded on a flattened plastic bag.

Maryann swept up a stray seed and added it to the pile. "You picked a big one. There was bound to be lots of gunk. Good job cutting open the top."

"Rob taught me how to use a knife." Jake was silent for a moment, then asked, "Mom, is there a God?"

"Jeepers! That's a tough question to answer. Why do you ask?"

"It's about a dog."

"Tell me," Maryann urged, wondering where Jake's question had come from and why.

"There's a little dog in town. Sometimes we see him crossing the playground like he's on a mission. He's black but has white speckles on his face and neck. We call him Talcum, but we don't know his real name. He's friendly. He wags his tail when he sees us, but he doesn't stop. He runs past us the same time everyday, when we're heading indoors after recess."

Maryann furrowed her brow. "Does anyone know who owns him?"

"Juan thinks he lives with the Clarks. Juan said he was Ollie Clark's dog before Ollie was killed by the motorcycle."

"I remember when it happened," Maryann said. "It was sad. Ollie was wish-boned on his bike near the Crossroads Market. That's why I warn you so often when you head up to school."

"Yeah, I know. But cycling here is safer than riding in the city."

"That's true," Maryann agreed. Moving to Connecticut had many advantages, Jake's freedom to roam one of them.

Jake continued his story. "Juan said Ollie had Talcum on a leash and was giving him exercise."

"Talcum must not have been hurt."

"I guess not."

"Why are you telling me this?"

"Because Juan said Talcum goes to the cemetery behind the church every day and lies on Ollie's grave. How does he know Ollie's buried there? Does it have something to do with God?"

"I don't think so, dear. Some animals simply have an instinct about those things. We saw the movie, *Hachi*. Remember? One day, his owner left by train but never returned. For the rest of Hachi's life, he went to the station every day and sat waiting. Hachi's love and loyalty were strong enough to pull him back, despite bad weather. It didn't matter that his owner didn't show up."

"Yeah, I remember. I felt sad." Jake pondered the story, then asked, "What about people, Mom? Do we have instincts the same as dogs?"

Maryann considered her reply. "Maybe, but in a different way. People do visit dead relatives, sometimes regularly."

"Why do they do that?"

"For months Nana went like clockwork to Pap's grave to bring him fresh flowers. It was a way for her to say a final farewell."

"Did she stop going?"

"Yes, eventually."

"Why?"

"Because her sorrow had healed. She didn't need to go to his grave as often. She had her love for him locked in her memory."

Jake considered his mother's explanation while continuing to scrape away at the pumpkin's insides.

"Did Pap go to heaven?"

"What do you think, honey?"

"I think he did."

"Why?"

"Because he was a nice man. Everyone liked him."

"I agree. Pap was a good guy. He was my father. I loved him. He did nice things for people and never asked for a thank you in return."

"Mom, what happens to birds when they die?"

"I don't really know. I don't want to sound silly about this, but maybe they just fall out of the sky or off a limb. It's a good question. You should ask Rob."

"I've asked Rob questions like that--about God and stuff. He always tells me God is ULAR."

"I know what you mean. Rob thinks the only true religion is the *Universal Law of Reciprocity*."

"What does that mean?"

"I can't explain it to you now. I have to get dinner on the table. It's a complicated answer, but when you think about it, suddenly it starts making sense. Let's talk to Rob about it during dinner. Hey! It's getting chilly out here. Want me to bring you a jacket?"

"No, I'm good. Is Rob's ULAR the same as God?"

"Not in the way most people think about God. But in some ways it's very God-like. Did you ever ask your father about God?"

"Yeah. I don't know if he was kidding me or not, but he said God was the almighty dollar."

Maryann snickered. "I can hear him saying that. But you don't believe it, do you?"

"No. George Washington's picture is on the dollar. I know he was called the Father of our Country. But I never heard him called God of our Country. Did you know he had wooden teeth?"

"I do know."

They became quiet, lost in their own thoughts. Jake continued scraping. Shadows were lengthening across the field. Maryann wondered when Jake would start asking other tough questions-- about babies, for example. Didn't fathers have the duty to explain reproduction to their sons? Was it up to her? Had Zachary said anything? Should she ask Rob to become the surrogate father in this situation? She smiled at the thought of Rob setting up an experiment for Jake, maybe with chickens, showing how it all worked.

"You've got the pumpkin nicely cleaned out. What are you going to carve for a face?"

Jake considered for a moment. He hefted the gourd to his lap, then twisted it looking for the best side. "I'm going to make a big question mark. It's gonna have a dot on the bottom, just like a real question mark." He laughed.

"Why are you doing that? Are you still wondering about God?"

"No. When kids come for candy, I want them to see it. The pumpkin's asking a question. It's saying: Why are you coming to this house? We have no candy! Go home!"

As the salad bowl was passed around the table, Jake asked Rob about God. Maryann admired Rob's effort not to sour any ideas Jake may have been forming about religion and the deities. Both had agreed to allow Jake find his own spiritual path, but it was impossible to remain neutral all the time. Children wanted to know what their parents believed. In due course, they would either accept or reject their parents' theology, juggling adult convictions to square with what they had experienced in life. Sometimes it resulted in devout children, sometimes it resulted in skeptical children.

"Hey, Rob, once you told me God is ULAR. Mom said you'd tell me what that means." Jake plunged his fork into a tomato wedge.

"Aye, so I did. When people refer to God, lots of images come to mind. You agree?"

"I guess."

"What do you imagine when someone talks about God?"

"I see an old man with whiskers. He's up in the sky. I can't tell whether he's sitting or standing, but there are lots of clouds around him."

"But you see a man," affirmed Rob.

"Yep. God's a man."

"Why isn't God a woman?" asked Rob. He glanced at Annie seeking approval then looked at Jake with questioning eyes.

"Because in the movies God's always a man with a deep voice and supernatural powers."

"So the movies have determined who God is?" asked Maryann, jumping in, annoyed.

Rob looked at Annie signalling her to ease back. Rob thought Jake's response was normal for a boy his age. Jake's idea of God was no different than others, many adults included.

"No, Mom. Not just the movies. Everyone at church refers to God as a man. They must know. All the hymns and sermons and stuff all say Him. That proves it."

Rob pinned Jake with a penetrating stare and asked the big question. "Is it possible, laddie, that whatever anyone thinks about God is just a superstition? Take a moment to mull it over, Jake, it's an important question."

Rob watched Jake construct a mashed potato dam as he considered Rob's question. Maryann appeared as if she was ready to supply the answer. She squeezed her lips shut.

"Yeah, Rob, I guess. I suppose God could be an invented person." Jake shrugged his shoulders, then destroyed his potato dam and ate a forkful.

Rob reinforced Jake's admission. "It's like leprechauns, Jake. You and I both know they're not real, but lots of people believe in them." Rob checked. "You do know leprechauns aren't real, don't you?"

"Yep, except on St. Patrick's Day," Jake said. He grinned at Rob as if sharing a joke and washed down the potatoes with a swig of milk.

"Okay, then, laddie. Now that we're on the same page and agree God might be an idea and not a real person--man or woman," he winked at Annie, "I'll tell you what I believe. It's only fair for you to know my thinking. You'll make up your own mind as you go along."

Rob fashioned his own potato dam, a smaller version of Jake's. He briefly considered how to convey his story, then unscrolled his theology.

"I know you know what the Golden Rule is, Jake. We've mentioned it before."

"Yeah, but I don't remember how it goes." He aligned his peas.

Rob explained, "Do unto others as you would have them do unto you. That's the rule in Bible-speak. Help others the way you would want them to help you, if you needed help. That's it in real-speak."

"Yeah, now I remember." Jake positioned his peas into the shape of a question mark.

"Don't play with your food, Jake," warned Maryann.

Hearing Annie's criticism of Jake's food handling, Rob tore down his potato dam. "When the Golden Rule is said that way, lad, it's what I call proscriptive. It's something you must do. But

I see the Golden Rule a wee bit differently. Here's my version." He put down his fork. "Don't do anything to others, you would not want others to do to you. In other words, don't harm anyone because you don't want to be harmed. You with me? Do you see the difference? Do you understand?"

After a futile attempt to balance peas on his knife, Jake reverted to more acceptable table manners, picking up his fork. "I get it. Your Golden Rule doesn't force you to help anyone."

"Correct."

"Isn't that selfish?"

"Nae. My rule doesn't prohibit me from helping. If I want to help someone, I can. It's my choice." Rob studied Jake's face to see if he was comprehending the small but real difference between the two philosophies. "As I said, the first Golden Rule is proscriptive, my version is restrictive. Am I getting through?"

"Yeah, I get it. When I'm down at the river with Andy, I remind him not to push me in the water because I'm not pushing him in."

"That's about it, lad. That's a good analogy. Anyway, when I say ULAR, it means my interpretation of the Golden Rule."

At last Maryann chimed in. "Honey, ULAR means Universal Law of Reciprocity. It covers all the ways people can choose to follow the Golden Rule." She had been locked outside the conversation for too long.

"Your mom's right. Getting along with others is another easy way to think of it."

Jake was quiet, trying to digest Rob's words as well as a piece of chicken skin. He discreetly removed it from his mouth and set it on the edge of his plate. "What's for dessert, Mom?" he asked.

"Berries, nuts, and coconut flakes--your favorite." She looked at her husband. "Rob, will you get it ready? I want to discuss one more thing with Jake."

"Aye, love, fixing dessert's one of my specialties, like preparing cross-section slides of earthworms and slugs. I'll be just a minute."

When Jake sensed Maryann was taking over the conversation he shuddered. He guessed he was in for a mother lecture. But he was wrong. Maryann began by asking him a question: "Honey, have you heard of the Ten Commandments?"

"Yeah, that bearded guy in the movies I told you about said them. What about it?"

"The Ten Commandments are the earliest list of dos and don'ts found in the Bible. Actually, they come from two books of the Bible, Exodus and Deuteronomy."

"Why do you know this stuff, Mom?"

"Because they're laws, and I'm an attorney. Laws are my speciality. Some of the commandments are old fashioned religious requirements like *honor thy father and mother*, while others are laws that are as correct today as they were then. Thou shalt not kill and thou shalt not steal are laws we obey today. Right?"

"Yeah, except for all the shalt stuff."

Maryann hesitated to consider how to spring her surprise. Jake appeared to be listening, reasonably engaged in her explanation, but unaware where she was heading. She continued.

"Here's the thing, honey. The Ten Commandments are intended to be obeyed exactly as they are titled--commandments.

They leave no room for people like you and me to think for ourselves. We are commanded to follow them. And the last commandment is especially troublesome: Thou shalt not covet thy neighbor's servants, animals, or anything else."

"What's wrong with that?"

"Not coveting something that belongs to someone else is perfectly fine. It's one item we're told not to covet that's bad."

"What's that?" Jake frowned. His eyes narrowed with concern.

"Servants, Jake. In those days the word servant was another meaning for slave. The ancient Israelites had slaves. Servants were not employees entitled to go home after an eight hour work day. They had no rights, no freedoms. I think both you and I agree slavery is evil."

Jake nodded vigorously.

Rob set the dessert dishes in front of them. In addition to the berries, nuts, and shaved coconut, he had drizzled each portion with maple syrup.

"I've dreamed up my own set of ten commandments," said Maryann. "I've been thinking about Rob's ULAR ever since we were married. Now I understand it. I've put my commandments in terms of Rob's ULAR. But I don't call them commandments. To me, they're life's rules."

"What are you talking about, Mom? I don't know what you mean."

"Neither do I," agreed Rob.

Maryann tasted a spoonful of dessert. "Mmm . . . good! The syrup's a nice touch, Rob. Mmm! Okay, here goes. This is my first rule: Don't kill others. You don't want others to kill you." Both males shared blank faces.

"I'll try again," said Maryann, hoping to clarify her position. "My second rule is: Don't cause pain to others. You don't want others to cause you pain."

Rob's face suddenly brightened. "Aye, I get it! You're making my ULAR less general by listing prohibitive behaviors. Understand what she's saying, Jake?"

"Huh?" said Jake.

"Here's a third rule," she continued. "Don't permanently injure others."

Suddenly, Rob joined her by reciting the second part in unison: "You don't want others to permanently injure you!"

"That's right, Rob!" encouraged Maryann. "You caught on! Now the fourth: Don't limit others' freedom! You don't want others to limit your freedom!"

"C'mon Rob," Maryann urged, "keep helping me. I'll say the first part. You join in on the second part. Listen to what we're doing, Jake. You'll catch on."

Rob nodded and Jake shrugged, as Maryann listed rule number five: "Don't stop people from having a good time!"

In unison: "You don't want people to stop you from having a good time!"

"Six: Don't lie to others!"

Now Jake piped in, answering his mother's call to make a three person response. "You don't want others to lie to you!"

"Good, that's it! Seven: Keep your promises to others!"

All three: "You want others to keep their promises to you!"
They were getting louder.

"Eight: Don't cheat others! You don't want others to cheat you!"

"Nine: Obey the law! You don't want others to break the law!"

Maryann took a deep breath and finished her version of the decalogue. Rob and Jake again joined her for the finale. "Ten: Do your duty to others!" she began. All responded: "You want others to do their duty to you!"

"There, we did it!" she said, smiling. "That's ten!"

"We win!" shouted Jake. The three secular theologians laughed and exchanged high-fives.

"What do you think, Jake? Do you understand my ten rules?" asked Maryann.

"Yeah, they're cool. But, Mom, we've already got enough rules around here. We don't need any more. Hey, Rob! Is there any more dessert?"

9

Mo

Tim, I hope you're not Catholic. No? That's good. Whenever I spell out the atrocities connected to Catholicism, my Catholic friends go ballistic, as if I'm inventing the truth. I'll get to the facts in a minute. But first a generality. In my opinion, the Roman Catholic Church is the most heinous crime family in history. It's more ruthless than the Mafia, more greedy than Midas, less kind than Idi Amin. It makes Adolf Hitler look like a pacifist. In the history of the world, the church is richer than any other private entity. No other organization even comes close. And it continues to amass wealth at an astonishing rate.

How could this monster have been perpetrated on humanity? I think there are two reasons, Tim. The Church promotes superstition and impedes knowledge. What do I mean? Well, superstition is easy to explain.

Before humans had the experience and insight they have today, they couldn't account for certain natural phenomena occurring in nature. For example, if a lightning bolt flattened a nearby tree, observers wondered why they had been spared. Had

killing a bear recently been a good or bad totem? Had they heard
a woodpecker? Maybe they saw a strange design in a pile of sticks
and rocks they had never seen before. Had the feathered amulets
they wore deflected the sky arrow?

As with all things, there was always a wise guy--perhaps a
priest--someone who sensed he could make a killing. I don't mean
a murderer. I mean someone with just a bit more insight who
knew he had suckers for easy picking. It was a killing all right,
but in riches: gold, jewels, spices, food.

"Give me the meat of your goat, and I'll tell you about the
arrow from the sky." That was the opening gambit of the hustler.
So the illiterate, uneducated, and superstitious gave the priest the
meat.

"Tell us, O Wise One," they implored. "Why were we not
killed by the arrow from the sky?"

"You were not standing on the spot where the arrow from the
sky landed," said the priest.

"How can we be sure to escape the arrow from the sky when
clouds again darken the sun?"

"Don't stand in a spot where the arrow from the sky might
strike."

"How will we know where that spot is?"

"Don't worry. You'll know. When the next arrow from the sky
comes, either you'll have picked the right spot or not."

This is the Roman Catholic Church. It is both the arrow from
the sky and a rapacious charlatan. It is history's most famous looter
and tormentor of the unassuming. It is the enemy of knowledge,
inquisitor of the skeptic, and denier of logic. It is the suppressor

of women by half-men who secretly fornicate with anyone--men and women alike--and rape innocent children.

A few years ago, the third highest criminal in the Vatican chain of horror, Australian Cardinal George Pell, admitted he and the church had made enormous mistakes in allowing thousands of Aussie kids to be abused by priests. He sorrowfully admitted he had not done enough to protect the vulnerable. He had sided with priests instead of believing the children. He remains under investigation. There's rumor he may have been as guilty as his gang of deviants. If he's nailed, I'd support capital castration. This band of devils publicly proclaim godly self importance, as if their destinies were preordained as a result of holy celibacy which, we know, is a lie.

Have you visited Italy, Tim? No? It's a lovely country filled with warm, expressive people. But they are people who for centuries were hoodwinked by the Holy See. It continues today. Same for Ireland with the magic of a pot of gold and leprechauns thrown in for good measure.

If you're ever on a planned tour in Italy, you'll visit enough churches to last a lifetime. Most will be large, ancient stone buildings, dripping with importance because of their gravitas. Inside, they will be overly ornate, guarded by scowling statues and hideous gargoyles. There may be smoke and incense. Sunlight will filter in through arched stained glass windows illuminating snarling animals, plump naked women, double-headed monsters, and scenes of torture. There will be images of confused people pointing in different directions. You'll see depictions of tormented anguish, rapturous insight, and holy bliss. Flat-faced saints will be holding bleeding hearts, jeweled crowns, or fat cherubs. There may be snakes and asses. You'll see feast scenes no serf ever enjoyed. In short, every macabre permutation for human suffering, gluttony, and stupidity will be portrayed in those windows. If you were to ask a priest on duty what it all meant, he would shrug and say, "You must have faith, my child. There is a donation box in the narthex on your way out. Give generously, my child, and faith will come."

Do you know who paid for all of it, the windows, the gargoyles, the church, the priest? Do you know who paid for the smoke, mirrors, and all the other excesses? In the past it was the lowly serf. Do you know who pays for the church's continued plundering? Today it's so-called enlightened people.

It's getting late, Tim. I've heaped plenty of scorn on the Apple Church and now on Catholics. You probably want to go home. No? You're willing to stay a bit longer? Okay, I'll try to be brief, but it will be hard. I can be an old windbag.

Here we are today, Tim, faced with a religion promoting ignorance and obedience. What obedience, you might ask? Do I need to remind you of the threat of Hell, the ignominy of the confessional booth, the fear of excommunication? Then there's the sin of premarital sex, the taboo of birth control, the crime of abortion, the shame of divorce. Everything's enforced by half-men who warn whole men and whole women about abstaining from vices the half-men covet or enjoy behind screens in the rectory.

Sadly, women are the targets of the church's perpetual misogyny. Women are forbidden to become priests and to enjoy the largesse of the half-men. Women are proscribed from making their own reproductive choices. Women are viewed by half-men as seductresses. Often, the half-men discount the allure of women in favor of the allure of other half-men. Yet, much of the church's good work, as little as it is, gets done by women. They are nurses, caregivers, friends of lepers, and founders of orphanages. They are advocates for the poor, the sick, and the infirm.

Tim, to me it's ironic the church diverted its attention from adoring the gentle son of a poor carpenter to venerating his mother. But in a way, this is a positive thing. Feminism finally has an ally in Marianism. Blessed be women, for they are the true way and the true light.

Boy! I've been ranting on and on. Let's wind it up today and get back together next week for more palaver. As usual, I've enjoyed our afternoon. Thanks for listening to an old fool, Tim. But before you leave, here are a few facts to chew on:

The earliest form of the Catholic Church didn't appear until the 4th century.

Through the Pope, the Roman Catholic Church is the third largest landowner in the world. The Crown of England is number one. The king of Saudi Arabia is second.

World-wide Church land holdings are approximately 177 million acres.

The Holy See has investments worth 10 billion to 15 billion dollars. It has financial stakes in banking, chemicals, steel, real estate, insurance, and construction.

The Vatican bank alone has holdings valued at 5 billion dollars.

The Vatican's yearly budget is about 300 million dollars.

The Church owns 26 thousand properties in the U.S.

The Church controls 6,800 institutions in the U.S., which include schools, nursing homes, hospitals, retreats, and insurance providers.

There are 244 Catholic colleges and thousands of K-12 schools in the U.S.

It's just a guess on my part, Tim, but I'll wager most of the misery and hunger in the world would disappear, if the Roman Catholic Church used its wealth to help people rather than protect priests who are sexual predators and women demonizers. Wouldn't it be in the spirit of Jesus, if the Church were to forego building more brick and mortar monuments, products of its greed? Wouldn't it be God's ultimate miracle, if the Church actually began serving people?

What do you think, Tim? Give me a call. We'll get together again next week. Now that I know your favorite beer, I'll have plenty in the fridge.

10

The Reformation

"It didn't last long." Jake inspected his pumpkin. It sat on a rock by the driveway. He lifted the lid, and fruit flies darted out. They had been aroused by the sun's warmth.

"I know, honey. When you hollow them out, they rot quickly. Last night's frost didn't help, either. Please go inside and change your clothes. We're due at the Hammonds' in forty minutes."

"Aw, Mom. Do I have to go?"

"Yes, you were invited. Phoebe will be there."

"I know, but she's in Mr. Lester's third grade class."

"Third grade or not, from what I've seen of her at Little League, she holds her own. You struck out twice when she was pitching."

"It wasn't fair, Mom. The sun was in my eyes."

"Hmm . . . as I remember, it was cloudy that day."

The parsonage originally was Greek Revival in design, but

years of alterations had added wings and modifications from different architectural eras. Two gabled dormers on either side of the roof looked like ears straining to hear gossip. A shed-roofed addition off the dining room was side-walled with vertical shiplap cedar. The original exterior six-panel Christian doors were hidden behind white aluminum storm doors. And, somewhere along the line, the exterior of the brick center chimney had been parged with white concrete waterproofing compound.

Rob knew smaller churches lacked the money to employ full-time janitors. As a result, repairs were hit or miss. Cleanups were done by volunteers pitching in. Few helpers were handy with tools.

Inside, Pete Hammond showed Rob two new bookcases in his office. They had been made by the Smit's son, Leonard, for his Eagle Scout project. He had access to power tools in the high school's shop.

Meanwhile, Maryann followed Trish into the kitchen to see what was cooking. Delicious odors drifted through the house. And Jake tailed Phoebe into the sunroom where *Battleship* was set up on the floor.

"Goodness!" said Maryann. "This smells fantastic! It's like autumn in a pot." She peered through the glass lid of the slow-cooker. "It's gotta be pork."

Trish nodded. "Yep. It's a rib roast I plan to section into six chops when done. Except I always use a crock-pot to cook it. It's swimming in lots of spices and cubed apples. Here's the recipe. Phoebe calls it, *Ma's Oink n' Apple Stew*." Trish gave the recipe to Maryann. It was printed on red paper in the shape of an apple.

"Thanks. I'll try it at home but with ingredients for four. I like having leftovers, and with two lads in the house, an entrée like this disappears fast." Annie folded the paper and stuffed it in her pocket. She uncorked wine, the MacKenzie family's contribution to the feast. Finally, with meal preparations complete, both families entered the dining room, their appetites whetted by the cool fall weather.

The Hammonds' table centerpiece was a plastic half-pumpkin, about 8" wide, and hollow like a diorama. Depicted inside was a Pilgrim harvest scene. At a tiny table sat two attractive male Indians and a beautiful Pilgrim woman. Behind the table in the center stood a Pilgrim commander-in-chief. He was gesturing to the sky as if saying a blessing. His words were printed on the apron of a white tablecloth covered with food for the feast. Pete Hammond played the role of the Pilgrim leader and recited grace: "Bless us, Oh Lord, and these thy gifts which we are about to receive from thy bounty, through Christ, Our Lord." Pete ad-libbed *amen*, which was not part of the diorama.

Hammond began separating the roast into chops. He joked it was like doling out loaves and fishes. Brussel sprouts and beets made their way around the table. When all the food was fully plated, Pete made a toast. "To our dear friends, the MacKenzies. I hope they remain within our fold for years to come. Together we can accomplish miracles. Let's eat."

Jake leaned on Maryann's arm and whispered, "Mom, what does *amen* mean?"

"Shh, honey. I'll tell you later."

Table conversation covered the change of daylight hours, Battleship strategy, and the fall's bountiful apple harvest. Pete asked Rob if he had any information about the resignation of Dr. Walsh, the School Superintendent. According to Hammond, Walsh resigned to become president of the New Paradigm Charter Schools. Rob wasn't able to supply any new information, other than saying New Paradigm was a subsidiary of the Gronk Family Education Initiative.

Trish questioned Maryann if she was involved in the dust-up over the Apple Church's appeal of their tax assessment. Maryann said Kitty Higgins, the town's first selectwoman, had mentioned it to her, but had not yet asked for help.

After pumpkin pie for all, plus ice cream for the children and coffee for the adults, the generations parted to pursue age appropriate interests. The kids resumed Battleship to experience the imagined pleasure of destroying vessels at sea. The adults drifted into the living room to consider bigger issues, like the Church of the Maligned Fruit.

"Hey, you two. I heard you attended Sunday service at the Apple Church," said Pete. He was frowning, as if he thought they had behaved improperly. There was an edge to his voice.

"Aye, we did," answered Rob. Suddenly, he sensed the conversation might have lasting consequences.

"What was it like?" asked Trish.

"Different," answered Maryann, jumping in. She was now on guard should any accusations or recriminations be on the horizon. Although she had asked Pete to officiate at her wedding because he appeared gentle of soul, since then she had learned Pete could explode at any time. Kitty Higgins said his temper was like dynamite connected to a hidden tripwire. Anything could set it off. Behind the pulpit he appeared quiet and taciturn, but in civilian life he frequently became pedantically aggressive. However, Maryann had seen no signs of erratic behavior at Conservation Trust meetings where Hammond was a member.

"What was different about it?" Pete probed.

"Well, for starters they worship Pippin, and the apple is their holy icon," said Rob.

"Do you mean Shakespeare's Pippin?" asked Pete.

"No. Same name but from different tribes. The Apple Church's Pippin comes from the Pantheon of the gods of nature. Pete, I swear it's crazy time on Appletree Lane." Rob sensed Pete relaxing hearing his indictment.

"So, you're not leaving us and becoming Pippinites." Pete spoke as if making a pronouncement.

"No. We're not becoming acolytes," Rob said. "We're not joining that cult." He disliked using the word cult, but there was no way to get around it. "We visited out of curiosity."

"And we got home with a dozen apples!" said Maryann brightly, trying to ease the tension in the room. "I felt as if I had stolen fruit from an orchard." She chuckled.

"Anyway, I'm happy you're still on board," said Pete. "I trust now you'll formally join our church?"

Rob looked at Maryann. A silent understanding passed between them.

"Pete," Rob answered, "we enjoy Sundays in church from time to time. It's an occasion for reflection or simply an opportunity to meditate. Sometimes you strike the nail on the head, as you did with that sermon about transgender rights."

Maryann interrupted. "And I enjoy the music, even if it's a small choir."

Pete became annoyed, apparently by Rob's tepid endorsement. "Do you have something against us, Rob?" His voice rose a notch. "Damnation! We're a mainstream church, not some loony cult. We do more than meditate."

"I can't speak for Maryann, but I certainly don't have any bad feelings about your church. I told you, I . . . we like to attend and be at peace."

Pete was visibly agitated. Trish left the room to stack the dinnerware in the dishwasher.

"Rob! This is a church, not an ashram. There's more to this place than convoluted mantras ending in *omm*. This is a church that worships Christ, the Trinity, and seeks the path to salvation."

Rob thought carefully about what he planned to say next. He wrestled with his instinct to respond frankly and risk capsizing the boat. Should he accept Pete's explanation or argue back? He noticed Maryann giving him a warning look.

"I understand your commitment, Pete. After all, this is your life's work, and you lead this church. The Christian fable is what you believe. But for me, the whole narrative is nonsense, no different than worshiping Pippin." He glanced at Maryann.

"What a preposterous story humans have generated." he continued. "Each faith believes in a god, the designer and ruler of the universe. Each god wants humans to adoringly fawn over him. God can be influenced by prayer and beseechment, and become angry when he is not adored to his liking. Pete, it's absurd fantasy! But humans are gullible enough to support the hoax and pay for all the trappings of disillusionment. It's the oldest and largest scam in history."

Hammond fumed. "How can you say that, Rob? How can you not believe in God and in Christ? You were raised in a Christian country. Most likely you were raised in a Christian home. You're denying your heritage! You're turning your back on the one thing that separates the wicked from the blessed! You've turned your back on Jesus!"

"Pete, I'm sorry. You say you're a mainstream Protestant church. You identify with Congregationalists, moderate Baptists, Methodists, Presbyterians. You all appear to be self-satisfied with your liberal causes, occasional sit-ins, and donations to food pantries. All that's laudable. It's the Christian myth that undermines everything. You're genuflecting to superstition. Your story is as weird as any cult. Your churches are simply bigger than cults like the Pippinites. You've been around longer, so people have forgotten your histories of narrow beliefs."

Hammond shoved back in his chair as if the Devil had been set loose by MacKenzie. He stomped his feet on the floor. He was livid and breathing heavily "How can you say this about us? How can you sully the name of Christ? It borders on blasphemy!"

Rob pressed on. "When I was a child in Scotland, I heard the same line. Believe me, Pete, adherence to Biblical truths was stressed more ardently over there than it is here. Bible gibberish morphed into impossible fables for me. Pastors spoke of the necessity and joy of faith. I was assured belief followed faith. Or did faith follow belief? It doesn't matter. It's all nonsense. It's all lies."

MacKenzie gestured imploringly. "Believe in what, I asked? Faith in what, I asked? Faith in a man who roams around after dying? Faith in a man who preaches peace, then goes haywire with bankers? Faith in a man who can heal the sick with his hands while walking on water at the same time? Can't you understand what I'm saying, Pete? It's all superstition and myth!"

Rob inhaled deeply and lowered his voice. "I don't know who the first scribe was to write the god story. But I'm sure it was as much science fiction to him as Ray Bradbury is to us today. Science was in its infancy then, so the scribe believed the manipulating necromancer when he told the scribe that the god story was true. Wizards pretend to know the truth. They have learned how easy it is to swindle the gullible.

"When science began to catch root and thrive, religion cut it off at the base hoping to kill it. Read your history, Pete. Fortunately, science has a deep tap root. Science is the enemy of superstition."

Rob was on a roll prepared to do battle for science and reason. He was itching to take on the Roxbridge Community Church and all the other mainstream dens of superstition. Infamous names and faces scrolled in his memory. He listed people he was certain Hammond knew: Joel Osteen, Oral Roberts, Jimmy Swaggart, Rex Humbard, Billy and Franklin Graham, Benny Hinn, Creflo Dollar, Pat Robertson, Jerry Falwell. All were members of the Protestant mainstream in one form or degree, and all were charlatan's perpetuating superstition.

"Pete, I don't mean to lump you and your church with

evangelicals. But you're all cut from the same cloth. You all have the same roots."

Sensing Rob was not ready to ease off, Hammond sat up preparing to deflect another round of insults demeaning the moderation of mainstream Protestantism.

MacKenzie continued. "Everything you are today--all your feel good causes, your contributions to Indian schools, your marches that defied Trump--is rooted in the genocide of indigenous people, the tacit toleration of slavery, and the intolerance toward churches unlike your own. I admit the Mormons are strange, but in their formative years mainstream churches like yours hounded them and slaughtered them. That's why they migrated west. Protestants are slumbering for the moment, waiting for the next ill-conceived crusade. In my opinion, many are sharpening their pikes ready to impale Muslims."

Rob stopped to catch his breath. "Pete, if you haven't heard of him, check out Rob Bell. He's a former hard-right, evangelical preacher who now counsels love, tolerance, and learning. While I don't agree with his continued belief in God, I respect his positions on moderation and kindness. All churches would do well to scrap their entrenched dogma and start focusing on the message of Christ."

Maryann looked daggers at Rob. She loved his intellect and willingness to take on fools. But they had been invited to a dinner party. In her mind, Rob had overstepped the boundaries of decorum. She jumped into the discussion.

"Pete, I treasure coming here on Sunday, but Rob has different ideas. I love his enthusiasm. He's a very special guy. Ask him about what he believes in, ULAR."

All three became quiet wondering where the conversation was headed. They could hear Trish in the kitchen rinsing the slow-cooker. Maryann regretted mentioning ULAR. She hoped Rob knew he had pontificated for too long.

But Pete was suddenly curious to learn about Rob's ULAR. He thought he might be able to catch Rob in an ethical blind alley. He might be able to get a modicum of intellectual revenge. He took a deep breath and continued.

"I think I understand your position, Rob. Of course, I don't agree. The atrocities you mentioned happened years ago. All that's forgotten now. Let bygones be bygones. It's water under the bridge. There's no reason to rush joining us. I'm sorry for getting upset. I should have known better." He hesitated then asked, "Tell me about your belief, Rob, what Maryann calls ULAR."

"It's the same belief you have, Pete."

"What do you mean? You just finished telling me how unlike we were." Hammond was agitated again.

"In seminary did you take a course in comparative religions?"

"Yes, it was required."

"Among all religions a few characteristics are universal. Can you think of any?"

Hammond considered MacKenzie's question, not wanting to fall into a metaphysical trap. He was aware Rob possessed a prodigious intellect. He answered, "Most religions are the product of a transformational character like Jesus, Muhammad, and Buddha. Do you want me to list all of them?"

"No. That isn't necessary," said Rob. "But not all religions spring from some superstar. Am I right?"

"That's true, but still . . . ."

"So, if a god-like prophet isn't universal to all religions, then what is?"

"All religions have rites and ceremonies." Pete was grasping for a common denominator.

"True, but is that adequate enough to support a belief?"

"Let me think. Hmm . . . all religions promise life after death. Either the life will be in paradise, or it will be in hell."

"C'mon, Pete! You know the heaven-hell duality isn't universal! Eastern religions like Taoism and Buddhism don't have prophets, believe in a god, nor believe in an eternal afterlife of pleasure or pain. Something else is universal. What is it?"

Hammond was struggling to solve the enigma MacKenzie had posed. He couldn't think past rites and prohibitions, heaven and hell, sin and redemption. Suddenly, he realized his religious training had been a litany of dualities. He couldn't come up with one stand-alone universal ethical belief. All his schooling had been about either/or. He didn't want to show intellectual defeat, so he carefully composed his capitulation. "So much is on my mind, Rob. We've been talking about religion, but our disagreements also involve ethics and morals. Why don't you tell me what's on your mind. Then I'll be able to tell you where you've gone astray."

MacKenzie calmed himself. He was annoyed. It wasn't because he was nervous about expounding on ULAR. He was annoyed by Hammond's condescending smugness. Hammond appeared to think Rob was out of his league arguing religion.

"Pete, I'm sure you know and understand The Golden Rule."

"Of course."

"In one form or fashion The Golden Rule is found in every religion. Sometimes it's expressed as a requirement such as, Do unto others, as you would have them do unto you. In this example, The Golden Rule is proscriptive. It requires action. But there's another version. It's prohibitive in intent. Don't do to others what you would not want done to you. In other words, leave people alone. If you want to help someone, that's fine. In fact, it's laudable. But it's your choice. You're not obligated to help, in the same way people are not obligated to help you. It would be nice if they did, but maybe they're not in a position to do so."

Hammond appeared crestfallen. He hadn't been able to come up with the essence of goodness. MacKenzie had outwitted him.

"You don't have to believe or agree with me if you don't want, Pete. But look up The Golden Rule and see how universal it is among all faiths and creeds. My ULAR is the *Universal Law of Reciprocity*. It's just a fancy term for The Golden Rule."

Jake used Rob's torch to illuminate his once proud jack-o-lantern. On Halloween it had scared some kids because they didn't know what to make of the question mark Jake used as a face. During the evening, while at the Hammond's, the gourd had succumbed to old age and lay pancaked on its rock. Signs of rodent teeth scarred the hollow husk. Jake poked the skin with his finger. *Tomorrow, I'll dig a grave and bury it*, he thought. *Sunday is a perfect day for a funeral.*

Inside, Rob poured a wee taste of scotch. Maryann declined to partake. He sat in the living room reconstructing his conversation with Hammond. He was angry with himself for having been argumentative. *Why get enmeshed in a debate over religion?* he thought. *Philosophical debates lead nowhere except to anger. Stick to what you do well! Stick to the facts!*

Meanwhile, Maryann was upstairs urging Jake to get ready for bed. It was late. *After this evening, I think I'll stay away from church for a few weeks*, she thought. *I've got to let tonight's skirmish be forgotten. I wonder if that's possible?*

Jake finished brushing his teeth, rinsed, and spat a sudsy mouthful into the sink. He wiggled his loose tooth. Rob had said he could pull it out. But the method Rob described sounded like torture. What did Rob say he would use? A block and tackle, a bag of sand, fishing line, and wads of gauze to stop the bleeding? And Rob had picked out a tree. Jake shuddered. Jeez! He declined Rob's offer.

"Hey, Mom. It sounded like Rob and Mr. Hammond were getting ready to fight. What were they angry about?"

"They have different ideas about religion, honey. That's all."

"I know Mr. Hammond believes in Jesus," said Jake. "He's a minister. What about Rob? Does he believe in Jesus?"

"You'll have to ask Rob. I can tell you, though, Rob's a very spiritual man. His main belief is The Golden Rule. Do you remember him explaining it to you at dinner?"

"Yeah. I remember. It's pretty cool. You give someone money, and they give you some money. What's wrong with that?"

"Nothing, dear. If we all followed The Golden Rule, the world would be a better place."

Jake mulled over his mother's assessment. "Yeah, I guess you're right." He remembered the question he had asked about amen. "Mom, you said you'd tell me what amen means."

"It means, so be it."

"So be it? What does that mean?"

"It means, the end."

"Why don't people just say, the end?"

11
Mo

I was honored to have been invited to the Seder, Tim. I'm not sure why I was included. Maybe it's because my last name sounds Jewish. It doesn't matter. The ceremony was delightful, even if it was a bit mixed up. Rabbi Marx is quite a character.

Has your family ever gone to the harvest fair at Temple El Shalom in New Milford? It's lots of fun, Tim. I know some children get spooked by the clown contest, but it's all in good taste. Between you and me, if kids really want to get spooked, they should try watching Republican politicians on C-SPAN.

The fair's always a good place for kids to buy holiday gifts for their grandparents. Everything's affordable. What grandpa wouldn't want a Chinese gyroscope? Or a nana getting new earrings from India? Precious kids, precious gifts.

At the Seder two dozen families were seated around the tables. I need to correct myself. They were Seder-Sukkot tables. It was held in the Stamp Room at the library. A long cloth hung from the ceiling like a tent. But I had the feeling of being in a barn or booth. How ironic that the dinner was on Tuesday, November 15, the end of the harvest season in Roxbridge.

Can you picture the Stamp Room's display case, Tim? Silvie Harwich filled it with her collection of Judaica. Years ago, she designed stage sets for community theater in New Jersey. Her husband, Harold, once played Tevye in Morristown for a production of *Fiddler on the Roof.* Now get this. Zero Mostel as Tevye was less than six feet tall. Harold's Tevye was 6-2. Mostel was heavily bearded. If you know Harold Harwich, he's as hairless as a block of ice. No matter. Harold has a cantor's tenor voice, strong and pitch-perfect, so his singing overcame any preconceptions I had about Tevye's stature.

As I said, the Rabbi's quite a hoot. He told one-liners and a story about a retired men's breakfast club. But he was serious about explaining the Seder. He said holding a Passover meal during Sukkot made some sense--something he said about birth and death. Anyway, I learned a lot.

Speaking of jokes, Tim, did you hear the one about the pig with three legs?

12

Stand-up Comedy

"We'll begin this evening's festivities with a blessing--the Kaddish. *Blessed are you, the Lord our God, King of the Universe, Creator of the fruit of the vine. Amen.*"

The guests took their seats. Rabbi Marx continued. "I like to start my educational Seders with a little humor. So, with that in mind and your permission, I'm going to tell you a story. Don't be afraid to laugh."

"A minyan of retired Jews from the temple meet once a month for breakfast at Gold's delicatessen. They call themselves *Retired Jews from the Temple.*"

Jake raised his hand.
"Yes, young man?" acknowledged the Rabbi.
"What's a minyan?"
"Ten men."
"Okay, sorry."

"The first thing the Retired Jews do when they get to Gold's is to visit the toilet. Then they file into a small dining room and sit in the same chairs they used the previous month. The table is loaded with bagels and lox."

Jake's hand again shot up.

"Yes, young man? You have another question? Oh, by the way, what's your name?"

"Jacob."

"My goodness. A name from the Torah. I haven't seen you at the temple. Are you Jewish?"

"No. I'm just a kid. Mom says sometimes I act childish. What's lox?"

Rabbi Marx laughed at Jake's interpretation of language. "Well, Jacob, lox is cold salmon. It's fish."

"Okay, sorry."

"The temple's Rabbi joins the Retired Jews. When everyone's seated and reaching for food, the Rabbi announces that this month the Trivardy topic is women. He reminds them Trivardy is a combination of trivia and Jeopardy. If the Rabbi gives an answer, someone must respond with a question. If he poses a question, all that's necessary is an answer. The Retired Jews have heard this before. They continue eating. The Rabbi consults a stack of 3X5 cards and begins."

"'First, an easy one,' says the Rabbi. 'The actress Joanne Woodward was married to what blue-eyed Jew?'"

"'Butch Cassidy!' croaked a Retired Jew with a half-full mouth of bagel."

"'You putz!' says the Retired Jew sitting next to him. 'It's Paul Newman! Butch Cassidy was a role Newman played.'"

Jake's hand waved.

"Yes, Jacob?"

"What's a putz?"

"It's a fool."

"Okay, thanks."

Marx resumed his story.

"The Rabbi plows ahead. 'This one's an answer,' he says. 'Ready? The answer is: get a prenuptial agreement.'"

"A Retired Jew with an eye twitch responded. 'What did the lawyer advise the millionaire to do before getting married?'"

"'That's right, Ben! Good! Here's one more. Which woman did the husband obey when he came to a Y in the road?'"

"The Retired Jews were silent. Many rubbed their chins or scratched behind their yarmulkes."

Jake interrupted. "What's a yarmulke?"

"A kind of hat. Actually, more like a beanie."

"Okay, thanks."

"'I don't know about you, Rabbi,' a Retired Jew said. 'But I'd damn well better obey my wife. Who's the other woman?'"

"'Siri.'"

Again Jake's hand. He was smiling.

"Jacob?"

"I know who Siri is, Mr. Rabbi. We have her in our car."

"That's good, Jacob. In my story the Retired Jews have no idea who Siri is." He continued.

"'Siri? Who's she?' asked Mort."

"'Mort, what kind of car do you drive?' questioned the Rabbi."

"'Ninety-nine Caddy.'"

"'Then you wouldn't know Siri. Anyone else not familiar with Siri?' There were weak gestures signaling mea culpa. 'Okay, we'll talk about Siri later. I'll explain it. For now, let's move on.' The Rabbi added sugar to his tea."

"'Is Siri American slang meaning Sarah?' persisted Rosen."

"'No, Rosen. I said, let it pass. Here's another one. The answer is: *I have no wife*. What's the question?'"

"A Retired Jew at the end of the table offered, 'What did Henny Youngman say when asked about his wife?'"

"'No, no, Cohen!' said the Rabbi. 'Youngman said "take my wife."'"

Marx checked to see if the Roxbridge folks were following him. He saw smiles but, so far, heard no yuks. The story continued.

"There were chuckles. One Retired Jew started coughing, a bit of bagel lodged somewhere in his windpipe. A hard back-slap dislodged it into his napkin. He wiped tears from his eyes."

"'Last one!' announced the Rabbi. 'What did the accountant say was the meaning of marriage?'"

"Again the group was stumped."

"After thinking it over, a Retired Jew who had worked for the government said, 'The meaning of marriage is defined in IRS Ruling 58-66, 1958-C.B. 60.'"

Rabbi Marx waited for the punch-line laughter he expected to hear from the dinner guests. People smiled but appeared puzzled. Finally, Harold Harwich, a Roxbridge resident and past-president of the temple acknowledged Marx's joke. "I get it, Rabbi! I get it, Rabbi! Very funny! Very funny!"

Laughter now circled the Seder tables. Not all understood the punch-line, but Maryann did. She was in charge of the MacKenzie-Caton income taxes. She had verified their marital status when she filed a 1040 for 2015. She had to be sure getting married before midnight on Hogmanay was legal.

"I hope I didn't take away from the solemnity of this occasion," said a smiling Marx. "It's not often I get to share our beliefs and customs with non-Jews, Harold and Silvie excepted. We have a fine ecumenical bunch here tonight."

Jake switched seats so he could sit closer to Peter and Paul, the Higgins twins. They were about his own age. When he slid in between them he whispered, "I've always wanted to sit between two putzes."

The Rabbi continued justifying his stand-up. "A little humor at times, even at a solemn occasion such as this, helps lubricate the rails of understanding."

Trains use grit on the rails, not lubrication, thought Rob.

"Humor is the most important quality we humans possess," said the Rabbi. "Our humor is what separates us from the animals."

Rob raised his hand.

"Sir? Do you have something to say?" asked Marx.

"Aye, Rabbi. To be sure, I do. I agree it's good to laugh. But the most important thing humans have over the animals are opposable thumbs." MacKenzie demonstrated his point by picking up a fork. He scanned the tables looking for support.

The Rabbi asked, "You're Dr. MacKenzie, right? Good point, sir. I'll see if I can work opposable thumbs into my stand-up routine. Mazel tov, to you Dr. MacKenzie! Is Jake related to you?"

"Aye, he's my wife's child, but I think of him as my own son."

"I can see where his curiosity comes from."

Finally, Marx explained why co-celebrating the odd combination of Passover and Sukkot made sense, at least for non-Jews. "Tonight is exactly the right moment to be enjoying the Jewish Festival celebrating the harvest. It's called Sukkot and falls in the middle of an autumn month the same way it would have occurred in ancient times.

"The drape above us represents harvest booths that would have been shared by Jewish families. Sukkot lasts for eight days. It is an acknowledgement that crops are dying for the season. In a way, it means death, not in a sad way, but in a pattern that is natural. It hints that rebirth will occur. During Sukkot families are free to enjoy the largess of the Earth."

The Roxbridge gathering was enrapt, thinking about American Thanksgiving only two weeks away.

Marx resumed his tale. "I want to play some music for you. I have it recorded on my computer. Listen carefully, then I'll tell you what it is." He hit the play key. Out poured a short, heavily accented orchestral piece. When it concluded he invited comments.

Taylor Peters immediately waved her hand. Taylor was in the sixth grade at the Roxbridge Regional Middle-High School. Her mother was the Roxbridge librarian. Her father owned a plumbing business. The Rabbi recognized her. "Yes, young lady, what do you think it is?"

"It's a Jewish hora dance. It probably celebrates Sukkot."

"That's an excellent guess. The piece is called *Harvest Dance*. Music like it might have been played in front of a family's booth, like we are under this drape. But this music is not Jewish in origin. It was composed by Hamish MacCunn, a Scot."

Seder guests looked surprised. MacKenzie nodded as if vindicated.

"It goes to show you," said the Rabbi, "that differing cultures celebrate yearly seasons in similar ways. This music makes us think of people holding hands in a circle dance. In fact, the dance steps in Scotland are almost identical to those in Israel."

Guests applauded. Many grinned at MacKenzie.

"Mazel tov, Rabbi," said Rob, when things had quieted. "That was a wee nifty piece of teaching."

Marx smiled, nodded his thanks, then preceded with the Seder.

"Passover is different," he said, using his best scholarly voice. "First of all, Passover is the story of the Jews escaping slavery in Egypt. The story is told through food. But Passover occurs in the spring, so it symbolizes rebirth. Sukkot, death--Passover, birth."

Marx knew the dichotomy between Sukkot and Passover

as represented by harvest and regrowth was a difficult concept to grasp, even for Talmudic scholars. They had been struggling with it for 3,500 years. Whether the Roxbridge folks understood was a guess.

Jake's hand waved.

"Yes, Jacob. A question?"

"No. No question. What you said is like when I plant tulip bulbs in October, and they don't pop up until April, or after the snow's gone."

"You're a smart boy, Jacob. That's exactly right." Marx felt a small love-lump grow in his throat for the little goy. He took a sip of water.

"As I said," he continued, "the Passover story is told through food. This is Karpas." He lifted a dish. "It can be any leafy vegetable. Tonight I've used parsley. I dip it in salty water, then let drops fall off. The drops represent the tears of the Hebrew slaves. This is how the Passover Seder begins. Go ahead, you can eat it. Next, I ask a question: Why is this night different from all other nights?'"

The guests carefully nibbled the parsley.

"Moving on we consider Maror. It is bitter herbs, a symbol of the wretchedness and harshness the Hebrews endured in Egypt. I use garden radishes. You can eat these, too."

As the guests nibbled at slices of radish, the Rabbi told another joke.

"God saw a fat man try to fit into heaven's gate. God said, 'You're too fat to fit in here with the rest of us.'"

"The man said, 'What should I do?'"

"God said, 'You have two choices, the one-step plan or the twelve-step plan.'"

"The man figured the one-step plan would be easier. 'What's the one-step plan?' he asked."

"God said, 'Stop eating.'"

"The man said, 'What's the twelve-step plan?'"

"God said, 'Stop eating.'"

At last Marx was rewarded. Smiles and giggles swept around the tables.

The Seder continued. "This is Charoset. It is chopped nuts, grated apples, cinnamon, and red wine. It represents the mortar used by Hebrew slaves when they built the Egyptian Pyramids."

The McIntosh sisters exchanged smug glances. They heard the words *grated apples*. Nan and Ann were the Apple Church's representatives to the Seder.

"Next we have Zeron. It can be a chicken wing or neck and sometimes goat meat. This was what was used as sacrifices in the Temple in Jerusalem."

Marx riffed into another joke.

"A man approached the gate to heaven but was stopped by God. 'Who are you?' asked God."

"'I'm Hyman Rickover, the inventor of the nuke submarine.'"

"'Oh,' said God, 'you're responsible for millions of cases of American heartburn.'"

"'No, not the grinder,' said Rickover. 'I'm the inventor of the nuclear submarine. I'm responsible for millions of cases of Russian heartburn.'"

The Rabbi was on a roll. He heard more laughter. Jacob's hand was aloft again.

"What is it Jacob?"

"I was in the Nautilus. It was the first nuclear submarine. It's in Groton. Rob took me."

Rob chimed in. "We went to see it when nuclear waste was a hot topic around here."

"I'd like to hear about that sometime," said Marx. "You and your wife have reputations as powerful environmental activists."

"Rob and Mom are heroes," affirmed Jake.

The Rabbi strove to wind up the event. "Sometimes six foods are part of the Seder," he said. "Tonight we are only discussing five. The fifth is Beitzah. It's a roasted hard boiled egg. It's a festival sacrifice and is a symbol of mourning."

Emboldened by Jake's questioning, Taylor Peters again raised her hand. "Wait a minute, Rabbi Marx," she said. "You told us Passover is about rebirth. How come Beitzah is about death?"

"No. It's not about death. It's about mourning. What's your name young lady?"

"Taylor. It seems to me mourning is a result of death. I don't get it."

Marx realized he and the girl were twisting into a Gordian Knot of dialectical theory and interpretation. It was part of the eternal Jewish struggle to parse every utterance, every word, every sentence.

"See me after the Seder, Taylor. We'll talk more about it." To escape the puzzle Taylor had posed, Marx told one more joke.

"God saw two men approach Heaven's gate. One was black, one was white. 'Who are you?' asked God."

"'We're the Brady bunch,' they answered in unison."

"'I thought I'd see you sooner,' said God. 'You were off the air after only five seasons.'"

"'No,' said the black man, 'not that bunch. Just the two of us. I'm Wayne Brady, and I do improv. Sometimes I play you.'"

"God said, 'Now I remember. You weren't very good at it, either. No miracles.'"

"Brady said, 'I tried.'"

"'Okay,' said God. 'Move along. You can get into Heaven. At least you tried.'"

"Then God looked at the tall white man. 'Who are you?' asked God."

"'I'm Tom Brady.'"

"'Oh, you're the guy who let the air out of the ball like a common criminal,' said God. 'What are you doing here?'"

"'I'm weighing my options,' Brady said. 'If I come here, I'll be sitting on the bench playing second string to you. If I stay down there, I'll remain God.'"

"God was shocked. 'How can you call yourself God?'"

"Brady said, 'Ask anyone in Boston. They know who God is.'"

★

Maryann was removing her makeup as Rob stepped out of the

shower. Her bathrobe was cinched around her tightly. Rob's habit of opening the window letting steam escape, also let in a draft of cold air. The mirror clouded over once the window was shut. She cleared it using her hair dryer.

"Aren't you all pink and clean?" she said, happily. "I'm sure we can get the water scalding, if we turn up the heater. My, my, you're quite the lobster man."

Rob toweled vigorously as if trying to expose a new layer of skin. Finished, he wrapped his arms around Annie's shoulders and kissed the nape of her neck.

"Aren't you going to shave?" she asked. "Your beard is scratchy."

"Aye. I'll be back after I'm in my pajamas. Save my place."

Maryann used her hair dryer again. When the mirror cleared, she studied her complexion. She didn't think she'd changed much in recent years. Only last week, someone told her she reminded him of the actress, Jennifer Lawrence.

She noticed a tiny mole above her eyebrow on her cow-lick side. The tuft of her hair and the mole spot looked like the two parts of a question mark. She thought of Jake's jack-o-lantern face. She touched the mole. *Damn!* she thought, *I've been using sunscreen. Why this? I'll have to make an appointment with the dermatologist.*

She had been told she was blessed with beautiful hair. It was a thick dark-blond mop showing highlights of sun bleaching. Sometimes it had a mind of its own, preferring to imitate a mushroom, rather than succumb to the will of her brush. Hair taming was just as difficult in the country as it had been in the humid city.

She saw no sign of skin-sag on her face. She gave her makeup collection a quick assessment. She pulled out shadow she planned to use in the morning. It was the best shade she had to compliment her hazel eyes.

Two weeks earlier, her dentist had done a thorough prophylaxis. Her teeth were white and straight. She smiled at herself and thought, *not too bad for a Pittsburgh babe.*

She stepped on the scale to learn the inevitable insult. "Jeepers!" she said, pleased. She was two pounds lighter. It wasn't much, but for her small frame, it was as if she had shed an arm. Jogging with the Roxbridge Road Rats was paying off. Up to now, she had continually been anxious about her weight, especially since Rob had given her a revised estimate of her height. If she was shrinking, she might as well do it east and west, as well as north and south.

Rob reappeared in his pajamas and slippers. He lathered his face and began shaving.

Maryann dabbed a spot of red lipstick on the tip of her nose. "What do you think?" she asked, thrusting her face at him as if she was a puppet.

"Good idea," said Rob nodding. "But that's not your color." He shaved on the right below his sideburn.

"If a Rabbi can act like a clown, so can I."

Rob grinned. His foamed face resembled Batman's Joker. "Aye. It was an odd religious experience. But I'd rather enjoy a few yuks than listen to the contrived seriousness of the Protestants or the enforced piety of the Catholics. Jews have been wrestling with the meaning of life for thousands of years. It's about time they laughed at the futility of their efforts." He began shaving on the left, again starting below his sideburn.

"I was proud of Jacob tonight," said Maryann. "He wasn't afraid to ask questions."

Rob laughed. "Nae, he wasn't. He's a wee mensch, that one."

"When we got home, Jake pointed out Rabbi Marx had used the word amen, just like Pete Hammond had done saying grace. He wanted to know if the Rabbi's amen was the same as Hammond's amen. Did the Rabbi's also mean so be it? We Googled to find out before he went to bed. For Jews amen means truly."

Rob orated in his best Moses voice. "Verily, I say unto you, truly! So be it! Amen!" He shaved his chin and neck.

Maryann ignored his nonsense and continued telling her Jake story. "He said the same thing you just did, Rob. Mom, there's a truly, a so be it, and an amen. Why don't all the religions get together and pick just one? Why not simply say the end?"

Rob nodded his head in agreement with Jake's analysis. "Actually, it's a grand question, love. If people are going to frolic in foolishness and legerdemain, why not unite and celebrate superstition as one?" He paused and squinted at his reflection. "What do you think, Annie? Should I let my mustache grow out or continue shaving my lip?"

"I vote keep shaving," she said. "Your once soft mustache has become bristly."

"Aye. It's a sign of aging. A clean lip it is."

13

Mo

You're here today earlier than usual, Tim. Instead of beer, how about some coffee? I have one of those special machines that makes single cups of any flavor. Mocha's my choice. You, too? Okay, give me a minute, and I'll be right back.

I was telling you about the Seder. It was an enjoyable evening. Jake Canfeld asked lots of questions. Nothing got past him. And Taylor Peters, Abby Peter's daughter, stumped the Rabbi. Women can become Rabbis now, but I don't think the Peters are Jewish. I forgot, you told me you didn't know everyone in town by name. Abby Peters is the town librarian.

Look at Ruggles stretch. First front end, then rear end. Circle once then collapse into a ball. It's his nap-time routine.

Thanks for asking, Tim. Lars is retired, like me. He lives in Morris on Bantam Lake. Smart guy. Got into MIT and majored In biomechanical engineering. After graduating, he teamed up with one of his professors. They designed a mechanical wrist and formed a company to market it. It was a very successful enterprise. They sold out to Gronk Industries. The patent is hiding somewhere in the Gronk labyrinth.

How did Lars get into joint replacement? That's a good question. Since he was a kid, he was drawn to guns. As he grew older, he became fascinated with the manufacturing precision found in sport rifles. A part of the firing mechanism called the sear holds the bolt back until finger pressure on the trigger releases it. As I understand it, finger pressure can be adjusted. Anyway, an assembly of micro-sears combined with teflon tendons made his wrist invention become reality. He and his partner made their product life-like. It can hinge up and down, rotate, and tolerate loads up to twenty-five pounds. It's not perfect, Tim, but it's damn near life-like.

Even though as kids we were close, I didn't realize how infatuated Lars was with guns. It certainly didn't come from our parents. They didn't allow firearms in the house. I started noticing his interest when we were about twelve. At the store, he was always leafing through hunting magazines. Then in high school, he joined the rifle club. There was nothing my parents could do about it. The club used a small range in the school's basement behind the furnace room. It was target shooting, nothing ominous. As the kids became more accurate and proved they knew the safety rules, their advisor took them to cornfields on weekends to shoot rodents. I can understand your disagreement with that decision considering your job. No, it wasn't authorized by the school. It was totally extra-curricular. Lars still has his high school orange vest and cap.

According to Lars, their advisor emphasized the seriousness

of gun usage and ownership. The first time out, he told them to consider what they were about to do--shooting at another creature, like a rabbit. If they made a good shot, he reminded them they had just ended a life. He asked them if they thought they had a right to end life. Lars says he'll never forget his first kill. He says to this day it haunts him, but he still hunts.

What's he doing now? After selling out to the Gronks, he retired. He hunts whitetails in the fall and gives gun safety lectures in schools. I think he and MacKenzie have crossed paths from time to time.

No, Tim. Lars has nothing to do with the NRA. He calls their leadership deluded power-hungry assholes--pardon my French. Sometimes he says they're fascists.

For a brief time, Lars considered buying a small business in Bantam on the lake. It featured winter boat storage and small engine repair. Lars has a knack of knowing how things work and how to repair them. But he backed out of the deal. After the Gronk buyout, money wasn't an issue. Time enjoying the outdoors was more important to him. Me, too, Tim. We're alike that way.

My sister? Q's in the cookbook business. No, not publishing--writing them. At Groton College she took a course in Nineteenth Century culinary activities. It was an elective in the history department. As part of the course, she visited Old Sturbridge Village and assisted the reenactors preparing a feast. That set her off on the quest to find the perfect pumpkin pie.

She's published three books so far, a fourth's on the way. No, Tim. She's no longer married. Her ex became fixated on paleo diets. That was enough to deep-six their marriage. She's not against eating meat, but she insists some root crops and green veggies ought to be part of the meal. A divorce based on food? Of course not. It was more than their differing culinary views. He left her for a woman involved with crossfit training. Need I say more?

I know. Thanks for reminding me, Tim. But in our family it's common knowledge. Connie Van Cortland went to Groton College, too. She's five years older than Q, so they never met. Good thing! My sister's a public school product, like you. Van Cortland's a preppy. Q said she'd like to kick Van Cortland in the ass for her campaign to reduce public school funding. That's salty language for a woman who spends her time rolling dough.

Ruggles! Come here, boy. Let Tim scratch your ears. Aren't they soft? You keep it up, he won't leave your side.

Did I tell you Ruggles got shot? No? How could I have forgotten that? And you didn't hear about it elsewhere? Amazing! News like that travels fast in this town.

Here's what happened. Last October, Lars and I were hiking the Rumsey Preserve. Lars visits quite often. Ruggles was with us. If you've ever been there, you know the trail makes a loop, about a mile around. Where you enter and when you leave you weave through a field of tall grass. Oh, good, you've been there, so you know.

We were half-way, up by the vernal pool, when we heard a pop. Then a minute later we heard another pop. The sounds weren't close by. We looked at each other obviously concerned, but decided to cautiously push ahead.

Lars told me he immediately knew we had heard gunshots.

He even sensed the weapon was a small caliber rifle, maybe a .22. Were we in danger? I don't know. It was almost deer season, but firearms aren't allowed on trust property. In fact, the land's posted. There were no more pops, so we kept going but talked loudly.

When we were nearing the hayfield on the way out, Ruggles took off after something-- probably a rabbit. We lost sight of him in the tall grass. All of a sudden, there was another pop, this one closer and louder. The sound came from the woods on the other side of the field.

Instantly, we heard Ruggles. He yelped in pain as if he had tumbled onto an in-ground nest of yellow jackets. We heard more yips. Lars and I knew Ruggles had been shot, so we hurried to the spot we last saw him. We ran as fast as our old legs could take us.

We saw the old fella in the grass. He was on his side twitching, arching his back, trying to stretch his muzzle to reach the wound so he could lick it. I held and comforted him, but he was crazy with pain. He was shot in the shoulder. Three inches higher and he would have been hit in the neck. He'd be dead.

Suddenly, we heard shouts heading our way. Two kids crashed out of the woods toward us. At first they didn't see us in the grass. But ten feet away they stopped dead in their tracks. It was the Higgins twins, Peter and Paul.

One was holding the rifle. I don't remember which. I can't tell them apart. Even though Lars and I are identical, that's no guarantee we can differentiate between other idents.

Lars jumped to his feet as if he was thirty-five again and snatched the gun from Peter. Or maybe it was Paul. He screamed at them: "What the hell are you doing? Guns aren't allowed on this land. What were you two numbskulls thinking?"

Meanwhile, I was comforting Ruggles. He was panting and in pain, but had quieted a bit. "Lars!" I yelled. "This is no time for the inquisition! We'll take care of those two later. I know where they live. Do you have your cellphone?" He did. "Phone Dr. Shea," I ordered. "Get him down here as fast as possible." I gave him the number. Shea was on the scene in ten minutes. I covered the wound with a handkerchief and applied pressure. Ruggles didn't lose much blood. Anyway, with Lars and Shea helping me, we carried him up to Shea's truck and back to the clinic.

What happened? As you might expect, Tim, the boys disappeared. Maybe they thought they could escape. But Lars had their rifle, and I knew their names.

Mickey Shea can work miracles. He sedated Ruggles, removed the slug, and repaired the wound. According to Lars, the bullet was a .22 short, so the damage was minimal. Still, he had been shot.

Ruggles. Come over here, boy. Show Tim your shoulder. That's a good dog. See? He has a bit of a limp, but he'll survive.

Peter and Paul? Yes, they were in a heap of trouble. The Higgins were cited for allowing them to hunt in the off-season. Kitty was angry as hell. You can understand why. She's the first selectwoman. Even at the small town level, politics rule. People accused the Higgins of being careless. Why hadn't they locked the gun away? I didn't say much to anyone. I was simply relieved Ruggles was okay. But you know how news like that travels.

I heard the boys paid a big price for their stupidity. I'm not clear how they were punished within their family, but it must have been severe. I know they had to pay Shea's bill. I'm sure that was painful, especially if Kitty dipped into their savings or made them forfeit their allowances. And they were grounded for three months.

Of course, the incident begs the question, Tim, why did they shoot Ruggles? They said they thought Ruggles was a coyote, and somehow shooting a coyote was okay. Stupid! Really stupid! Twelve year old minds!

Go ahead, boy. You can go back to sleep. Good dog.

It might have been all over then, but the incident aroused sleeping resentments. Remember, Tim? One group argued that not allowing guns on Trust property was unconstitutional. They refused to change their opinion even when it was pointed out that the Rumsey Preserve was private land. Hikers were permitted on it but had to follow posted rules. Another group stood firm and argued that firearms of any form were wrong. A more moderate bunch counter-argued that small caliber rifles were essential tools in rural communities where rodents can decimate crops. Still another faction pointed out that marksmanship was an Olympic event. Opinions were all over the place. A big can of sardines had been opened.

I don't think Roxbridge has heard the last of this. Lars said he would visit more often and offer his two cents. He is, after all, an expert in the field.

It's sad how the gun debate has divided our nation into two camps--pro-gun and anti-gun. It's the same for other things--pro-choice vs. pro-life--religion vs. secular humanism--conservative vs. liberal--rich vs. poor. Our country is split into polar opposites on everything. No one compromises any more. No one listens to the other side. And as positions harden, the arguments become less rational and more emotional.

I don't know where it's all headed, Tim. I don't think the result will be good. I'm so old, I may not find out. However, you're young, so get involved. Do your homework. But don't hate the other side. Work together to find a solution.

C'mon. The sun's way over the yardarm. No more coffee. Let's have a real drink. Let's drink to friendship, Tim. You're a tolerant guy. You've been patient listening to an old man.

14

In Bed

"It's chilly tonight. Get closer. Warm me up." Maryann pulled the covers over her shoulders.

"Aye, 'tis a bit unseasonal. Want me to close the window?"

"No, I like fresh air, and it's a good excuse to snuggle."

"Lassie, I don't need an excuse to snuggle. Scootch over here."

Maryann curled into Rob's embrace. He wrapped her in his arms. They nested like spoons. "Did I tell you about Aunt Alice?" she asked over her shoulder, laughing silently.

"You've told me lots about your family," said Rob. "What did Alice do?"

"Whenever she eats Chinese food and gets a fortune cookie, she adds a tag-line to the fortune."

"What do you mean? Tell me."

"If the fortune is, *Today you'll make a new friend*, she adds, *in bed.*"

If the fortune is, *You will be rewarded with riches,* she adds, *in bed*. Get it?"

Rob laughed while burying his face in her hair. "Bloody

brilliant! Those cookie fortunes are always so inane. Alice's come up with a way of making them even sillier." He thought for a moment. "Here's one: *It's better to eat an eggplant than to suck an egg in bed.*"

Annie laughed. "I remember! That's what the granny said at the Hartford hearings about the nuke waste storage problem."

"Aye, something like that. Remember the reaction of the crowd?"

"They went nuts. It was a good tension reliever."

"Lassie, I know another way to relieve tension." He kissed her neck.

"Aye, laddie, but first, I need your advice about how to explain the Middle East turmoil to Jake. He's been asking questions."

Rob chuckled. "You mean you want to talk politics right now? I'd like to talk about something else."

At that moment, Annie could not be dissuaded from her quest for knowledge. She had been accused by friends of always being in pursuit of truth, justice, and the American way. She touched Rob gently assuring him their magic moment was imminent. He twitched. She planned to inhale his warmth and nearness. She and he had become we. But first she wanted Rob's advice.

Knowing she would not be satisfied until he helped resolve her politics, he asked a question: "Is Jake concerned over the hostilities between Iran and the Saudis?"

"No, I don't think he's asking about any specific conflict. It seems to me he's simply trying to make sense of some of it." Annie pulled Rob's arm tighter around her.

Rob sighed. "That's a bloody hard story to tell. There are so many combinations and permutations. Och! I don't know where to begin."

Annie was silent for a moment, figuring out a way to compartmentalize the competing conflicts in the Middle East. She decided to create a mental file similar to a plan she would outline for a client. She interlocked her fingers with her husband's.

"Sweetie, this is what I know," she said. "Here's how I see the issues. Tell me if I'm on the right track. Be honest."

"Aye, I will. Are these the ideas you're going to share with Jake?"

"Maybe, if I can decide which story will best help him understand." She rolled to her back and positioned his arm across her chest. "In some ways," she continued, "the Middle East story is no different than histories of other disparate groups trying to live together, but often failing miserably. You know from Scotland how the clans feuded. Norsemen pillaged Ireland. Napoleon invaded Russia. The Axis Powers set their sights on world domination."

She turned and kissed Rob lightly on the tip of his nose. "All these stories mostly have geopolitical roots--land grabs, fossil fuel greed, race domination, and slavery." She felt Rob bury his nose in her neck. She got goosebumps.

"But there's another factor, Rob, that's just as worrisome. I think I can help Jake understand what's going on, if I explain the events in terms of religious intolerance."

"That's a good idea, love. It's as valid an approach as any other." He nibbled on her earlobe.

"How does this sound, Rob? What if I explain the Middle

East in terms of Sunnis versus Shiites? I can compare it to Catholic versus Protestant--evangelical versus secular humanism."

"I'd leave out evangelical versus secular humanism," he advised. "That's a tough dichotomy to explain. Keep to one religious dispute. Since you're helping Jake understand the Middle East, tell him how Islam became divided into two sects. Divinity schools are still wrestling with that one." He turned her face toward him and kissed her softly.

Annie returned Rob's kiss sensing his growing desire. She knew it was time to begin exploring his body with her hands. She propped herself on an elbow, touched her nose to his nose, and said, "Religion 101 will have to wait until tomorrow, my laddie. Right now I want to have a tactile dialogue with you."

Rob caressed her. "Lass, I love it when you talk dirty in bed."

"Rob and I had a serious conversation last night, trying to figure out how to explain the Middle East situation to you." Maryann sipped her coffee watching Jake sort a handful of Cheerios arrayed on his toast dish He made eight piles of seven. "Here's what we decided," she continued. "It's so complicated over there, I'm going to keep my explanation to the differences in Islam between Sunnis and Shiites. Have you heard of them?"

"Sure. They're on CNN all the time." Jake slid Cheerios from one pile of seven to make seven piles of eight.

"I didn't realize you watched the news that much." She stirred sweetener into her coffee.

"Only when there's nothing else to watch."

Jake's face suddenly brightened. "There, that proves it!" he announced, pointing at his dish. "No matter how I arrange the Cheerios, 7 X 8 = 56 and 8 X 7 = 56." He laughed, then stuffed half the ovals into his mouth.

Rob was watching Jake's manipulations. "Laddie, you've demonstrated what some people call multiplicative inverses. Seven times eight is the same as eight times seven."

"I know, I get it," agreed Jake. "You helped me a year ago with multiplication. I got better. But it never made sense to me until now. There it is! I can see it! Cheerios showed me how multiplication works."

Rob continued his explanation undaunted by his competition with breakfast food. "In the multiplication table for the ones through the nines, there are eighty-one combinations. At first it looks daunting--a lot to memorize. But if you understand multiplication inverse, memorizing becomes much easier."

"What do you mean?" asked Jake.

Rob explained. "If you agree 7 X 8 = 56 and 8 X 7 = 56, then you have two equations resulting in the same answer." Rob saw Jake's eyes widen as if he had just discovered electricity.

"There are thirty-seven inverse equations in the ones to nines table. If you memorize thirty-seven, you'll also know thirty-seven others. But it can get even easier."

"How?" Jake's brow furrowed. He appeared to be making mental notes.

"I'm sure you know the ones, twos and fives," said Rob.

Jake nodded.

"If you eliminate them from the thirty-seven, that leaves

twenty-one. Six of them have no inverse, so they have to be learned without a mirror image. That leaves fifteen equations with an inverse. The six without an inverse take a wee bit of memory work, but it's a lot easier than tackling eight-one."

"That's cool, Rob! I can do that!"

"Sure you can, laddie. I know you can. I'll help you. We'll copy an inverse chart from the internet. There are plenty to choose from."

"Thanks, Rob," said Jake shaking his head in wonder and admiration. "I'm gonna be a math wizard."

Maryann interrupted smiling broadly. "Okay, Einstein. How about a brief lesson on the Middle East. You asked me about it."

"Sure, Mom. Wait until I get more Cheerios."

When Jake returned to the table with a bowl of cereal swimming in milk, Maryann began. "As I said before the multiplication lesson, middle eastern history is complicated. Israelis are against Palestinians. Tribes are fighting tribes. There are countries against countries, especially where oil is concerned. And a hundred years ago, the countries we know today didn't exist. Arbitrary boundaries were carved out in the Middle East by the British and French after World War I. It's a mess."

Jake spooned cereal into his mouth.

"Unfortunately, belief versus belief also played a part. Nowhere was this more evident than in Islam." She checked Jake to see if he was tuned into her lesson. For once, he was listening intently as he ate.

"To illustrate the magnitude of the split between the Sunni and Shiites, I'm . . ."

Jake interrupted. "Wait a minute. How many Muslims are there?"

"About 1.6 billion."

"Wow, that's a lot! What about Christians?"

"Two point one billion."

"Sounds like Christians outnumber Muslims," he said.

"Yes, but only in total numbers. Christians are divided into Catholics and Protestants."

"How many Catholics are there?"

"About 1.2 billion."

"So, there's more Muslims than Catholics."

"That's right."

"Protestants?"

"Nine hundred million."

"Jews?"

"Fourteen million."

"Holy smokes! That's less than I thought."

"It was a surprise to me, too," admitted Maryann.

"How do you know all those numbers, Mom? That's a lot to remember."

"I found the numbers on the internet, made a list, then memorized them. It's the same way you're gonna learn the multiplication tables--memorizing."

"Okay, I guess if you can do it, so can I."

Jake continued probing. "How are the Muslims divided up? How many Shiites? How many Sunnis?"

"From what I've read." said Maryann, "there are about a 1.5 billion Sunnis and 340 million Shiites. The Shiites are mostly in

Pakistan, India, Iran, and Indonesia. The Sunnis are spread out all over the world."

Jake digested the numbers then asked Maryann, "Of all of the religions, which one is growing fastest?"

"Islam," said Maryann.

"Stupidity," mumbled Rob.

"Hush, Rob. Don't vent your disgust in front of Jake. You're usually tolerant."

"Don't worry, Mom. I agree with Rob. I'm an ULAR man, too. You give me money, I give you money. Rob makes sense."

Rob joined Maryann in a big laugh. Her eyes teared. It reminded her of the time the church brochure showed up. They laughed so hard then, they were lucky not to injure themselves. She had had an attack of the hiccups, she remembered.

She blotted her eyes and continued talking with Jake. "I love you Jake," said Maryann warmly. "You're a funny guy, even if you're my son."

"What did I say, Mom?"

"Don't fret it, Jake. I'll tell you later." Her chuckling persisted.

Rob continued with the story. "Islam can be traced back to 600 CE. CE means Christian Era. That means Islam started six hundred years after the time of Christ, assuming all the dates and times are accurate. A prophet named Muhammad received holy revelations from the angel Gabriel. With the message of Gabriel's revelations, he won over the hearts of an increasing number of followers. Many of his revelations had to do with peace. They were written in the Quran."

"Is that like the Bible?" Jake asked.

Maryann answered. "It's not like the Bible, but it does contain Islam's holy writings."

"Muhammad died in 623," said Rob getting back on track, "and disagreement arose as to who should succeed him. Some believed a new leader should be picked by a consensus of the people. Others thought Muhammad's cousin, Ali, should take over. As it turned out, instead of Ali, by vote the title went to Abu Bakr, Muhammad's close friend and advisor. Those people became Sunnis. Eventually Ali was assassinated, and he became a martyr. His followers are known as Shi'ah. The word is a contraction of *Shiat Ali,* which means followers of Ali.

"The story is much more complicated than that" said Rob, "and spans hundreds of years. But there you have it, lad. Islam split over who should be in charge."

"Sounds pretty stupid to me," said Jake, shaking his head. "You said Islam's about peace."

"True," agreed Rob. "When one Muslim greets another he says, *Peace be unto you.* The response is: *And unto you, peace.*"

"Then they kill each other!" groaned Jake.

"No, not quite like that," said Maryann, shaking her head. "There are billions of Muslims in the world who practice peace and tolerance. In a way, they are ULAR people, too. The philosophy of the Golden Rule is part of Islam. Much of the killing you hear about involves narrow-minded people who think their ideas are the only correct ideas. There's an old saying that illustrates that kind of thinking: *It's my way or the highway.*"

Jake sat staring silently at the last few Cheerios floating

randomly in his bowl. Maryann wondered what was floating in his head.

"Mom, do Muslims say amen?"

"Yes, I think they do, or something like it."

"Then they're like Christians and Jews. They all have ways to end their preaching. But I think my idea's best."

"I don't remember, honey. What was your idea?"

"They all should say, the end."

Guns

★

The Second Folio

The Amendments to the Constitution of
the United States of America

Bill of Rights -- Amendment Two

"A well regulated Militia, being necessary to the
security of a free state, the right of the people to
keep and bear arms, shall not be infringed."

Bill of Rights ratified effective December 15, 1791.

15

At the Library

"Good morning, Abby." Maryanne slid the library's copy of *Under the Banner of Heaven* onto the counter.

"Hi, Annie. Did you run this morning?" Librarian Abby Peters arranged Jon Krakauer's book on the re-shelve cart.

"Yes. They did the 5K today."

"Many runners?"

"I didn't count. Maybe seventy-five. It's pretty consistent from week to week. It's a beautiful morning. Will you be able to get outside and enjoy it?"

"Since I opened the library today, I'll be able to leave at 2:00."

"Any plans?"

"I'm taking Taylor for a haircut. She doesn't want me to chop off her ponytail, so she's agreed to get it trimmed."

"Where do you go?"

"Hair-Less in New Milford."

Maryann looked around. "Is Taylor here with you? By the way, I guess congratulations are in order now that she's been bumped up to eighth grade. Are you okay with that?"

"George and I talked it over. We recognize she's intellectually beyond her age group. Fortunately, she's never lorded it over kids her own age. It's a risk, I suppose, but having her advance a grade seems to make sense at this time. She's here, Annie. She's in the adult non-fiction section looking for *I Am Malala*. I told her I'd help her find it, but she said she could do it herself. She's stubbornly self-sufficient."

"She's a special young woman, that's for sure," Maryann acknowledged. "You said she's looking for books in the adult section. Does she have a school assignment?"

"Yes. She's supposed to write about someone she admires, and why. The person can be from real life or from literature."

"And Malala was her choice?"

"Actually, she's picked three heroes. Like most girls her age, she adores Anne Frank. But she's equally captivated by Liesel Meminger, the protagonist in *The Book Thief.* And now, Malala. Her report's going to be about all three, their similarities and their differences."

"Jeepers! That's a tall order, even for a college freshman."

"I know. I tried to talk her into focusing on one person. But she insisted all three were important to her in their own ways. She won't listen to me."

Maryann considered Taylor's challenge. "Would you like me to say something to her?"

"That's fine with me. She admires you. Maybe she'll listen to you, but don't count on it. She's my pride and joy. Sometimes I think she's too smart for her own good."

"Rob and I got a big kick out of her stumping the Rabbi at

the Seder." Maryann laughed. "By the way, Krakauer's book was great. Rob suggested I read it. Lots of Mormon mysteries have cleared up for me. Now I understand what Rob's been saying-- Mormon beliefs defy logic."

"Same is true for the Pippenites," said Abby. She shook her head in disgust at the new church in town. "I don't care what people say," she continued, "if you worship the apple you're certifiably insane."

Maryann nodded in agreement, chuckling. "Out of curiosity, Rob and I went to a Sunday service to see for ourselves. Crazy stuff! At least they're focused on the apple and not on the serpent. Last thing we need in Roxbridge is snake worship."

Maryann saw Taylor entering the main room. "Here she comes. Hi, Taylor."

"Like, hi, Ms Caton."

"Taylor, please call me Annie."

"Okay, Ms Caton."

"Good luck in eighth grade."

"Thanks, Ms Caton.

"Your mom told me what you are up to with your report. Aren't three heroes too many to write about all at once? Why not save spares for future reports?"

"I know like what I want to say about them. There are plenty of other people to consider for the future. So . . . like . . . I'm going to stick to my decision."

"Okay, your choice. Who else might you write about someday?"

"Rosa Parks, Eleanor Roosevelt, Geraldine Ferraro, Erin Brockovich, Joan Benoit. I have a long list."

"As I recall Joan Benoit was a marathoner. She was an Olympic champion. Am I right? That was awhile ago."

"Yes. Her time was like 2:24:52 in 1984. She's married now. Her full name's Joan Benoit Samuelson."

Abby interrupted. "Taylor's a list maker. She has all those statistics in a ledger."

"Any divers on your list?" asked Maryann hopefully.

Taylor smiled and nodded her head. "Three. Like Greg Louganis, Mickey King, and you."

Mayann grinned as if she had been anointed. "Thank you, Taylor. That's a nice compliment. I was an okay college diver, but nothing like King and Louganis. What about you? Do you have a favorite sport?"

"I like running. Someday I want to do a marathon, like Benoit. Dad took me to a 10K. I loved it."

Annie smiled understanding Taylor's interest. "I'm running Saturday mornings in the Roxbridge Road Rat Series," she said. "Why don't you join me someday? You'll probably run me into the pavement, but I'll try to stay with you."

Taylor shrugged her shoulders. "Okay. Like we'll run together. I won't leave you, if you don't leave me."

"You said that like a lawyer. Let's meet next Saturday morning at the starting line in the park. They take off at 8:00."

"Will Jake be with you?"

"No. Jake will be home in bed."

★

"Taylor said she had a good time this morning. She was impressed by how nice everyone was to each other. She said it was like a club of old friends. Two girls from the high school talked with her."

It was the next Saturday. Abby Peters was spraying the library counter with disinfectant. Maryann smiled contentedly, as if a long shot she had wagered on came in first place.

"She's a natural, Abby. She has such long legs and a light toe strike to her stride. This morning I realized how tall she might become. She's taller than I am now, and she's only twelve."

"She'll be thirteen in two months. But, yes, we knew when she was a baby her growth markers showed signs of tallness. Is tallness a word?"

Maryann laughed. "It is now." She became reflective. "The reason I came in today is to see if you have a copy of the children's classic, *Misty of Chincoteague*?"

Abby lit up. "Oh, I love that story! Yes! We still have a battered copy in the children's section. It's shelved under H."

"That's right," remembered Maryann. "Marguerite Henry. I'll be right back."

"Boy, this is one of the earlier prints. It has Misty's brown eye and erect ears looking straight at me--no one else, just me. At least that's what I thought when I was a child. Look, she has eyelashes!

She was the pony every little girl wanted, and some boys, too, like my brother Fred. I want Jake to read it."

Abby agreed. "I felt the same way. The story of Assateague and Chincoteague, the pony roundup, and pony penning day made me feel like I was one of the Beebe family. I wanted to live there."

Maryann nodded in agreement and reflected on her memory. "I have to tell you how Misty affected Fred. When I was eight, I sliced my finger cutting an apple. Mom and Dad drove me to the emergency room to get it sewed up. See? I still have the scar." She presented her finger for appraisal. "A bunch of crazy stuff must have happened on Friday night, because there were lots of emergencies on Saturday morning. We weren't going to get out of there quickly." She gave the book to Abby for stamping.

"Mom phoned Fred to tell him we'd be late. She must have called three or four times and couldn't get him."

"Was he out of the house?"

"No, he was there. The line was busy each time Mom phoned, so they knew he was home. They weren't worried. Even as a kid, Fred was reliable. When we got home, Mom asked Fred who he was talking to on the phone. He said Aunt Beebe. Mom said, 'What?'

"I think Fred thought he was in trouble, because he rapidly began telling a story of how he had talked to the Beebes in Virginia. He said he called the operator and told her he wanted to talk to Grandma Beebe on Chincoteague Island. I guess the phone operators had lots of kids do the same thing, so they were prepared. They connected him." Abby handed the book to Maryann.

"He said there were no grandma and grandpa, but there was an aunt, a real life aunt. He talked with her for about thirty minutes. He told us how real life facts differed slightly from the novel, but only by just a little. He said he was sorry to make us worry. He checked out the bandage on my finger." Annie looked at her finger again.

"Mom and Dad were skeptical about his story, but they didn't want to ruin whatever fantasy he had about Misty and the Beebes. Fred was positive he had talked to a real live Beebe.

"When the next phone bill arrived, sure enough, there was the call to Chincoteague, Virginia. Mom and Dad knew Fred had talked with someone. He said it was a Beebe. But they weren't convinced despite the phone bill. So Dad tried the number, and . . . voilá! . . . he got to speak with Aunt Beebe, too. For years they joked about Fred's imagination and curiosity. In the end, one thing they realized was they shouldn't leave us at home alone."

Abby grinned broadly. "What a sweet story, Annie. I love it. I have a similar problem about leaving Taylor at home alone. George made reservations for the two of us to celebrate our fifteenth anniversary on Block Island. Trouble is, he went ahead without thinking about Taylor. When I asked him what we were going to do with her, he said she's old enough to stay home by herself."

Maryann laughed. "Uh-oh, that's a problem! Maybe I can help. I'll invite her as a guest while you're away for your romantic weekend. She's a great kid."

"Thank you, Annie. I really appreciate it. I love my husband. He's the most considerate guy. But sometimes all he thinks about is copper tubing and bathtubs." She shook her head in happy resignation.

Maryann nodded. "Rob can be the same way, especially if he's preparing lesson plans. Give me a call with the details. It'll be nice to have Taylor as a guest. Jake will have to shape up."

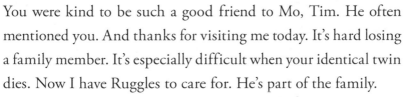

16
Lars

You were kind to be such a good friend to Mo, Tim. He often mentioned you. And thanks for visiting me today. It's hard losing a family member. It's especially difficult when your identical twin dies. Now I have Ruggles to care for. He's part of the family.

Mo told me he filled you in on my background. I'm a nuts and bolts kind of guy. Mo was a philosopher. I went to MIT; he went to Columbia.

I assume you knew Maryann Caton. Yes, she was a sharp attorney. Roxbridge was lucky to have her working for the town. Maryann attended Columbia, too, for both undergraduate and law school. Mo and Maryann were forty years apart but shared similar adventures going to school in New York City. The biggest difference in their experience was the makeup of the college. When Mo attended, all the students were men. By the time Maryann was a freshman, the college was co-educational.

Tim, did Mo tell you we have a sister? That's right, good memory, Curly-Q or simply Q. Her given name is Kerliss. How she got from Kerliss to Q, is complicated. I like to joke that it was a hair-brained scheme.

She and I decided to keep Mo's house for a while. It's easy for me to check on it, since I live close by in Morris on Bantam Lake. Q will be able to visit from time to time to enjoy the woods. Eventually, we may donate it to the Conservation Trust. Our property backs up on the Miller preserve. Adding ten acres on Bumpy Lane will allow a second public access into the preserve.

Ruggles is healed from his wound. He's doing okay. I know Mo told you I was with him the day Ruggles was hurt. Poor dog was shot for no reason, except for the carelessness of two twelve year olds. I'm sure the Higgins' rifle is now securely locked away. I hope other homeowners learned from the incident and have secured their guns. Shotguns, pistols, rifles--it's all the same. Don't let kids get them. Nearly three children die every day from guns.

Locking up firearms is not a bad idea for adults, too. Why let a heated argument become a crime because a gun is within easy reach of an angry spouse? Some people think their constitutional right to own a gun means they're not obligated to use common sense in handling them. All of a sudden, a limited constitutional guarantee has expanded to mean we are an armed nation. Now we can pack heat wherever and whenever we want. You can blame the NRA and their legion of toady politicians for that. The NRA is now starting to run slick ads promoting insurrection and the overthrow of our government. What they're suggesting is a rerun of Hitler's night of the long knives, only this time an attack on our democracy with assault rifles. The sad thing is, Tim, there's a large group of fascists living in the U.S. ready to go to battle.

Do you own a gun, Tim? My advice is don't bother. Unless you're willing to stay alert and follow all the rules, a gun is a tragedy waiting to happen. Too bad home insurance companies don't charge exorbitant premiums for gun ownership. I've heard some companies don't ask if a homeowner owns a firearm. I'm guessing they've been bullied by the gun lobby.

You might think I'm totally anti-gun by what I've said. That's not true, Tim. A firearm is a marvelous tool. Guns allowed the early immigrants to tame the forest primeval. Sadly, that also meant decimating the indigenous folks living here. I don't condone that, but I do understand how it occurred. The history of white Europeans stealing from dark-skinned people is well documented. Our actions were due to arrogance because we thought it was our divine right.

I've been a gun fancier for as long as I can remember. You can track the history of the Industrial Revolution by following the evolution of firearms. I admire the tight tolerances of machined parts. The change from smooth bore muskets to rifled barrels was a stroke of genius. A Scot discovered that fulminate of mercury, when struck, created a small explosion that could propel a projectile. It marked the end of pouring gunpowder down a barrel. Eventually, it meant the disappearance of powder horns and ramrods. Theoretical physics and chemistry turned into reality.

Oh! I'm sorry you have to leave so soon, Tim. I'm sure I was boring you. Too much science, right? No? You'd like to discuss the gun issue in depth? Okay, fine with me. I'll give you a call when I'm back in Roxbridge. Next time I'll have refreshments. Mo's cupboards were bare today.

Before you leave, Tim, give Ruggles a good scratch. If you do it right, you can get his back leg to move as if he's strumming a banjo. There's a special spot on his side. It's his on button.

17

Dunblane

Nineteen years before Robert and Maryann met in the Guggenheim Museum, in Scotland a horrific event occurred shocking the world. On March 13, 1996, forty-three year old Thomas Hamilton entered a classroom at Dunblane Primary School and murdered sixteen children and their teacher. Fourteen others were wounded. Only one child escaped bullet-free. In two minutes, a lovely Scottish cathedral town was turned into a slaughterhouse.

New York City newspapers covered the tragedy on their front pages. They detailed that Hamilton had been a Scout leader, may have photographed children at a youth club he managed, and had a large collection of firearms. In fact, he used four guns on his rampage that day, saving the final bullet for his own head.

The New York Times printed statements from Dunblane residents. A rescue worker was quoted: "It was like a scene out of a medieval torture chamber. There were literally piles of dead bodies, most of them just little kids. Blood was spattered all over the floor and walls. There was blood everywhere."

Ron Taylor, the school's headmaster, lamented: "The scene that met us in the hallway was utterly devastating, utterly appalling. Evil visited us yesterday, and why, we will probably never know."

Especially saddened by the tragedy were Scottish citizens and people of the Scottish diaspora living elsewhere in the world. Modern Caledonia was a country where it was rare to have a shooting crime occur even in cities. And other than carrying the burden of genocidal memories from past English occupation, modern Scotland was a peaceful place where pride in family and neighborhood were dominant themes.

Robert MacKenzie was no less shocked than anyone else when he learned about the Dunblane murders. He was twenty-six at the time and had just completed his doctoral studies at the University of North Carolina. He had attended Dunblane High School as a commuter from Balmaha. He didn't know any of the families who had borne the tragedy, but he still grieved for them, feeling their pain while living thousands of miles away.

As was his custom when wrestling with emotions he could not express in speech, MacKenzie turned to the companionship of his writing journal.

I was shattered by what happened in Dunblane. Those poor dear children! How is it that the innocent, the vulnerable, and the unprotected always seem to bear an unfair share of the world's misery? I remember writing a poem for Mrs. Cameron when I was in high school. How was I to know my poem would be a requiem for Dunblane bairns?

I played the pipes one spring day / To celebrate
The first of May / Windows at last opened wide
Dancing children came outside / To jig and reel
Breathe clean air / To feel the sunlight in their hair
Winter's gloom fades by June / As I play and play
Another tune.

Happiness never lasts. Moreover, its very existence is dependent upon sadness and grief. Without darkness and misery there can be no joy. Ironically, the equation can't be reversed. There is no corollary. Happiness is not the harbinger of sorrow.

Evil begets sorrow. Evil begets sadness. Evil begets misery. Evil begets grief. Even when evil has been temporarily subjugated, its malevolent legacy is persistent guilt.

Happy times are too short. They bloom like daylilies for one sun-up, then die. I need to lock away the perfume of happiness for the long winter of sadness.

God protect the children.

R. M. 17 March 1996

18
The Meaning of Money

"My mom told me to give you this." Taylor Peters handed Maryann another red paper apple recipe.

"Thank you, Taylor. Welcome to the MacKenzie manse. Your room's upstairs to the left. You'll have to share the bathroom with Jake. But, you'll be able to lock him out. We checked. Why not take your bag up now?"

"Okay, Ms Caton. I'll be like right down."

Maryann called up to her. "Your mom's note was a recipe for Apple Brown Betty, but you probably knew that. I have apples. Want me to make some?"

"That's my favorite!" Taylor shouted. "I'll like help you cut up the apples."

★

A rainy Saturday afternoon was the perfect time to stay inside and play board games. Earlier in the morning, under grey threatening clouds, Maryann and Taylor had completed the

Roxbridge Road Rats five-miler. Returning home, they showered, then began working in the kitchen.

Earlier, while the ladies ran, Rob and Jake nailed rungs up the trunk of an oak tree. The ladder went as high as the spread of the lowest limbs, a pattern of branches that would eventually support a tree house. Jake said he would attach a rope to the structure and shinny up. Other kids could use the rungs for ascending.

In Connecticut, the rain held off until noon. However, beginning a day earlier on Friday, wet, gusty winds halted the ferry service to Block Island and abraded the Rhode Island coastline. As a result, he Peters's romantic fifteenth anniversary had been cut short by a day.

The Apple Brown Betty turned out as might be expected--deliciously decadent with just a hint of health.

"Brilliant!" exclaimed Rob.

"I love it with ice cream!" acknowledged Maryann.

"So cool!" said Jake.

"It's like really good, Ms Caton," agreed Taylor.

"So, who's Brown Betty?" asked Jake.

"I'll tell you later," Maryann said.

She turned her attention toward her guest. "Taylor, honey, I told you to call me Annie. Enough with the Ms Caton stuff. When you're here, you address Rob as Rob. From now on, if you say Ms Caton, I'm pleading the fifth. No response."

"Like, I'm sorry Ms . . . Annie. It's just that . . . like . . . you're a lawyer."

"Good! I got an Annie out of you." Maryann explained her home status. "I'm not a lawyer at home. Rob, tell Taylor what you call me."

"Annie."

"See? He doesn't call me Ms Caton."

"How about you, Jake. What's your name for me?"

"So, I don't remember."

"You remember. C'mon, fess up."

Jake pondered his reply. "So, I'll have to think about it." He popped a piece of Apple Brown Betty in his mouth. "I'll tell you later."

Maryann changed subjects. "We often play board games around here, especially when the weather's like this. Rob calls days like this dreck. He and I are going to play Scrabble. Do you want to join us?"

Immediately, Jake gave the thumbs down sign.

Taylor weighed her options. "Like, I read a lot. There's only me at home. I've tried playing chess against myself, but when I get to the other side of the board, I remember what I had been planning on the first side. I like can't out-fox myself."

"There are chess games on the internet," suggested Rob.

"I know. But like I'm only allowed an hour a day on the computer. I bank my time for typing reports."

"Do you have a tablet or cellphone?" asked Maryann, conveying her curiosity to Jake in the chance he might start using internet tools available to him for serious reasons other than *Grand Theft Auto*.

"No. Like I told you, I read a lot."

"You used the word bank when you described how you save up time. How 'bout a game of Monopoly with Jake. He's always bragging about how good he is. He calls himself the real estate agent from hell."

"Aw, Mom! You're exaggerating," Jake said laughing.

Taylor shrugged her shoulders and nodded, agreeing with the idea. Even though Jake was two years younger, he was entertaining enough to tolerate for a few hours.

Rob and Maryann set up Scrabble in the living room. Jake and Taylor staked out Monopoly claims at the dining room table. Jake insisted on using the wheelbarrow token, arguing he always won using that piece. "I need it to haul my loot to the bank."

Taylor thought it over then selected the battleship. "I think girls can become like boat captains," she said firmly.

The games began. Soon enough the children's conversation wormed its way into Annie's brain. She stood up. "I'll be right back, Rob. I want to try something."

Rob watched as she dug through her purse and pulled out two bills. She went into the dining room. "I have ten dollars," she said to the children. "All I hear out of you two are *so* and *like.* Both words are useless most of the time. You don't have to use them in your conservations. If either or both of you can get through the game without saying so or like, you get to keep the money. It's not bribery," she justified, "it's only a linguistic experiment." She plunked five dollars in front of each. "Wanna give it a try?"

The eyes of both children opened wide. "So, all we've got to do is not say so and like?" asked Jake.

"That's right," agreed Maryann. "Trouble is, you've already lost, Jake. You just said so to begin your last sentence."

"Aw! C'mon, Mom. That's not fair. You didn't say start."

"All right, I agree. I'll say go. Are you willing to try, Taylor?"

"Sure."

"Okay. Go!"

Back in the living room seated at the Scrabble board, Maryann concentrated on the children's language so intently, she soon was thirty-one points behind Rob. At first the children whispered, assuming their conversation couldn't be heard. But eventually they began speaking in regular tones, words Maryann recognized. As far as she could tell, up to now, there had been no sos or likes.

After forty-five minutes a lull quieted the dining room. Jake sauntered into the living room looking pleased with himself.

"What's up, Jake?" asked Rob. "Taylor getting the better of you?"

"Naw. As long as I have the wheelbarrow, I always win." He stopped for a minute as if considering his choices.

"Hey, Mom," he began. "I know you're doing an experiment with us about so and like. But it's unfair."

"Why's that, honey?"

"Because you didn't give yourself a challenge. What's good for the goose, is good for the ga . . ."

". . . gander," said Rob, finishing Jake's sentence.

"Yeah. That's it, gander." Jake looked stumped. "What's a gander?"

"It's a male goose," said Rob. "Often they stand lookout checking for predators like raccoons or coyotes."

Jake laughed. "I get it. They take a gander around searching for gander danger."

"Aye, laddie. That's so true."

"C'mon, Mom. Take the challenge. You, too, Rob."

"What kind of challenge could that possibly be?" she asked, as if dismissing a jester after a pratfall.

"There are things you both say that drive me bonkers."

"Really? What are they?"

"Two things. You say, 'I'll tell you later,' and 'I'll think about it.'"

"I say those things?" she frowned. "Do I say them often?"

"Yeah. Both you and Rob say them. You're making me nuts." Jake crossed his eyes to prove his point.

Maryann was quiet for a moment. "Jeepers, I never realized it. I guess you're right. I'll have to think about it." Returning to Scrabble for a moment she added an *re* to *quiz* for a triple word and double letter score. "One hundred two points!" she announced. "Take that Rob! I'm up by seventy-one!" Triumphantly, she high-fived Jake.

"Sure, Rob and I are in," she said grinning. Then she gave Rob a warning look signaling he had no choice in the matter.

19

Lars

Did you bring your copy of the Constitution, Tim? Great! I have the same edition--Bantam Classic. It's funny the publisher has the same name as Bantam Lake where I live. Or maybe it's kismet.

I always have a copy handy, Tim. There are times when social evenings deteriorate into arguments over what is or is not the law. It's surprising to me how many of my lawyer friends don't have a clue. This little book helps straighten things out. The only time we arrive at loggerheads is over the concept of *textualism* versus *contextualism*. Sometimes *textualism* is referred to as *originalism*.

Let's see if I can clarify each term before we get into a more complicated debate. Okay, Tim? Textualism, or in other words originalism, is a narrowly focused way of thinking about the Constitution. It means applying the text only as it was originally understood, based on life at the end of the Eighteenth Century. This view implies the Constitution is a dead document. It does not evolve along with society. It has no flexibility. That was Justice Scalia's belief, unless the application of that reasoning got in the way of some decision he was arguing.

In contrast, contextualism is the theory of an evolving Constitution, a document that allows for a changing and more modern society. Justice Breyer was a contextualist. However, in all fairness, none of the Justices, neither conservative nor liberal, have rigidly held to their positions. Sometimes they surprise us with their opinions. Excuse me for a minute, Tim. I need to get fresh water for Ruggles. Last time, I said I'd have libations when you returned. How about it, Tim? You'll have a glass? Good choice. If we're going to tackle the Constitution, especially the Second Amendment, some whisky on ice is a good idea.

Years ago, MacKenzie tipped me off. Tullamore Dew is an Irish blend, but it's damned good. At first he thought he was being disloyal to Scottish single malts, but you can't deny taste. I'm sure he was forgiven by the Loch Ness monster or whomever he offended. Rob and I became good friends long before Mo's passing.

Let's talk first about the society in which the U.S. Constitution was written. You probably know much of the theory of the Constitution originated in the Federalist Papers. Historians have argued the papers are a great compendium of political science.

From October, 1787, to May, 1788, Alexander Hamilton, James Madison, and John Jay wrote eighty-five letters to the citizens of New York in an effort to convince them to support a central government. They wrote under the pseudonym, *Pluribus.* There are five main themes in their papers--federalism, checks and balances, separation of powers, pluralism, and representation.

The men were attempting to sway New York's strong colonial government that ultimate security rested in combining forces with other strong colonial governments. It's the classic meme--strength in numbers.

Not all colonies were buying it. Their experience with Britain taught them to be wary of central governments, especially monarchies. Although George Washington was recognized as a hero for his participation and perseverance in the Revolution, there were those who feared he'd become another King George. As we know, it didn't happen, but that was the thought at the time.

Today, people forget that the ratification of the Constitution occurred eleven years after *The Declaration of Independence* was signed in 1776. That's a long time for people to be stewing about what was to become of their grand experiment, a new country free from England. It was resolved in 1787 with the signing of the Constitution. The agreement of only nine colonies was necessary for ratification.

Hold on, I'm getting a refill. You too, Tim? Tullamore Dew is delicious. MacKenzie was right.

I don't think Mo would mind knowing I'm using his favorite chair. Reuse and recycle, right? In this case, it's continual use by his brother.. Anyway, where was I? Remind me, Tim.

Oh, yes. Soon it became evident that individual liberties needed to be spelled out. People worried that a strong central government could usurp freedoms they enjoyed in their states. But it wasn't until 1791, four years later, that the Bill of Rights was ratified. The rights are in the form of Amendments to the

Constitution and range from the first, freedom of speech and religion, to the eighteenth, prohibition. If the eighteenth hadn't been repealed by the twenty-first, we wouldn't be enjoying our drinks.

Today there are twenty-seven amendments. The last was ratified in 1992. That one's about politicians not getting paid until they're elected. It says nothing about hidden money they get from PACs and lobbyists.

Oh, by the way, what do you think about the Clark Elementary School over in New Milford being sold to the Gronks? It's been sitting idle for years. Finally, the New Milford Board of Education found a buyer--Reload Armaments, a division of the Gronk Family Industries. I heard Duke Dowd, an NRA board member was named President and CEO. I learned about Dowd when I was a member of the NRA. He's called Dead Eye Dowd. I don't have to tell you what it means. Use your imagination. Very funny, Tim! No. Dead eye doesn't mean he has partial vision. It means don't be on the wrong end of his rifle scope.

The New Milford facility is slated to manufacture Slicer magazines. They have a fifty round capacity and fit a variety of U.S. legally manufactured semi-automatic weapons. They also adapt to automatic assault weapons Gronk makes overseas. That's a questionable practice, if you ask me. But here's the thing. The New Milford property is large enough, so that the company has applied for a permit to build a firing range behind the plant.

Beyond the so-called bullet-proofed facility, looms the west side of Granite Hill which, you know, sits entirely in Roxbridge. If they get permission to operate, I hope they figure out a way to limit gun elevation, so no rounds fly over here. People scramble all over Granite Hill. Mo was up there only a month before he died.

Thundering Moses! I've gotten off track. Come back next week, Tim, and we'll get into the Second Amendment itself. We'll see if we can figure out what it means. It's stumped historians and constitutionalists up to now. I don't care about all those opinions. Let's see if you and I can arrive at an interpretation of our own based on common sense.

That's fine, sir. Put your glass in the sink on the way out. I'll take care of it later.

20

Sandy Hook

"Six of us decided to take a detour today and rerun the same twelve miles to Sandy Hook the Road Rats covered in 2012. We parked two cars there to bring us back to Roxbridge." Annie untied her running shoes.

"You ran the whole way?" asked Rob. "Up to now, the longest you've run is five miles. You must be knackered."

"Yep. I'm beat. I think I'll soak my feet. No, better yet, I'm gonna soak my whole body."

"Then Taylor must have run in Roxbridge by herself."

"Heck no! She did the whole bloody thing with me. Yikes! I said bloody. I'm starting to sound like a Scot."

Rob laughed. "To sound like an authentic lassie, you'll have to learn how to roll your r's better."

"Then I'm dead. I've never been able to get my tongue wrapped around rural." Annie put her bare feet on Rob's lap. He began massaging them.

"Try not to wrap your tongue around the r's. Let them roll out of you like a cat's purr. No problem with me, if you can't master it. By now you know I love you no matter what you sound like." He pushed his thumbs into the tendons of her insteps.

"Ouch! That hurts! Ease up, laddie!"

"I'm sorry, your highness." He gently massaged the spot he had just rolfed. "Taylor ran the whole twelve miles? Amazing! She's only twelve."

"No. Her birthday was two weeks ago. She's thirteen now. She reminded me of that many times."

"There'll come a day when she won't be so eager to tell people she's older."

"You're right, dear. But that's a few years away." Annie thought about the run. "Here's the good news. She never said *like* the whole trip. When I put five dollars on the table during Monopoly, I think I made her an offer she couldn't refuse."

Rob laughed and tickled Annie's feet. "There's more to it than that, love. She admires you, Annie. I can see it in her eyes. You've become a hero to her. I had two people like that in my life--Uncle Willie and Pipe Major Angus."

"When the Road Rats jogged to Sandy Hook in 2012, it was only two weeks after the murders had occurred at Sandy Hook Elementary," explained Annie. After her soak, Maryann continued retelling Rob about her morning run. They were in the kitchen. Rob had made tea. Maryann was recuperating. Earlier, while soaking in the tub, she realized her twelve miles amounted to 20K, a new system of distance measurements she would have to learn, if she was to continue running: 5K = 3.1 miles; 10K =

6.2 miles; 12.4 miles = 20K. She had been toying with the idea of keeping a running log and recording her daily mileage. But she also was aware that logs can turn running into compulsive behavior. *In fact*, she thought, *a log might not be a good idea.* She resumed telling Rob what she learned about the Sandy Hook shootings.

"The course we followed today mirrored the run the Road Rats took in 2012. Their effort was only ten days after the shootings. A Road Rat regular, Bruce Skoog, organized the event and set off with one hundred twenty runners. Through Bruce's efforts, the Road Rats collected more than $5,000 to donate to the Sandy Hook Memorial Fund. They were among the earliest contributors to the charity. 'Before we leave Roxbridge,' Bruce had urged them, 'let's agree. No discussions about guns today. Okay? No pro-gun, no anti-gun sentiment. Save your breath for the twelve miles and the hills. Today let's be pro-run.'"

"I remember the day of the shootings, love," said Rob. "I was teaching a lesson about the rain cycle to a bunch of fourth graders in Hoboken, New Jersey. I was at the Kelley Elementary School. It was a nice place. It appeared to me to be inclusive. It had children of all ethnic and racial groups.

"While there, by chance I learned Kelley's minority population was higher than the average in New Jersey, and their teacher-pupil ratio was lower than the average. They accepted all students: bilingual, special education, and children receiving lunch assistance. No charter school cherry-picking at Kelley. Their arms were wide open to everyone. It was a good place for kids to feel safe and be nurtured. Oops, I'm sorry for getting off track. In Connecticut in a similar setting, the school sanctity I witnessed in Kelley was shattered."

Rob took a breath to calm himself. "Again, I'm sorry, I went off on a tangent about Kelley. But that's where I was when Sandy Hook occurred."

"That's understandable, honey. After what you told me about Dunblane, I can understand why you were upset. This time, the tragedy was close to home."

"Aye, that's true. Dunblane shattered me, of course. That's where I grew up. But Sandy Hook was in the country of my choice, just down the road. I began to wonder, is there no place safe from this savagery?"

Maryann nodded her head in agreement. "It gets to the issue of mental health, Rob, how as a society we persist in neglecting mental health initiatives. It's convenient to ignore dangerous deviances. Look at who our country picked to be President. He was so far to the right of the bell-curve of normalcy, he was off the charts. He was bound to self-destruct. Our country elected an insane person. Shame on us!"

Rob rubbed his forehead in bewilderment. He looked at Annie and once more realized how much he loved her. Their shared beliefs and understanding of the human condition were incontrovertibly entwined. He could not imagine his life without her.

"The gunman in Newtown was seriously deranged," he said. "No therapist would ever have denied that. It was his mother who refused to accept the signs of his mental illness and allowed him to wander around without therapy."

Annie could tell Rob was becoming emotional. He was

gulping, words catching in his throat. "Rob, dear, his mother was wacko, too. She encouraged a mentally unstable child to become familiar with guns. The .22 caliber rifle he used to kill her was an entry level gun she gave to him. It was the kind of firearm you give to kids to teach them marksmanship and safety. It was ironic he used it to kill her."

"Aye, Annie. The whole story is so, so sad. He killed her and then took the assault weapon she owned and turned it on children. Nobody knows why, honey. He left no notes. The only clues are hidden in the troubled relationship between mother and child. The mother turned out to be unstable. The child certainly was so. What a nightmare!" Rob blotted a tear off his cheek. "Honey, I'm sorry for becoming emotional."

"That's okay, dear, I understand. Tragedy is the price we pay for allowing untreated mentally ill people to live among us," she said. "Those two needed professional help. Twenty children dead. Six adults cut down trying to protect them. The murderer and his mother gone. The facts are hard to comprehend. My biggest fear is that it's likely to happen again." She pushed her feet into her slippers, kissed Rob on the forehead, and left the room.

Rob thought about Annie's departing prediction. Aye, he agreed, more shootings were inevitable. Too many people were mentally unstable. Too many people were irrationally angry. Too many people owned dangerous weapons. It was a formula for disaster. He admitted to himself that as he aged, he would have little impact changing these trends. But he also vowed to continue the love and tolerance he had for friends and family.

Being the best father to Jake and the most devoted husband to Annie were his life's missions. He remembered the parental strains he had witnessed in his youth. As a result, for him there was nothing more divine than a close-knit family.

21
Lars

Tim, I understand perfectly. We'll lay off the hard stuff today and stick with coffee. Sometimes a headache is the price you pay for enjoying a few drinks. We don't need that today. We're considering constitutional language. That's enough to generate a migraine.

Yes, Ruggles is here. He's outside on a line. He needs some vitamin D.

I'm glad you returned with your copy of the Constitution. If you had forgotten, I was prepared. I found a duplicate at the end of The Federalist Papers. It was included as an addendum. Now I have two. I'm doubly armed. Armed! Oops, bad pun!

When I give this talk, people wonder how I became an expert on the Constitution. The truth is, I'm not. For years I've been educating people only about the Second Amendment because it's the foundation of a fundamental right I happen to cherish--gun ownership. But I don't believe in unregulated gun ownership. I think common sense should prevail. I'll get into that when we revisit textualism, originalism, and contextualism.

The NRA proclaims that guns don't kill people, people do. That's true in the case of .22 caliber rimfire target rifles. But even then there are exceptions--single murders. That was the case in Newtown when Adam Lanza shot his mother with a target rifle. But no one uses a bolt-action Remington for mass killings. That's when bad actors get their hands on AR-15 Bushmasters to murder people in large numbers. That's wrong. In that case the gun's as much of a murderer as the perpetrator using it.

'The Second Amendment is frequently titled, The Right to Bear Arms. In fact, the Amendment has no title. To begin our discussion, it would be helpful if we read it together. In your Bantam Edition it's on page seventy-seven. I'll read it aloud. You follow along.

A well regulated Militia, being necessary to the security of a free State, the right of the people to keep and bear Arms, shall not be infringed.

As we agreed the last time you were here, Tim, the first ten amendments were written to protect the rights of citizens living in the states. There was no guarantee that this right extended to the federal level. The federal government was nascent, mostly unorganized.

The Second Amendment is about weapon ownership. In 1776, the American army was a coalition of colonial volunteer fighters. Many soldiers stayed on the battle lines for only a short time before returning home to tend to crops and family. When they mustered out, they didn't turn their muskets into a U.S. armory, as is the case today. They owned their weapons. Their flintlocks were tools they needed back home as they contended with the non-military dangers of their time: marauding Indians, bands of highwaymen, pillaging fur-trappers, dangerous animals, fraudulent land speculators.

As a colony resident, they were required to own a firearm. Whether fighting for Rhode Island or reinforcing the federals, the presumption was their personal weapon would accompany them into battle. Powder and lead had to be supplied by the combatant. Centrally stored colonial munitions were rapidly confiscated by the Redcoats as the war became hot. In a nutshell, successful federal action was predicated on the goodwill of colonial militias to work together beyond their home boundaries.

At the time, the idea of an all-powerful and globally dominant America could only have been an impossible dream. Even after the revolution, England was ascendant. Other than getting a black eye in America, at the beginning of the Nineteenth Century, Great Britain ruled most of the earth and all of the seven seas.

Tim, let's take a brief look at the Second Amendment's phrases and words. Here's where language comes in. We'll parse the written words starting with the first four, *a well regulated Militia."*

This refers to state militias. In the early federal system on a wartime footing, colonial militias were amalgamated to form a national force. The federal government had no standing army of its own and no power to conscript colonials. Federal fire-power was dependent on the good-will of colonial volunteers.

Sometimes, amalgamations are for purposes of military efficiency and thrift. In other cases, governments overreach to acquire more control. Nowadays, in our country the state militias--our national guards--are second cousins to federal forces, the Army, Navy, Air Force, and Marines.

Moving on, Tim, let's consider the phrase, *security of a free State*. Since the word *State* is capitalized, I think it's fair to assume the phrase refers to an entity larger than any one of the original colonies. This theory falls under the idea of contextualism. What the word State meant at first--a separate colony--evolved over time to mean all of America. By the time the Bill of Rights was ratified, the idea of the United States of America had become well understood. Fealty to the new nation often eclipsed state loyalties in places like Vermont and New Jersey.

Let me diverge for a moment, Tim. Sadly, we know federal loyalties took a backseat to state allegiance as the Civil War approached. Robert E. Lee demonstrated stronger devotion to Virginia than to the country he had sworn to defend. It drove him to become the ultimate traitor. A West Point education and oaths to serve the United States disappeared in his misguided effort leading the secessionist military. Whether scholars are ready to admit it or not, his actions validated slavery, at least to the landed gentry in the South.

The southern poor foolishly jumped into the fray with nothing to gain. They had no slaves. But they had a warped image of southern gentility and dixie loyalty. To my mind, Tim, Lee and the rest of his band of officers weren't heroes. They were all traitors.

The South likes to call the Civil War, The War of Northern Aggression. Can you believe it? South Carolina fired the first shot attacking Fort Sumter. Hell! It happened on April 12, 1861! That's just seventy-seven years to the day before my birthday in 1938. I'm an April twelfth baby. Then the Confederates had the cojones to blame the North. After the southern atrocities at Andersonville, we should have hung the whole lousy mess of them.

Aside from the federal army, in your opinion, Tim, is there a clear hero in the Civil War calamity? Yes, I agree. We both know who he is--Abraham Lincoln. With his desire to let bygones be bygones, he urged reconciliation and forgiveness between the North and South. Lincoln was a tragic figure in many ways. But in my opinion, he was a Christ-like hero in all ways.

Jeez, Tim! I went on a roll. I need to get back on track. But first I'll refresh our coffee, and then we can consider the word *arms*. Okay with you? Now I need to stand and pace. I hope you don't mind. It helps me think. I've been sitting too long.

★

What does arms mean in the Second Amendment? In order to learn, Tim, refer to any textbook describing weapons of the Eighteenth Century. The word arms found in the Second Amendment does not only mean guns. It includes weapons in a much broader definition: knives, swords, spike bayonets, and spears. Firearms back in the day meant muskets, the blunderbuss, Brown Bess, and pistols, to name a few. Both swords and flintlocks were the arms referenced in the Second Amendment.

Those were the weapons of the time. As such, they were what was referenced in the Constitution. I argue we ought to think of arms in the original sense using textualist logic. There was no evidence that arms of that time might evolve into today's weapons. When an originalist leaning justice ignores the original meaning of arms and votes in favor of high-tech weaponry, he or she has trashed their judicial philosophy and shown themselves to be opportunists.

When we get together next, I suggest we discuss how war antiques have morphed into Twenty-first Century hi-tech killing machines. Okay? I may have to revert back to whisky to open that can of worms.

To finish up today, consider the final phrase, *shall not be infringed*. It seems pretty clear the federal government can't deny ownership of a weapon. It also means the federal government can't co-opt a state's requirement to own one. If a state decides, it can vote to change its ownership regulations, but the feds can't mandate nor prohibit it. If that was to happen, it would ultimately be up to the Supreme Court to decide if the regulation was constitutional. Although no longer necessary, many states hold onto their weapon prerogative, still nursing a nagging fear of an intrusion by the central government.

Case in point: Texas, 2015. Governor Greg Abbott ordered the Texas National Guard to monitor a U.S. military training exercise in the Lone Star State. The operation was called Jade Helm. I don't know where they get those crazy titles. Anyway, poor, deluded Abbott feared the exercises were part of a secret plot to impose federal military rule on Texas. He said other states were in danger, too. If I could guess, the only hardship Texas faced was a sizeable loss of beer enjoyed by the troops when the war games were over.

In a way, the Fourth Amendment prohibiting unreasonable

searches and seizures, supports the Second Amendment. If you have a firearm in your residence, neither state nor federal authorities can barge in your front door and seize your weapon. The critical word in this case: unreasonable. One person's unreasonable is another's reasonable due to a whole bunch of factors. Harboring a criminal, plotting an insurrection, hiding a murder weapon, and threatening a neighbor are all reasonable justifications to search for and seize a weapon. All it takes is a warrant from a judge granting permission. In certain imminently dangerous situations, a warrantless seizure of firearms can be done to protect the public.

Phew! Enough for today, Tim. Write down any questions and concerns for when we meet again. In addition to trying to arrive at answers to your questions, we'll continue thinking about the concept of originalism. How does it apply to the Second Amendment? As I said earlier, next time I'll uncork the the good stuff. We may need it to deal with a range of opinions more complex than a Rubik's Cube.

Have a safe trip home, young man. You know by now to ignore any gunshots you might hear driving by Granite Hill. They're from that damned firing range in New Milford on the other side of the ridgeline. Sometimes the sound carries on the breeze. They're supposed to be closed at this time of day, but there are always a few hard-asses unwilling to go home. They spoil it for everyone.

22

Plumbum Mortiferum

"George Peters phoned," called Maryann. "He said Taylor is on her way here." Annie was on a mission to clean the two second floor bathrooms.

"Is he driving her?" Rob asked from their bedroom. He removed the last of the bedroom's incandescent light bulbs and screwed in an energy saver.

"No, she's cycling. He said she wanted to talk with me. When I asked what it was about and he told me, I said she'd have to ask you."

"Me? What does she want to know?"

"I'm not sure, but it has something to do with lead."

"Lead? Like lead in the periodic table?"

"I think so. We'll find out when she gets here. Oh, by the way, George thanked us for watching her while he and Abby were in Rhode Island. They had a lovely time. The wind quieted enough to let the ferry run on Saturday. He also said since staying with us, Taylor's stopped using the word like. He wondered if we had anything to do with it."

Maryann moved to the second bathroom.

"Did you tell him you bribed her?"

"No. He said she started listening to herself on tape. I'm sure that had more to do with it than my five dollars."

Taylor Peters stood on her pedals as she pumped up the driveway. Her ponytail poked through the rear of her helmet and bounced like a mare's tail batting away horseflies. It flew left and right with each push on the cranks. Sometimes it spun in circles.

Maryann saw that Taylor was looking more and more like her dad. George Peters was tall and lean and had a complexion that always darkened in the summer. He purposely accented his coloring by wearing yellow shirts advertising his business, Peter's Perfect Plumbing. Printed on company trucks below the business name was their pitch: Having stoppage problems? Call us. We'll plunge right in.

Taylor reminded Maryann of the CNN newscaster, Erin Burnett. Maryann thought Burnett was beautiful. Her eyes sparkled, and she had a full mouth that appeared to be perpetually smiling. Her face was well balanced with a strong nose. She was blessed with rich and healthy, long dark hair. Maryann thought Taylor had a chance to look like Burnett as she matured, although her nose hadn't yet made up its mind what it wanted to do. Also, Taylor was likely to be taller than Burnett when her growing spurts called a permanent time-out.

Maryann realized she had fallen into a trap ensnaring many people. It was more lazy thinking. Describing someone by comparing their looks to a TV or movie personality was brainless effort. Once she had been told she looked like Jennifer Lawrence. She admitted to herself there was some resemblance, but her short stature always muted any pleasure in the comparison.

"Hi, Taylor. Much traffic today?"

"Only two cars, Annie. Oh, and a pickup pulling a livestock trailer. It was filled with sheep."

"Your dad called," affirmed Maryann. "He said you wanted to talk with me about something. Lead, I think he said. What's it all about?"

"A bunch of older kids at school said they want to demonstrate in New Milford at the gun range. They're going to try and shut it down. They asked me if I wanted to join them. I might. But first I want to know about lead. I know the range is a dangerous place. It probably should be shut down for that reason alone. They said there's also the issue of lead. I want to know how lead fits in."

"I'll get Rob. He'll be able to tell you."

"Yes, Taylor, I heard about the demonstration. The teachers were talking about it at lunch." Rob flattened cardboard light bulb boxes and stacked them for recycling. The old incandescent bulbs went into the garbage. He washed his hands.

"Yeah, Rob. The kids are planning to get students from other schools to join them. New Milford High School is especially interested."

"Annie can help you understand your rights and obligations if you demonstrate. But why are you asking about lead?"

"When I was at the library with Mom, I saw a book someone returned. It was called, *Toxic Truth: A Scientist, a Doctor, and the Battle over Lead*. It caught my eye because on the cover there's a photo of a baby chewing on a crib. Mom let me check it out. It's a pretty good story, but there's science stuff I don't understand. I heard of lead poisoning but didn't know how complicated the topic is. There's lead all over the New Milford range property. It could get into the Berkshire River."

Rob studied her for a moment, measuring her maturity. "I'm not an expert on lead poisoning," he said, "but I can give you a few facts. How much do you know?"

"Dad told me lead was in the solder he used years ago. Lead makes solder easier to melt. He said in 1986, the EPA banned lead based solder. Now he uses solder with tin and silver or tin and anthony."

Rob laughed. "It's antimony, not anthony. That's right. Lead in solder can leach into water and poison it. If you have an older house, you may have lead-solder pipe joints. In that case, homeowners are advised to let the water run for ten or fifteen seconds before drinking it. Running helps to flush the pipes."

"Our house was built when I was in first grade."

"Then you're all set, Taylor. You live in a newer house."

"What does lead do, Rob? Why should we be worried about it?"

"Excellent question. As I said, I'm not a poison specialist, so there's no point in my speculating about how lead interacts with human tissue. Just let me say ingestion can cause nervous system damage and stunted growth in children. Look at the uproar lead in city pipes caused in Flint, Michigan. What a mess! I do know it can damage adult kidneys and sometimes causes reproductive problems. I assume you know about reproduction, Taylor?"

"Of course."

"Until scientists started making a connection between lead and human illness, many products containing it were routinely manufactured. Pewter plates and mugs used in colonial time contained lead. It was added to gasoline to make engines run smoother. Household paint dries quickly with lead as an additive. I'm guessing the book you found tells the story of the discovery between lead and poor health."

Taylor buckled and unbuckled her cycling helmet thinking about what Rob had said. "What about bullets, Rob? Aren't they made of lead?"

"Aye, the projectile part, the slug. The National Park Service lobbied both congress and President Obama urging them to outlaw lead in national parks. Fishing sinkers, too. It seems there was enough spent ammunition lying around that birds, animals, and fish were suffering. One of the last things Obama did before leaving office was to ban lead ammunition and sinkers in national parks."

"That's good!" said Taylor. "Too bad it took so long."

Rob shrugged in resignation. "The sad thing is, Taylor, when Trump became President, he and his cabinet reversed many of the laws protecting the environment. Lead is allowed in the national parks again."

She slumped as if she had been punched in the stomach. "That stinks! That makes me mad! I'm definitely going to the protest and carry a no-lead sign. I'll have to think up a good slogan."

★

"Rob told me you're going to New Milford to protest at the gun range." Maryann was sitting in the kitchen practicing knitting. She didn't sew, but maybe working with wool would prove therapeutic. Winter was nearing. New toques would be appreciated.

"Yes, I'm positive. Now that Rob told me about the dangers of lead, I'm going to protest against it. I figured out a sign I'm going to make. Three men are standing side by side. One is covering his mouth, one is covering his eyes, and the third is covering his ears. Each one has a letter printed on his shirt: E-P-A. The caption is: Let the EPA Eat Lead." She looked at Maryann for approval.

"I love it, kiddo!" laughed Annie. "Nothing seditious about that sign. Go for it."

"What does seditious mean?"

"Doing or saying something that causes people to riot, especially against the government. Your sign's not calling for an insurrection, you're merely inviting the EPA to lunch."

"Annie, what are my rights about demonstrating? Will I get in trouble?"

"There's no way to predict what might happen, honey. If you stay within the law and obey police orders, you should be okay. I'll be right back. I'm getting my copy of the Constitution."

★

"The major body of the Constitution deals with how the government of the United States is organized. Our system of government is divided into three parts. Do you know them?" Annie quizzed Taylor, probing to learn the depth of the young woman's knowledge.

"Yes. I read about it." Taylor ticked off her fingers as she named them. "Executive branch. That's the President, the cabinet, and all the agencies. The judicial branch is the courts, judges, and departments like the FBI and Attorney General. The legislative branch is congress. Its job is to make laws and pass rules to keep the country running."

Maryann nodded her head in agreement. "That's good. You understand. But your right to demonstrate is not defined in the organizational part of the Constitution. It's in the Bill of Rights--the first ten additions to the Constitution."

"I've read the Bill of Rights, too" Taylor said. "We went over them in civics class."

"You have? Good for you! Good for your teacher! Let's look at it again. As far as free speech and the right to demonstrate, it's all there in the First Amendment. Go ahead. You read it." Annie handed the Constitution to Taylor. She held it close to her face and read out loud:

Congress shall make no law respecting an establishment of religion, or prohibiting the free exercise thereof; or abridging the freedom of speech, or of the press, or the right of the people to assemble, and to petition the Government for a redress of grievances.

Maryann asked, "How many guarantees do you see in this amendment?" She looked down at her knitting and puzzled over a knit--knit, purl--purl combination. Since she was making no progress with hats, she had switched to scarves. She waited for Taylor's response.

Taylor studied the text. "Let's see: freedom of religion, freedom of the press, free speech, and two more. There are five."

"Yes," said Maryann ripping out an errant purl. "The one that gives you the right to go to New Milford and demonstrate is . . . ?"

". . . freedom of speech!"

"Sure, it's a no-brainer. And the fourth guarantee is about assembly. You are allowed to get together with like-minded people to demonstrate. The fifth right gives you permission to seek the redress of grievances. Here's what that means. If you're harmed by government actions and think you can prove it, you may sue the government for damages. But in all five rights, they must be pursued peacefully. That's what the first amendment says."

Taylor considered Annie's words for a moment. "That means I can demonstrate in New Milford about lead even though others may be demonstrating against an unsafe gun range?"

"Yep."

"Cool!"

"Just don't do anything stupid," warned Annie. "If the other group gets unruly and breaks the law, you get out of there. You don't want to wind up in the slammer."

Taylor agreed. "You're right. I don't have time for that. I have homework to do."

23

The Cartoonist

"Hey, Mom. I've decided to become a cartoonist. Look!" Jake handed Maryann four sheets of paper. On one he had neatly drawn three side-by-side rectangles. He explained how he had figured out how to use the computer printer to make replicas. That way he didn't have to redraw the boxes every time he had a new idea. He said he planned to keep one master page in reserve.

He gave his mother the three completed cartoons. "These are my first," he said. He watched Maryann's face for a sign of a smile. She studied them trying to get the joke.

"I'm a little slow today," she said. "Explain them to me."

"When we lived in New York, you said we were going to the sticks when we came to Connecticut. That's why I named my cartoon, *Sticktown*."

Suddenly, a wide smile spread across Maryann's face. "Of course! I get it now. I couldn't figure out what all the up-down lines were cluttering up the pictures. Now I see. I should have paid closer attention to the title."

Each box depicted a fifth grader's concept of a dense thicket of saplings. Two sets of bulging eyes protruded from between trees. The trees looked like pretzel sticks aligned vertically. The eyes expressed the concerns of the speaker and the listener.

Eyes in the first box said to the other eyes, "Mom told me we were moving to the sticks." Eyes in the middle box asked, "Are you happy here"? Worried eyes in the third box said, "I'll be happy when I can find my way home."

Jake showed his second cartoon. The layout was the same as the first, but the gag line was different.

First box eyes said, "Hey, Jake. You own a gun?" The reply from the second box was, "No, but I sure hope to get one." Third box eyes said, "Until you do, we'll use my shotgun. It's double-barreled. We can share."

By now Maryann was chuckling. She was surprised to learn Jake had an understanding of subtle punch lines. Up-to-now, his jokes had always been broad puns or gags. To her, these new cartoons were nuanced and conveyed insight. Apparently, Jake had an ear for language.

"I have one more, Mom. Then I'm getting to work and make others. I have lots of ideas."

"Okay, dear. Let's see your last one."

First eyes said, "Hey, Mom. You said you'd take me to the gun range." Second eyes responded, "I said I'd think about it later." Third eyes said, "Time's up, Mom. It's later."

By now, Maryann had progressed from a chuckle to a belly laugh. She remembered Jake being annoyed with her for using evasive language. She had promised not to say, *I'll think about it,* and *I'll tell you later.* That was when Taylor had been a house guest.

"These are good cartoons, honey. But two of them are about guns. I didn't know you were interested in firearms."

"I'm not sure if I'm interested in guns, Mom. Some kids in my class told me their parents took them to the firing range. I'd like to see for myself. I may not like it, but I might."

"I have to admit. Your thinking is good," said Rob, entering the room. "I'm not a gun fan, but you have a right to decide for yourself. You didn't have the chance to pick your name when you were born, so now's the time to decide about other things."

"If I could have picked my own name, I'd have chosen Tarzan," said Jake. He laughed, then skipped upstairs to resume his cartooning career.

"Hey, Rob," said Jake returning to the first floor. "You used to write lots of poems. Remember the one about dinosaurs? You recited it when we were in the back field looking at nature."

"Aye, laddie, I do."

"You dreamed up any more?"

"Aye, I have. One."

"What's it about?"

"With all the talk about guns around here, I made up a silly poem about weapons."

"Read it."

"A *please* would be nice, lad."

"Okay, please read it."

"Better than that, I'll recite it. It's called, *I Love Guns.*"
"Cool!"

I want to shoot a gun today / To aim and pull the trigger
To feel the recoil on my arm / I thank God for my finger.

I hear the blast in my ears / The ringin' of delight
No matter that I'm goin' deaf / I'm ready for a fight.

Ricochets careen around / No tellin' where they'll fall
I stand behind the firin' line / Safe behind a wall.

Protect our right to own a gun / It's an institution
I'm a brave militia-man / States the Constitution.

"It's funny, Rob. You're good at writing poems. Now I'm really excited to go to the firing range. Maybe they'll have a bazooka I can try."

24

Lars

Last time we talked, Tim, we agreed to meet again to continue to discuss the concept of originalism as it applies to the Constitution. To reiterate, sometimes the term textualism is used. In order to understand how either term is connected to firearms, we need to figure out what the two words actually mean. But before I begin lecturing you, how about some beer and nuts? Wait a minute, last time I said we'd have some good stuff. You'll need some fortifying to survive my rant. Besides you're leaving Roxbridge, so it's let's make it a kind of going away party.

Here's my take on the puzzle, Tim. In my opinion, originalism refers to the meaning of words or phrases as written by whomever the authors were at the time they were written. In our case, we're talking about the framers of the Constitution. I think I alluded to this the last time we met.

So, for example, if one of the framers said arms, he was

referring to the weapons in use at that time. If he said press, he was referring to printed newspapers, broadsheets, letters, and books. Radio, television, social media, and all other forms of what today is considered press would have been as unthinkable to the framers as men walking on the moon. Likewise, modern arms such as assault weapons, machine guns, machine pistols, and sniper rifles were beyond the ken of men of that era. Those tools hadn't been invented. Arms to a framer meant a single-shot, muzzle loading, smooth bore musket, a knife, or a sword. I think all reasonable people would agree with my analysis. You and I came to that understanding last time.

Originalism means what was understood by people at the time the Constitution and Bill of Rights were written. The latter was approved in 1791. The Constitution was not written with science fiction in mind. There was no mention of the internet, rocket ships, supermarkets, or nuclear bombs. You with me, Tim?

Okay. Then along came the Constitution interpreters. They were scholars who looked closely at the meaning of what was written. Depending on their political philosophies, they either held to a strict meaning of the words insisting word interpretation must be limited to original intent. Or they insisted the words had to be applied to an evolving society, changing as science advanced and the culture matured.

Sadly, we have lower court and Supreme Court Justices who flip-flop all the time in their philosophies. If an issue comports with a justice's political views, he or she will take an originalist position or, maybe, an interpretive position. It depends. The justice vacillates between two legal philosophies to suit his or her personal preferences at the time. It's not unusual for a justice to cite original intent as the reason for a decision one week then change ships the next week and embrace modernism. In my opinion, that approach is lazy and weak-minded jurisprudence. I can think of a deceased justice who arrogantly boasted his thinking was superior to the thinking of his fellow justices, even though his logic had about as much consistency as a melting stick of butter.

It sounds as if I'm picking on the men and women on the Supreme Court. I admit, to a degree I am. But my disdain for philosophies of convenience applies to others--political scientists--certainly politicians. Add religious demigods to the list. All try to sway us with manifestos that suddenly disappear when a more promising ideology comes along.

As I've mentioned, I admit I'm a supporter of the second amendment. I believe in the right to own a firearm, particularly when that firearm is used as a practical tool. I do not support unfettered access to modern weapons only suitable for murdering masses of people. So, in that case, I support the originalist view that guns ought to be limited to those most closely replicating arms in use at the end of the Eighteenth Century. That leaves plenty of models available for bird and deer hunting, target shooting, and self-defense, if you feel threatened.

I do not support the National Rifle Association. The NRA is nothing more than a shill and mouthpiece for the weapons industry. NRA executives are paid handsomely to lobby for the unrestricted right of gun manufacturers to produce whatever killing tool is most profitable. You may not agree with me, Tim, but I think the NRA and others of similar persuasions are evil.

This bunch of outlaws makes all reasonable and responsible gun owners guilty by association. I don't like it.

My dear friend! You've been a great companion to Mo and me. Mo mentioned your name many times, Tim. And for many of the hours I've spent watching over Mo's house since his passing, you've been generous with your time listening to another old man. I'm sorry you're leaving, but happy for your new job. I hope working in Massachusetts will be as good as working in Connecticut.

Before you leave town, I wonder if you'd do me a favor? I understand you know Raul Black through professional association meetings. My sister, Q, will be visiting here from time-to-time. May she phone you to get Mr. Black's phone number? I don't have it. She's worried about what's happening in Connecticut schools. Like you, Black's a public school educator with actual front line experience with kids. I think you know he lives here in town.

Q went to the same college as the new State Commissioner of Education, Constance Van Cortland. Q's furious with Van Cortland's negative comments about public schools and her praise for the private sector, including charter schools. My sister went to public schools, as did Mo and I. Van Cortland's a private school product. It would be helpful if my sister could share her concerns about Van Cortland with Mr. Black.

Yes, you will? Great! I'm delighted you'll do that. I heard Raul's a great guy with a sweet family. I'll tell her to phone you next week when she's in Roxbridge. I hope you get to meet her before you leave. Then you'll have met all three Kleins.

Charter Schools

★

The Third Folio

"Human history becomes more and more a race
between education and catastrophe."

H.G. Wells

25

The Parent-Teacher Conference

"Good morning, Mrs. MacKenzie. Welcome! Please come in." Helen Dawson stood.

"Thanks, Mrs. Dawson. Where would you like me to sit?"

"I have a chair ready for you. Why don't you join me here at the table."

Helen Dawson, Jake's fifth grade teacher, swept her hand over the round table in front of her. She sat. Three extra chairs were positioned around the circle in case others planned to attend. Meetings could become confrontational if both parents showed up accompanied by a lawyer or child advocate. *Why start off with insufficient seating?* Dawson reasoned.

"I'm sorry the seats are so low," Helen said. "They were designed for children. Adults have to be prepared to talk over their knees." Whenever Helen saw Annie MacKenzie, she always admired Jake's mom for her spunkiness and youthful beauty. Today was no different.

"That's not a problem for me," Annie said grinning, "but if my husband was here, he'd be like a praying mantis sitting on a thistle, all legs and joints trying not to get impaled on a flower spike."

Dawson laughed. "Yes, I know Rob. He and I are on the school board's curriculum advisory committee. The high school's in session today, so I figured he wouldn't be with you. Oh, by the way, Mrs. MacKenzie, please call me Helen. I'll feel more comfortable that way."

"Fine, Helen. In return, I'm Annie. If we're going to work together this year, let's do it as a team rather than parent versus teacher."

"I agree wholeheartedly, Annie. You voiced my sentiments exactly. I wish all parents felt the same way."

Dawson slid a folder of Jake's papers in Annie's direction. "These are samples of Jake's work up to this point. I've saved papers that best illustrate the progress he's making, as well as one that shows an area needing attention."

Helen sensed Annie was anxious to open the folder. "Before we look at Jake's work," she said, "if you don't mind, I'd like to ask you a few questions."

Annie's eyebrows rose. "Okay, that's fine with me," she said, wondering what was coming next.

"Parents know their children better than anyone," Helen began. "They want what's best for their kids. Most parents have an idea what direction they'd like their children to follow--what dreams to pursue. All want their children to succeed and be happy."

Annie nodded vigorously, pleased with Helen's astute understanding of the relationship between parent and child. "I agree, Helen. You're absolutely right about that." She glanced at the folder.

Helen continued. "What interests or talents do you see in Jake? I'm sure you know what makes him tick. What do you see that gets in the way of his intellectual growth?"

Annie laughed. "What makes him tick? Oh, my! Everything makes him tick, except homework. But he's getting better with that. Last year with Ms Baldridge at the elementary school, and now this year in the middle school with you, seem to have changed things."

"Yes, I see growth there," said Helen smiling. "His assignments are handed in on time."

Annie detailed Jake's pursuits. "My boy's very inquisitive. He asks lots of questions, almost non-stop. Rob's piqued his curiosity about science in general and the environment in particular. He loves hiking Conservation Trust properties, and he climbs every boulder he sees. Oh, yes. He's started collecting *Far Side* cartoon books. Jake has a weird sense of humor, so he understands Gary Larson's irony and whimsy."

"Does he see much of his real father? Sometimes he appears wistful when family issues are discussed."

Annie shrugged. "His father died in a car accident. He doesn't talk about it. Rob's wrapped his arms around Jake as if Jake was his own son. Rob's the father every kid should have."

"Oh goodness! I didn't know. Jake's said nothing. I'm so sorry to hear about it. Please accept my condolences, Annie."

"Thank you, Helen. We all seem to be doing fine, including Jake."

After a moment of silence thinking about Jake's loss and apparent coping, Dawson probed deeper. "Do you watch much TV? Does Jake have access to electronic devices?"

"No, not much TV in our home. Rob and I urge Jake to read. All three of us usually have a book going, and we discuss what we're reading during meals. And as you probably know, when Jake's not reading or fooling with his cartoon books or miniature Scottish soldier collection, he's constantly drawing."

Helen smiled and nodded, recognizing Annie's astute understanding of her child. "Annie, you've found the right formula to help Jake shine even brighter. You and Rob are attentive parents willing to help him succeed. You encourage him to read," she said smiling, "and I'm continually amused by his drawing and cartooning. In my opinion, Jake's got talent, and it's not hidden. But the biggest advantage for Jake is your willingness to work with his teachers. You and I want exactly the same thing for him: his intellectual growth, his willingness to consider history as more than facts and dates, and to develop a curiosity about what might happen in the future."

Helen paused to consider Annie's reaction to what she just said. "Both you and I have roles to play in educating Jake. Up to now you've been willing to share the responsibility with his teachers. That's perfect!"

Annie's face shone with pride and happiness. Helen sensed she had delivered a message any parent would want to hear. *If only more people were involved in their children's schooling,* she thought, *partnering with teachers rather than seeing them as adversaries.*

"Thank you for being so kind," said Annie. "I agree we need to be a team. Rob and I support you. He especially knows how difficult teaching can be when parent involvement is missing."

Annie briefly considered where they stood with Jake, then asked an important question. "Is there anything more we can do now to keep Jake growing?"

"There is," replied Helen. "That's why I asked you to bring Jake to school with you. I assume he's here somewhere?" "He's out on the playground climbing on the apparatus."

Helen laughed. "Oh, yes . . . the rock climber! When I'm on recess duty, I constantly remind him to use the equipment the way it was meant to be used. He acts like he's a contestant on American Ninja Warrior."

Annie frowned. "Unfortunately, that's one of the few shows he's seen on TV. I'll get on his case about it."

"Good, Annie. I don't want him getting hurt. But, I admit, he's fun to watch."

Helen switched topics. "I have a suggestion. Let's get Jake in here and set up a goal for him to pursue for the remainder of the year--just one goal. We'll discuss the idea with him, and if he agrees, we'll write it up. All three of us will sign-off. Does that make sense?"

Annie appeared doubtful. "I'm a lawyer, Helen. If we have a mutually agreed upon goal, each of us will have to spell out our responsibilities in detail. A written goal can get long and complicated, like a contract."

"Then let's not make it a contract," suggested Helen. "Let's keep it simple. My responsibility is to teach, your responsibility is to encourage, and Jake's responsibility is to try."

"I don't know," said Annie sounding skeptical. "I don't know whether Jake will buy into this."

"There's only one way to find out, Annie. Please round him up and come back in. I have an idea for a goal he's capable of accomplishing."

Annie placed her hand on Jake's folder, anxious to see what it contained. "Don't you want to go through his work with me before I bring him in?"

"No. I think the three of us ought to do it together."

When Annie was gone, Helen had a few minutes to reflect on the meeting so far. What a lovely mother Jake had! She was so easy to deal with.

Helen was glad she had learned the art of listening and compromising. As a result, her parent-teacher conferences rarely reached loggerheads. Fellow teachers told her horror stories of meetings that had turned into shouting matches and threats. Almost always the cause was the teacher hardening his or her position, feeling threatened, and not understanding the parent's point of view. For some teachers, no amount of training resulted in better meeting management.

Jake barged into the room, Annie trailed behind. "Hey, Mrs. Dawson," said Jake, in an outside voice, "am I in trouble?"

Annie shushed him. "Please quiet your voice."

Helen laughed. "No, Jake, not at all. Your mom and I have

an idea to discuss with you, something you can try for the rest of the year."

"Am I failing? I thought I was doing okay. Rob helped me improve my writing."

"Your writing's improved a lot, Jake," Helen agreed. "Annie, now you can look at the samples of Jake's work I've saved." Annie opened the folder. Jake peeked in. "You can see he has the multiplication tables memorized."

"Seven times eight equals fifty-six" interrupted Jake. "Rob taught me about multiplicative inverses."

"Hush, honey, let Mrs. Dawson finish."

"Jake was especially observant when we used microscopes to study swamp water. He gets high praise from Mr. Flynn in P.E. and Mrs. Bernard in art. Their evaluations are in the folder. But the last example is where we ought to consider our goal. Jake, tell your mom what the assignment was."

"Oh, yeah, I remember. We read a story about the life of Frederick Douglass. Then we wrote a report about him. That's my report, Mom." Jake pointed at the paper Annie was holding. "It was for English and history. 'Two birds with one stone,' Mrs. Dawson said. Hey! I thought I did okay?" Jake looked surprised at Helen, as if he had been double-crossed.

Helen watched Annie's reaction, then answered Jake. "You did pretty well," she affirmed, "but you can do better. I'll explain it to you." She put Jake's work in front of him, pointing to paragraphs as she spoke.

"Through the whole paper, Jake, you listed all the dates and facts accurately. That's excellent! I found only one comma in the wrong place and one period missing. That's good work, too. I make those mistakes all the time. You with me so far?"

"Sure, but what did I miss?"

"The assignment was to write about Douglass, and what you thought of his struggle to escape slavery and become a famous abolitionist and orator. You got his life's details fine, but you didn't offer your opinions or feelings about the man's accomplishments."

"Sometimes people tell me to keep my opinions to myself!"

"Does your mom say that?"

"No."

"Does Rob say that?"

"No."

"Well, I don't know who's saying that to you, but your opinions are valuable. When you write, I want you to express your feelings and opinions about the topic. That's your goal."

"Really? I won't get into trouble opinionating?"

"No, you will not." Helen laughed.

Annie enthusiastically jumped in adding her approval. "Thank you, Mrs. Dawson! What a good idea!" She turned to Jake. "Do you have any problems with Mrs. Dawson's suggestion for a goal--when writing, express your opinions--like we do at home when discussing books?"

"No! Heck no! I'll give my opinions about everything. I've got lots of opinions." Helen sensed the matter was settled to everyone's satisfaction. The team bumped fists. A goal had been established.

On her way out of the classroom Annie whispered to Helen, "Good luck, girl, you're gonna need it." Both laughed at their mutual understanding.

Annie hurried to catch up with Jake. Striding side-by-side, he expressed his opinion to her about how the meeting went.

"I guess I'm doing good, Mom."

"You're doing very well, Jake."

26
Curly-Q

"Lars told me a little about you, Mr. Black, but he didn't mention how long you've worked in Millbury."

"Eight years, Ms Klein. That's when the assistant superintendent's job opened up. Until then, Superintendent Jack Crawford handled just about everything: hiring, staff development, curriculum up-dates, reporting to the board of education. When the district enrollment topped twelve hundred students, the job became too much for one person. That's when I was hired. Before that, I was a school principal in Norwalk."

"If we're going to spend any time together, Mr. Black, I insist you call me Q."

"Fine with me Q. But it's a two-way street. I'm Raul."

"Got it! Lars told me you were close to completing your doctorate. I assume it has something to do with education."

"Of course. I'm a PhD candidate at Columbia's Teachers College. My thesis is titled: *Organizational Patterns in Middle School.*"

"Then you're the perfect person to fill me in on all the charter school stuff that's making the news. I assume you know about Betsy DeVos in Washington and Constance Van Cortland here in Connecticut?"

"Of course. I know who they are. I'll try to bring you up to date on the charter school mess. It's a complicated and contentious story."

"Before that, tell me about yourself. Lars said your job focuses on curriculum development, staff training, and student testing. He learned that from Tim Gallagher, a principal in Danbury--the one who gave me your phone number."

"Yeah, I know Timmy. He has a new job in Massachusetts. He's a good guy."

"I did all the things you mentioned when I was hired, including out-of-district placements. Since then, another person's been added to the management team--director of special services."

"Is he responsible for struggling kids--children with unusual needs?"

"Yes, but he's a she. Dr. Marcie Davenport oversees special education, speech and language remediation, children on the autism spectrum, and out-of-district placements. Thank goodness that's off my plate."

"How do out-of-district placements work? It must be an expensive business."

"It is, Q. But if we can't provide help in the district for children with extraordinary limitations, we have an obligation to locate suitable outside services. Help can be either part-time or full-time depending on the youngster. With so many nasty syndromes identified these days, local schools are overwhelmed providing individualized instruction. We're lucky to be able to partner with institutions like the American School for the Deaf in West Hartford."

"It must be difficult budgeting every year not knowing what problems might surface."

"Very difficult, Q. That's why we're so cautious with our behavior diagnoses. What appears to be beneficial for a child must be balanced by the rising costs of special placements and the pressure they place on the annual budget. Our district needs to buy books, paper, crayons, mow the grass, repair roofs, and pay for salaries and benefits. That's on top of out-of-district costs."

"Wow! Big job! Do you like your work?"

"I do. It can be frustrating at times, but there also are great rewards when I see our kids ready to go on to college or move into the business world. Many are foregoing the expense of college to become entrepreneurs or help in environmental campaigns. With some money saved and real world experience under their belts, attending college at a more mature age is paying off. Hey! Speaking of entrepreneurs, have you seen Lars recently?"

"No, but he's coming down from Morris for a cook-out this weekend. Why don't you and your wife join us? I'm testing barbeque recipes for a new book: *A Connecticut Healthy Diet: Nutrition in the Nutmeg State.*"

"Thank you, we'll be here."

"Great, I'm already looking forward to it."

"Your book title sounds like food for the winter season-- nutmeg and eggnog."

"It does, doesn't it? No, it's about including spices in our diets.

Many are antioxidants. Nutmeg is reputed to ease systemic pain, soothe indigestion, detox the body, cure insomnia, and prevent leukemia. Pretty good snake oil, huh? There's a long list of reputed medicinal benefits."

"Boy, I'll say! Who knew?"

"I wonder if there is a spice that straightens hair. My mop is driving me crazy. Maybe It's the weather. So many curls, so little time to tame them."

"There are varieties of hot peppers that will straighten anything, Q. But your do's stylish. Be happy you have hair. Look what's happening to me."

"I think bald guys look great, Raul, especially when they have a trim beard like yours."

"Thanks for the compliment and the cook-out invitation. Can Bonita and I bring something? Some wine, maybe?"

"If you want. But I'll be serving gin slings."

"What are they? Like gin and tonic?"

"No. Gin, ice, a lump of sugar, and a sprinkle of nutmeg. The drink was popular for one hundred years before gin and tonic and martinis took over."

"If you're serving those bad boys, Bonita and I definitely will be here."

"Great, Raul! I'll plan for you. What about your children?"

"My Aunt Lola will be happy to have them. It's taco weekend at the Ruiz hacienda."

"One day, when I'm in Roxbridge again, I'd like to meet your children. Maybe we could have a picnic in the Rumsey preserve."

"They'd like that a lot, Q. Isn't that where Ruggles was shot?"

"Yes."

"Where is the old guy? I didn't see him when I arrived."

"He's living with Lars. It's turned out nicely for him. Now he has Bantam Lake for swimming and wading. And there's always a good mud hole to roll in."

"Like a hippo."

"Exactly, Raul. Changing the subject, in your opinion what's all the hoopla over charter schools? Betsy DeVos and the conservative right have touted them as the great remedy for the failing public school system. That leads me to ask two questions: first, are public schools failing; second, how do charter schools measure up? You're the educator, Raul, what do you think?"

"As I said, it's a complicated and contentious issue. I'll tackle the second question first. Charter schools have been around a long time. You know them by different names: prep schools, private schools, independent schools, church schools, for-profit schools, and so on. There have always been academies independent of the public sector. But up to now, they functioned without public tax money relying, instead, on tuitions and donations."

"I understand, Raul, like Choate. How do they measure up?"

"There are also two answers to that question; how they measure up institutionally with other like schools, and how student academic results compare with student results from public schools."

"Sounds something like comparing apples to apples and apples to oranges."

"Exactly. For any secondary school to be worth its weight in salt, it must meet criteria set by accrediting agencies, like the

NEASC, the New England Association of Schools and Colleges. Similar agencies are in other parts of the country. The associations establish standards of excellence for schools to attain. Schools are visited periodically to see if the standards are being met. Accreditation means a school's graduates have met certain requirements and are considered ready for college admission. Needless to say, schools like Choate and Taft do very well. They're prestigious prep schools."

"Right, I know about Choate. I live in Wallingford."

"Where about?"

"Near Quinnipiac University."

"I know that area. I took a course there a few years ago. Anyway, comprehensive public secondary schools have a variety of paths for students, Q. Not all are ready for college. Not all want to go to college. Not all can afford college. Many independent schools--call them charter schools if you like--compare favorably with public schools. I mentioned Choat and Taft. Others do not."

"What about student achievement?"

"That's the second part, Q. First of all, only about five percent of students go to private schools. So measuring student achievement in private schools produces little statistical evidence to compare with public schools. And some charter schools hide their results. If that's not enough, private schools can limit their enrollments to a narrow range of children: no special needs students, no disruptive students, no students needing free lunches. Again, some kids do great in private schools, others do not. Public schools deal with them all. Choate is a fine place, but it's expensive and caters to influential families with high achieving children."

"I know. Like Jack Kennedy."

"Right. The sad thing is that when compared with other nations in reading, math and science, the U.S. is far down the list: twenty-fifth in science, twenty-fourth in reading, thirty-ninth in math."

"That doesn't sound good. What countries are at the top of the lists?"

"Comparing larger countries to ours, Japan is second in science, Canada second in reading, Japan fifth in math."

"Why such big differences? Is there any way for us to improve?"

"The differences result from many factors. Each state has its own set of requirements. They vary widely. Education in the U.S. is universal, so poor kids and children with special needs are taught shoulder to shoulder with all others. We have a diverse society, Japan has a homogenous society. We have a multitude of ethnic, racial, and religious groups. Canada is smaller in population and, I think, has fewer social differences."

"Except for the cultural divide between Quebec and the other provinces."

"I hadn't considered that. Maybe. But much of public education in the U.S. is managed at the local level where narrow parental beliefs and politically minded school boards can create curricula and learning conditions that are anti-intellectual. They select history texts that gloss over slavery, set rules that exclude gays or transgenders, spend far too much money on football."

"And put kids at risk for getting concussions."

"You bet."

"What about the Common Core debate?"

"It's been determined that if the Common Core was fully implemented, U.S. test scores would yield significant gains. And yet, the Common Core was reviled by Trump, Betsy DeVos, and other weak-minded conservatives. In a nutshell, our diversity is also our Achilles' heel."

"Would you say Trump University was a charter school? I know it was for adults and for a very specific purpose, but still...."

"I'd say Trump University was a scheme designed to swindle people out of a lot of money. It was a gigantic hoax."

"Fortunately Trump was nailed."

"Yep, twenty-five million dollars. I hope it was enough to reimburse those who were swindled. His status as a free man is still to be determined."

"Right! He's appealed his convictions. I'll bet he's trying to cut a deal, the nasty man."

"Probably. I hope it's a deal over which prison he's sent to--max security in Colorado or the gulag in Russia. He has connections there."

"You're a funny man, Raul. I'm sorry to keep diverting you. Back to education. Are there any clear success stories on the charter school front?"

"There sure are. For example, the work Jeffrey Canada is doing in New York City is heroic. His Harlem Children's Zone and Academy are proving that impoverished black kids, if given an opportunity, can achieve as well as middle-class white kids living in suburbia. His enterprise doesn't have the word charter appended to its title, but that's what it is."

"So, Raul, from what you're saying, I take it some charter schools are successful, others are disasters."

"Yes, Q. That's exactly what I'm saying."

"Do you have an opinion about the little school here in Roxbridge, the Johnny Appleseed Academy? You know, the one that's affiliated with the Church of the Maligned Fruit?"

"The report card's not in on them yet, Q. But any organization that narrowly focuses on one myopic idea, in this case the sanctity of the apple, has to raise some eyebrows."

"What I'm riled about is Constance Van Cortland, Connecticut's Commissioner of Education. She and I attended the same college. But before that, she was raised in a private school setting. I went to public schools. She seems to be cut from the same cloth as DeVos. She could do some damage here in Connecticut."

"Possibly, Q, but local control and reason have the power to combat any foolish schemes she dreams up. The one I'm worried about is the reduction of the free and reduced lunch program. Some kids presently meeting the eligibility requirements may be dropped if Van Cortland changes the threshold for family income. It will be especially hard on families with more than one child. We'll see what happens."

"Raul, how does this all fit with vouchers? Are charter schools and voucher programs the same?"

"More good questions, Q. But I need to get to daycare and pick up my two. Can we save it for another day?"

"Of course, Raul. I'm just beginning to get an idea of the

complexity of the whole issue. We need to talk more. I'll see you on the weekend, when I'm up from Wallingford."

"Okay, Q. ¡Hasta la vista! ¡Que tengas una buena tarde! Have a great evening!"

27

A Question of Ethics

"Dr. Livingstone, I presume." MacKenzie laughed. He put down his red pencil and gestured to an empty chair at the table.

"Cut it out, Mac, not yet. Graduation's in ten days."

MacKenzie pushed aside the pile of papers he was grading and made room for Jen Livingstone. He was finishing off a tuna sandwich in the teacher's lounge. She had a banana and a container of yogurt.

"You're a bloody PhD!" he insisted. "It's only a matter of wearing your robe and picking up your diploma." He congratulated her with a broad smile.

"A question, Mac. Did your life change when you got your PhD? Did you think about yourself differently?" Jen pried off the yogurt lid and stirred the blueberry puree into the culture.

"Nae," said Rob, "not really. The degree was useful for advertising my bona fides and opened the door to some interviews, but for the most part, I don't think about it. When I do, I remind myself it's not a mark of brilliance. It's a result of perseverance."

"What title do you prefer being called?"

"Title? That's for the peerage in England. I respond to Rob or Mac--sometimes even 'hey you.' The students have to be a bit more formal, but Dr. Mac is fine with me."

"I'm afraid I'll get kidded about being Dr. Livingstone, the way you did when I came in."

"Jen, nobody's gonna mistake you for a Nineteenth Century missionary lost in the jungle." He glance around the room. "You're much too pretty a lass for that," he said quietly. "Enjoy your new title. You earned it." He nodded toward her lunch. "By the way, did you know you were eating milk fermenting as a result of bacteria cultures?"

She laughed. "Yes, I know. And the blueberries are fruit seeds picked from bushes."

Chuckling at his own silliness he said, "I didn't have a chance to ask you. How did your oral defense go? What was the title of your dissertation again--something about ethical behavior in the public sector?"

"It turned out fine. I was nervous at first. There were three inquisitors. Then I realized they weren't out to get me. They were only probing my breadth of knowledge. I relaxed. The title of my thesis was *Expected Ethical Behaviors by Municipally Financed Managers*."

"Phew! That's a big topic. Student advisors usually try to get their doctoral candidates to narrow their field of investigation."

"Yes, in my case, too," explained Jen. She peeled her banana and bit off an end. "My topic was too broad at the beginning. But by the end I narrowed the subject to local government employees like school administrators and town hall employees. I stayed away from law enforcement. That's a whole dissertation by itself." She dipped a piece of banana in the yogurt and popped it in her mouth.

"Wow!" said Rob, showing surprise about Jen's project. "Now thinking about it, I realize what a big task that must have been."

"It was. For a measuring tool I had to adopt an ethical framework already existing or develop one of my own. That required studying philosophy and applied ethics. Whatever employee action I wanted to look at had to be measured by some peer accepted framework. Issues such as loyalty, fairness, obligation, truthfulness, and contract fulfillment required consideration. Then I needed to obtain a cohort of willing subjects, test their responses to a questionnaire of my design, and pore over public records and newspaper articles to see if what they answered on their questionnaires matched their actions in real life. Of course, I had to promise anonymity." Jen folded her banana skin and stuffed it in her empty yogurt container.

"Let me take those," said Rob eyeing her refuse. "My classes are composting waste vegetable matter, and I use small plastic containers to start seedlings."

Jen laughed. "Be my guest. You're the reuse-recycle guy."

Rob asked, "You were an undergraduate major in political science, right? That's why you teach civics. I can see how your dissertation fits with civics issues."

"Yep. At Wesleyan I majored in government with a minor in history. So when I decided to take the alternative route to teacher certification, teaching social studies--civics to be specific--seemed like the right choice for me."

"Why are you here teaching in a public school?" asked MacKenzie. "You told me you went to private schools as a kid."

"I did. Both my parents were private school educators, Mom an English teacher, Dad a math guy. They worked in some pretty toney private schools in New York City. We had a rent stabilized apartment in Riverdale. I attended their schools as a benefit of employment."

"My step-son, Jake, was at Dalton through grade three."

"It's a fine school, if you can afford it." She hesitated, thinking. "I was a good student and did well, so I received scholarship assistance to attend Wesleyan. For most of my youth I was surrounded by kids of privilege and wealth. Same for college. Getting certified in Connecticut meant I could teach a wider array of children than those I grew up with. Even though Litchfield County is well-to-do, there are pockets of poverty. Someday, if I get enough courage, I may head to an inner-city school where there are more minorities, more poverty, and bigger challenges."

"Whatever you do, lass," Rob reassured, "you'll do well. It's bloody terrific to see young dedicated people become teachers."

He looked at the wall clock. "I want to talk more about your ethics research. I have more questions. But now I need to get to my next class. We're recording seed counts from different varieties of grasses to determine which is more efficient for reseeding burned over meadows. And I'm trying to convince the Apple Church kids to show some interest in science other than maximizing orchard yields."

"Good luck with that," laughed Jen. "I'm having a struggle getting them to see there might be two sides to an issue. All they want to discuss is which is better--red delicious or golden delicious."

"Aye. That group's a wee bit narrowly focused. Very strange."

★

Maryann uncorked a bottle of MacKenzie Estates red. Rob sliced a baguette of French bread. Spaghetti sauce bubbled on the stove and angel hair pasta neared completion--al dente. Jake was at the table chuckling over a Gary Larson book of cartoons.

"What do you know about Dr. Walsh's departure, Rob?" asked Maryann. She kissed him on the cheek. "There must be some rumors going around."

"Aye, a few. He's leaving to become president of the New Paradigm Charter Schools." Finished with bread slicing, Rob pulled the butter dish out of the refrigerator. "It's a for-profit scheme being pushed by the Gronk Family Foundation."

Maryann shook her head. "It's amazing how much clout the conservative right has these days."

"I don't know about the conservative right, lass." Rob shrugged his shoulders. "To me it looks like nothing more than a money-making scheme."

"What are they up to?" asked Maryann.

Rob listed New Paradigm's initial foray into for-profit education. "They're opening or operating four schools. Here in Roxbridge they have the Johnny Appleseed Academy. In New Milford there's the Redstate Preschool and Kindergarten. It's scheduled to start in the fall and add an additional grade level each year. A Jewish school, Left Bank-Right Bank Schull, just opened its doors in Goshen, of all places."

"Why's Goshen a surprise?"

"It was the name of the location in Egypt the Jews vacated during the Exodus. You'd think they'd have chosen a better school site than the name of a place they were escaping." Rob chuckled and centered the salad bowl on the table.

"You said there are four schools."

"Aye, Annie. The last one's in Litchfield. Its name is Light of the East Madrasa. I can't believe there are that many Muslims living in Litchfield, but I suppose they'll draw from surrounding towns."

"Yikes! What a lineup!"

"Aye, that it is. But I can't detect any one spiritual theme other than resistance to public schools. If anything, they're focused on political messages rather than spirituality, either conservatism or liberalism."

Jake looked up. "What's a madrasa?"

"A type of school for Muslims," said Maryann.

"Sunnis or Shiites?" asked Jake.

"Wow! You remember the difference!"

"Sure. You think I'm stupid or something?"

Maryann laughed. "No, my son. I'm just never sure what you're taking in and storing in that head of yours."

"Don't worry, Mom. I've got the whole Muslim thing figured out."

"We need to get him on the Israeli-Palestinian peace

negotiating team," laughed Rob. He winked at Jake. "What's your favorite Larson cartoon?"

"It's the one with the doctors operating on a patient. Suddenly a piece of meat flies out of the guy's gut and lands on the floor. The boss doctor says to the other doctors, 'Keep your eye on that chunk. We may need it later.'" Jake laughed. "That's so cool!"

Teachers filed out of the staff meeting heading to the parking lot. Rob walked alongside Jen Livingstone on the way out. After mentioning the meeting, he restarted their earlier conversation about ethics.

"Lassie, shorter meeting today, wouldn't you say?"

"Yes, thank goodness. I need to get to the store. I like the new meeting structure. Standing meetings are forcing shorter reports and requiring forms no larger than an index card." She laughed.

"Aye," agreed Rob, nodding his head. "Adopting a corporate meeting format has helped keep things moving along. At first I wondered whether the teachers' union would agree to meetings without chairs. But they're fine with it. They can escape earlier, too. Unfortunately there's always a jokester hoping to get a few yuks."

Jen chuckled, "When Andy Anderson called Trump an ape, I almost lost it."

"I did, too," agreed Rob. "That used to be my line. Say, Jen, changing the subject for a minute, we were talking about ethics the other day. What do you make of Phil Walsh's departure? If you have a few minutes, I'd like to hear your opinion."

"Only five minutes, Rob, then I have to go." She unlocked her car door and stowed her canvas book bag in the back seat. To Rob, she appeared as if she was ready to divulge a secret.

"I know I'm just starting out, Rob, and I may be overstepping my grounds, but I say, good riddance!"

"Och!" said Rob, his eyes wide. "That's a harsh judgement! How come?" His curiosity was piqued.

"It's simple. Walsh didn't do his job. I'm guessing he violated his terms of employment. That's a legal issue, Rob, a breach of contract. In doing so, he didn't keep his promise implied in the contract. That's a moral failure. Honesty, obligation, dedication to your employer; they're all part of the job, and he failed each." She looked at a flock of birds swirling over the soccer field.

"His time out of district lobbying for charter schools and courting voucher proponents were blatant conflicts of interest. His behaviors were legitimate causes for termination of employment. He should have been fired. He was lucky to leave here before the axe fell."

Rob was amazed by Jen's insight and understanding of the problem. "I agree with you, lass. I've thought the same thing since I started here. Phil comes across to some as erudite and a deep thinker with defined convictions. But I was never able to discern his convictions. I thought he was pretty shallow. He reminded me of a sidewalk superintendent telling everyone what to do, but not knowing a rake from a hoe, and never lifting a shovel. I'm relieved he's gone. Now I hope he doesn't do any damage to undercut our efforts here in Roxbridge."

"Yes, that would be a shame."

"Piece of advice, Jen, keep your opinions to yourself. You can trust me to keep my yap shut. Although I think most staff agree with you, it may not be everyone. You're new on the job and have a great future. But some of the old-timers become annoyed when a newbie speaks out. Although the REA would defend you if you were pressured to leave, you don't want to go through that trauma."

"Thanks for the advice, Rob. You're right. Mum's the word."

Rob smiled. "Mum's what I call my wee Scottish mother." His smile turned into a chuckle. "Off ye go, lass. Get thee to the store."

"Not to the nunnery?" she asked, laughing with him.

"Nay, lassie. The supermarket's punishment enough."

Rob suddenly imagined himself a wise father advising his young adult daughter. It was a pleasant feeling.

28

The Right is Wrong

Maryann turned off the radio. She grimaced, shrugged as if apologizing, and looked at Rob. "Maybe it's my imagination," she said, "but the alt right seems to be gaining greater traction."

Rob frowned. "It's more than the alt right," he said. "It's a new form of fascism. As far as I'm concerned, the bloody idjits who promote hate philosophy are worse than dogs. I call them the *wrong right*. What a bunch of lizards! They make Neanderthals look like Rhodes Scholars."

"Did you read the article about the school initiatives being pushed by the Commissioner of Education? Van Cortland's trying to undo all the positive changes that have been made in recent years. Yikes! She's trying to under-cut the efforts Connecticut's made in equalizing school funding. Her legislation is shocking! Can I read the list of her actions to you?"

"Aye. I may know about them, but tell me anyway."
"Okay. She aims to short-change the inner cities by diverting tax monies to charter schools and a voucher system. She filed a suit titled, *Van Cortland v Bridgeport*. The Connecticut Education

Association has filed a counterclaim on behalf of Bridgeport children, *CEA v Van Cortland*."

Maryann continued. "Then--my God!--she sued to make mandated school innoculations unconstitutional. That case's called, *Van Cortland v AMA.*

"Finally, she's promoting two outrageous ideas. The first is to require all public school students to wear uniforms. The second's a lobbying effort to get the legislature to name Peter Pan the state's official peanut butter. If adopted, Peter Pan would be the only brand served in schools."

Rob laughed. "That's how much she knows! The nincompoop doesn't realize that nut products aren't served in school cafeterias--too many nut sensitive kids."

"And too many nut jobs managing the Department of Education," Maryann added. She sighed. "More of us need to become allergic to those fools. They're wrecking proven public policy and practice."

"I predict things will get better," said Rob. "Midterm elections are coming up. If the polls are accurate and predictions true, we're gonna have a new cast of characters next fall. You agree, lass?"

"Yep, Rob, I do. But you never know. Look at how wrong the polls and predictions were in 2016. We wound up with the orange man. Remember? The day we met you equated Trump with an orangutan."

"Aye, that I did. And to this day I'm sorry for insulting orangutans the way I did."

★

"Except for *The Scottish Music Hour,* Rob, and the classical music station, you rarely listen to the radio." Maryann was thumbing through *The New Yorker,* on the lookout for cartoons Jake might enjoy.

"Aye, lass. Most of it is worthless shite like television."

"That's why I recorded this, honey. It was playing on that conservative station broadcasting out of Meriden. The program's on every afternoon after that windbag, Rush Limbaugh."

"Is it worth hearing, my love, or will I be wasting my time?"

"Both," Maryann said. "It's a tune worth hearing because it's so incendiary. At the same time, it's three minutes of your life gone forever."

"I guess I can spare three minutes. Go ahead and play it."

Maryann pushed the play key on their cassette recorder. A DJ announced the next song.

Okay, all you gun totin' right-wingers out there in liberal-land. Next up is a great new tune from our own Celtic alt-right music scene, the patriotic group, Stomp and the Purple Pants. From station WRWB, here is *God, Guns and Charter Schools.*

Rob shook his head in disgust as the throat-searing sounds grated his ears. It was music of defiance, hatred, and anger--a tune with no redeeming values. To him it was atonal pornography.

God, guns and char-tair schools / God's me road map, guns me tools
God, guns and char-tair schools / Fook da data, science ghouls

Heed yer God, do not tink / Public schools really stink
Proudly wear yer u-ni-form / Conform ya jerk, dat's da norm

God, guns and char-tair schools / Ammunition is me jewels
God, guns and char-tair schools / Eddie Eagle, bird dat rules

Heed yer God, do not tink / Public schools really stink
Proudly wear yer u-ni-form / Conform ya jerk, dat's da norm

God, guns and char-tair schools / NRA, I pay me dues
God, guns and char-tair schools / NEA's a bunch a fools

Heed yer God, do not tink / Public schools really stink
Proudly wear yer u-ni-form / Conform ya jerk, dat's da norm

God, guns and char-tair schools / Salute da flag, dem's da rules
God, guns and char-tair schools / Disobey means dunce's stool

Heed yer God, do not tink / Public Schools really stink
Proudly wear yer u-ni-form / Conform ya jerk, dat's da rules.

Maryann stopped the recording. "Pretty sad. I'm afraid that's where our country's heading."

"Aye, what crap! The lyrics are rotgut, there's no melody, and Stomp and the Purple Pants have no musical talent. I'll make a prediction, Annie. It's always risky business, but in this case certain--that bunch will never perform their hog swill of a tune at a public school graduation. If my prediction is wrong, I'll clean the toilets for a year. Stomp and the Purple Pants are in the same category as shitecans needing a good flush."

29

Our Home

"This is my home. This is your home. This is the home of everyone who ever lived. This is the home of everyone who will live in the future. This is the only home we have."

MacKenzie slowly paced across the front of his classroom reciting his short speech. As he changed directions, he watched his class of high school juniors fidget at their desks. Clearly, a few appeared edgy when he called the Earth *home*.

Holding aloft a sixteen inch diameter inflatable globe and using it as a visual reference seemed to him to have more impact than referring to the Earth as our home using words alone. He had employed this technique when teaching college students a year earlier at WestConn. The planet prop helped dramatize his message. The fragility of tiny Earth floating within the unfathomable depths of the universe became alarmingly apparent.

MacKenzie had decided to use his favorite lesson introduction a week earlier after hearing a cluster of students argue that a space colony could save humans from the environmental crises that seemed to be overtaking the Earth. Foremost among the crises, he overheard, was climate change. One student argued that climate change and global warming were different names for the same problem--a planet under stress that threatened human existence. His friends agreed.

Then and there, MacKenzie decided to deviate from lessons already scheduled. In the next week he had planned to enrich the unit he was currently teaching, Water Conservation and the Rain Cycle, by filling matching containers with loam, clay, and sandy soils, adding identical amounts of water to each sample, then measuring rates of evaporation by weight. He planned to position a third of the containers under heat lamps, a third in darkened sealed boxes, and the control third sitting on open-air shelves in the back of the room.

However, hearing his students speculate about living and surviving somewhere in space made him realize their optimism needed a touch of reality. This was a teachable moment--an occasion when set lesson plans were ignored--when astute creative teachers know exactly what to do. It was time to refute childish misconceptions with evidence supported by data.

"I detected a wee bit of unease in the class when I said, 'this is the only home we have.' Am I correct in my observation, lads and lassies?" He waited for a reply. No one uttered a sound. Students exchanged nervous glances.

"I've observed that you all seem to understand the environmental problems facing humans," he said, "but I don't think you've come to grips with reality. There are no easy fixes. There are no simple solutions to the mess we've created."

"But, Dr. Mac," said a boy, "if we could build a colony on Mars, then the human species might survive."

"Aye, Ron, that's true in science fiction. But when you add up the costs and consider the roadblocks, the possibility of preserving human life in space is a dream, not reality."

"Wait a minute, Dr. Mac! Do you mean to tell us we'll never go to Mars?"

"That's not what I said. A small group of brave explorers may touch down on Mars someday--as happened on the moon--and a few may be lucky enough to survive and return to the Earth. But a large mission to build protective housing, harness the sun's power, discover water, and produce food will never happen in my opinion The engineering and logistics for such an undertaking are staggering."

"Then all the stuff we hear about space exploration is bull," said a boy on the left.

"No, lad, that's not right either. Space exploration's going on right now, but by robots, not humans." MacKenzie searched faces. The group appeared enrapt. He continued teaching.

"Here are the problems for humans wishing to live beyond the boundaries of the Earth: First, it's obvious that food and water are necessary for any extra-terrestrial voyage. Second, fuel and propellants are limited to what can be carried. There's no filling station dispensing petrol on Mars's Main Street. And, third, the cost of the fuel necessary to lift us off Earth and propel us into orbit or hurl us into the solar system is staggering. The rate we're presently using fossil fuels--even supplemented with new energy sources such as gas from fracking, solar and wind energy--will someday produce fuel shortages. It's simply a matter of time."

"But if we use solar and wind energy, gas supplies might be extended," said a girl hopefully, nervously fiddling with her braid.

"Aye, lass, using renewables would help. But finite resources are not infinite. Someday the so-called bottomless supply of convenient energy will run dry."

"Maybe someone will invent an anti-gravity machine," suggested another student. He pretended to be elevating off his chair.

"That's already been done," interrupted a ginger-haired boy with an arch of freckles across the bridge of his nose. "It's called a pogo-stick." The class laughed.

"Aye, Desmond," said Rob trying to stifle a loud guffaw. "And don't forget the trampoline, bungee jumping, and the circus clown shot out of a cannon." Rob's outlandish examples resulted in more laughs. "The problem with everything we've tried so far is gravity always pulls us back to terra firma."

Rob allowed the laughing and kidding to continues for a minute, then refocused the class on the subject they were broaching--human extinction. What a dangerous topic to raise with kids! Professional ethicists, demographers, physicists, and the clergy wrestle with the problem. For those with little or no imagination the fall-back position was, God will save us. MacKenzie knew salvation was within reach, but not by God, only if humanity recognized and accepted it's harmful contributions to global degradation and changed behaviors. Without that, future scenarios were bleak.

"Finally, my friends," said MacKenzie, "there are enormous distances involved in space travel requiring years to get someplace relatively habitable. Does everyone agree that our moon's not the answer?"

Heads nodded in affirmation. "But it's close enough to get there and back," said a girl wearing a pink hoodie.

"Yeah," agreed her friend, "but it's made of rock, not cheese." More laughs bounced around the room.

"Stephen. Do you have something to say?" Rob called on a student usually quiet during "what if" discussions, like the one they were now having.

"What should we do, Mr. MacKenzie? If we won't be able to save ourselves by building a colony somewhere in space--as you predict--what should we do? What chances do we have to survive?"

Stephen's was the question MacKenzie had anticipated. It was the question that allowed him to call on his class to become engaged in environmental causes and political activism. The answer to Stephen's question had the power to ease student anxiety and help them understand the need to take charge.

"Your question's a good one, Stephen," answered MacKenzie with conviction. He peered at the class hoping to convey his seriousness. "I think you all know the answer to Stephen's question, lads and lassies. You all must become engaged in causes that actively work to protect the Earth. You must vote for Earth conscientious representatives. There's still time to heal the planet, but you must participate.

"Notice I'm using the word *must,* I didn't say *might,* or *if you have enough time,* or *if you want.* Those are weasel words and phrases--words that imply you have a choice to get involved or *things are not that bad* and can wait.

"You can't wait. If you want to keep the Earth habitable, you must become actively engaged now. Don't put it off. Start today, not next week."

A hand waved in the rear of the room. "Yes, Lisa?" called MacKenzie.

"It's almost two-thirty, Dr Mac. Can't we wait at least until tomorrow?"

He chuckled. "Of course, lass. But begin healing our planet starting tomorrow when you wake up. Don't put it off. Reuse and recycle. Plan for Earth Day. Teach younger kids the importance of a clean environment. Do it by example."

The class was quiet. Then Stephen spoke just before the dismissal bell. "Thanks for the pep talk, Mr. MacKenzie. I needed it. We all needed it. We can make a difference. Count me in."

"You're right, laddie. You really can make a difference. The health of our planet rests with your generation. Now come up here, Stephen, and help me end the lesson. Hold the globe high, lad. It's our blue-green jewel among the stars. Make sure everyone sees how beautiful it is."

Stephen proudly held the globe aloft, the same way his teacher did at the start of the lesson. Once more MacKenzie recited his favorite speech. "This is my home. This is your home. This is the home of everyone who ever lived. This is the home of everyone who will live in the future. This is the only home we have."

30

Eighth Grade Civics

"I think you all know you're gonna get a double dose of me." Jen Livingstone was in front of her eighth grade class of thirteen and fourteen year olds. She moved to the chalkboard and wrote reminders of the year's topics.

"Here's a brief outline of what's left to be done by June. In high school we'll build on what we've learned this year, and we'll study the topics in more depth. So far we've covered the Declaration of Independence, read and discussed Lincoln's *Gettysburg Address*, and taken a brief look at the Bill of Rights. Anyone remember where we found the Rights?"

"They're part of the Constitution, Dr. Livingstone," answered a boy digging through his pockets.

"You're right, Todd. Good memory." Livingstone nodded to him. "What are you searching for?"

"A pen."

"I'll give you one. For now keep your mind on what we're discussing." She forged ahead.

"Up next we're reading *Ruby Bridges Goes to School* and the story of Rosa Parks. One is the civil rights tale of a school girl, the other is about an adult. Eventually we'll include Martin Luther King, Jr. These are compelling histories of African Americans fighting to overcome white hatred and bigotry. As the year continues, we'll consider these stories in the context of gerrymandering and voter suppression." She hesitated. "Anyone know what gerrymandering is? Who's heard of it?" Livingstone saw a surprising number of hands aloft. She called on Taylor Peters.

"It's when voting districts are changed to give preference to one group over another," explained Taylor. She added a question. "How do they get away with that stuff, Dr. Livingstone?"

"You're right about the definition of gerrymandering, Taylor. People get away with it because other people are too poor to sue and bring the issue to the courts. Sometimes the affected parties are physically threatened if they try do something about it. Folks with less political clout feel intimidated. There are other reasons, too, but the bottom line is we must fight injustice and make sure everyone has equal protection under the law--voting laws as well as criminal laws."

Livingstone said nothing for a minute, then completed her outline of Roxbridge Regional High School civics. "In high school you'll study the Federalist Papers and learn how they influenced the writing and adoption of the Constitution. You'll get to meet *Pluribus*. Don't bother asking, I'm not telling. You can look him up on your own.

"We'll look at voting districts here in Connecticut to see if they've been fairly drawn. We'll study the modern Supreme Court. I plan to use two excellent books by Jeffrey Toobin."

Taylor raised her hand and interrupted. "Is he the political analyst on CNN?"

"He is. One book is titled, *The Nine*, the other's called, *The Oath.*"

Taylor persisted with her questioning. "Am I allowed to get a head start on reading them?" The class groaned.

"Of course, Taylor, but you have a few years to go." "I know, but I like to begin early." More groans.

"Okay, that's fine. Read them now, if you insist."

"Which book should I start with?"

"Start with *The Nine*. It has good information about Justice Sandra Day O'Connor, and it predates *The Oath*. Read them in historical sequence."

Livingstone changed the subject. "I have an offer you can't--or at least shouldn't--refuse. I received permission to do this. When you're in high school, I'll increase your final grade by half a point, if you promise you'll register to vote when you turn eighteen. If you've already reached that magic age, register before the school year ends. We'll celebrate with a party, and I'll let you guys plan it." Murmurs of "cool" and "neat" swept the room.

"I don't want any Roxbridge kids graduating not knowing how our government works. Everyone needs to understand their duties as citizens. Everyone must vote. ¿Comprende?"

Livingstone watched some heads nod. Other students jotted notes.

"Make everyone swear on the Bible that they'll register," suggested a prim and proper girl, a recent transfer to Roxbridge from a parochial school.

Another student faulted the idea. "No, let's keep church and state separate. We should swear on the Constitution."

"Excellent idea," affirmed Livingstone smiling widely. "When the time comes we'll pick a date and make it into a ceremony followed by a class party."

"With refreshments?" asked popular Sierra, who always took over organizing social events.

"Of course. But it's still a few years away."

"Yeah," Sierra said, "but you can never start planning a party too soon. Taylor wants to begin reading high school books now. I want to select a party theme."

"Okay, Sierra, start planning," agreed Livingstone. She conveyed her smile to each and every student in the room. "When you plan, remember to include plenty of red, white, and blue bunting."

★

Dr. Livingstone was facilitating a discussion in her eighth grade course: *Civics One: An Introduction*. The class was plowing through a cursory examination of the Bill of Rights. Her plans called for a deeper in-depth analysis in high school. The second installment of civics was titled: *Toward an Educated Citizenry*. Both were part of the Roxbridge social studies curriculum requirement, split between the middle school and the upper grades.

Livingstone made sure all district students graduated with a solid knowledge of how the United States government worked. After her teaching, they would be able to list the Constitutional mandates which were the foundation of a free society. In addition, she guaranteed a final grade "bump-up" to every graduating senior who registered to vote. Her plan was approved by the board of education.

"Taylor, you told me you were planning to join our high schoolers when they picketed the New Milford gun range. Did you go?"

"Yes, Dr. Livingstone," answered Taylor. "The demonstration was neat. There were other middle schoolers and bunches of older kids."

"I read in the newspaper the event was estimated to have drawn about a thousand students. Do you agree with that?"

Taylor squinted as if trying to re-assemble the throng in her memory. "I don't know, Dr. Livingstone. It may have been that many, but I have no way to judge. For sure, there were lots of kids."

"We'll get to your report in a minute, Taylor, but the reason I'm asking about crowd size is that reports of actual people counts or falsified numbers can influence voters. Remember the hullabaloo after President Trump's inauguration? He claimed that millions had attended the event, and it was the largest crowd ever to witness an inauguration. That boast was meant to persuade his followers that he had huge support among all Americans. But when aerial photos of the Mall were published, the images showed it was a small crowd--maybe a third of the number who had attended Obama's two ceremonies."

"I remember," said Taylor. Other students nodded in agreement.

"Trump's claims were false news" continued Livingstone,

"perhaps lies. Former FBI Director, James Comey implied Trump was a serial liar. It's what happens when power corrupts people. And Trump's not alone caving to dishonesty."

"On TV they call it fake news," someone added.

"No matter how it's define--fake or false--it's untrue. Dr. MacKenzie urges you to collect data to support your science discoveries. Right? In this case the aerial photos were the data proving Trump was wrong. Yes, Jeff. Do you have something to add?"

Jeff Snyder lowered his hand. "Hey, Dr. Livingstone. Isn't it disrespectful to call the President just Trump? After all, he's President Trump or Mr.Trump. In fact, he says he has a PhD, so he's also Dr. Trump."

"The PhD part is a lie, Jeff. It's false news. I don't know where you heard it, but it's not true."

Livingstone considered the impact her next sentences might have. Would she be overstepping her role and unfairly influencing her students by expressing an opinion? But Jeff had raised a good issue--crumbling civil discourse in American politics. She decided to respond.

"Why not refer to the President simply as Trump?" she asked. as if surprised by Jeff's question. "After all, that's his name. It's more respectful than, "the Donald" or "the dotard". And remember, he called his opponents derogatory names during the primary and presidential elections. I'll remind you: Lying Ted, Little Marco, Crooked Hillary. I'm all in favor of hard fought campaigns, but I expect the candidates to speak civilly about each other. For me, there's no place in American politics for name calling by the candidates. The media may resort to sassy cartoons and heated language. That's freedom of the press. But the men and women representing us ought to function at a higher level.

"Trump shows no respect for anyone," she went on. "As a consequence, he deserves no respect in return. When I talk about him, I say Trump--that's his name. I'm not purposely disrespecting him. But sometimes he goes too far. It seems he'd like to be called King Trump or Czar Trump or Lord Trump. To me, he's just Trump. There you have it, Jeff. Now you know how I feel about the man who is our President. I apologize if I've stepped on anyone's toes. But that's my opinion. You are entitled to yours."

Again Livingstone worried that she had exceeded the bounds of impartial teaching. She often wondered: where are the boundaries of responsible teaching defined? What are the boundaries, if any? How thin a margin is there between impartiality and indoctrination? Did ethical issues regarding indoctrination impede instruction, especially for a civics teacher working in a public school? Must she remain politically neutral--a cypher--for the rest of her teaching career? She acknowledged that her own ethical framework remained under construction even as she taught newly forming young adults

But Livingstone was certain of one thing. She had not voiced support for one party or the other, one candidate or another. If anything, she had expressed two moral imperatives--the need for civility in public discourse and the astonishing importance of the Constitution as the foundation of democracy.

Livingstone's students had listened quietly, providing no clue whether they agreed with her or not, nor for that matter, if they understood what she had said. She redirected the discussion. "I'm still waiting to hear your demonstration report, Taylor. What happened in New Milford?"

Taylor rubbed her jaw. "Kids marched in a huge circle in front of the gun range. We heard gunshots drifting from inside. A few customers were annoyed they couldn't enter. They could, of course. No one was stopping them. But they respected the picket line, didn't cause any trouble, and left."

"Did anyone block the entrance?"

"No way! Gunners could enter, if they wanted." Livingstone nodded positively. "That's good." She scanned the class. "You're all entitled to demonstrate peacefully. However, it must be done legally. Obstructing commerce could be treated like a crime, even if it's done by youthful students. 'We didn't know' is not an excuse."

"Yeah, I've seen plenty of that stuff on TV," said a freckle-faced boy.

"Then you've also seen the way the police handle obstructionists. They get arrested and are hauled off to jail." Livingstone expressed her displeasure of such tactics with a hand wave, as if she was erasing a chalkboard.

"But what if we strongly disagree with something?" asked Taylor, concern on her face. "Aren't we allowed to sit-in and disobey?"

"Legally you are, within limitations. Everyone understand?" Livingstone was serious. "You are obligated to follow the law. I admit sometimes laws are immoral or just plain wrong. For example, at one time laws existed preventing a person from marrying someone of another race."

Sun-Moon interrupted. "Then I wouldn't be here," she said indignantly. "My dad's white. My mom's Japanese. That law stinks!"

The class agreed, laughing. Someone said, "Sun-Moon's a figment of our imagination." More laughter.

"Okay, class. Settle down," warned Livingstone while smiling, "Sun-Moon's a living, breathing, beautiful eighth grader." She touched Sun-Moon on the head. More laughing.

Taylor's hand flew up. Livingstone called on her. Taylor asked another thorny question. "How about abortion, Dr. L.? Are pro-abortion laws immoral?"

Livingstone answered by deflecting the question. "I don't want to get into an abortion discussion. Many people believe abortion is immoral. Others believe laws preventing women from choosing for themselves are immoral. It's become a huge divide in this country. Some issues are too contentious to discuss in class. You'll get plenty of opportunities to debate abortion as you make your way through life."

She had an idea. "Let's try an experiment. I'll give each of you a 3X5 index card. On it write either 'for' or 'against'. Don't let your neighbor see what you write. Don't sign your name. Turn the card over. I'll come down the aisles and collect them. 'For' means you're in favor of laws allowing abortion. 'Against' means you're not in favor. There are twenty-two in class today. I'll sort them into two piles. We'll see where we stand on the issue."

After collecting the cards, Livingstone positioned herself in the front not allowing the class see her make two piles. She was careful to make sure they couldn't judge the outcome by watching her hands move. Sorting completed, she turned to the class and announced the results. "In this hand," she held up her right, "I have eleven 'againsts'. In this hand," she held up her left, "I have eleven 'fors'.

"There you have it," she said. "We're equally divided. Our split opinions makes abortion a possible topic for debate when you're in high school. Meanwhile, learn more about it. Check with Dr. Mac about the biology involved. If we do debate this topic in the future, we must do so civilly while respecting other opinions. No name calling."

Livingstone walked to center front. "Sometime in the future, most likely when you're in college, you ought to take a course in philosophy. That's the place to start debating abortion in depth. Of course, before that, talk it over with your parents and the spiritual leader of your place of worship. Try to learn what the procedure entails. As I said, study biology, listen to both side of the debate. Then make up your minds." Livingstone collected herself. "Phew, abortion's beyond what Roxbridge middle school civics is about. By the way, I'll shred these cards so everyone's vote will remain a secret." She slid the index cards into her briefcase.

"Let's get back to the gun range demonstration. Taylor, do you think picketing accomplished anything?"

"Yes, Dr. L, I think it did. In the afternoon an employee handed out copies of a news release. It said the range would continue to operate, but the management had a contract to roof-over the open-air wing. That will keep lead inside rather than falling into the Berkshire River or landing on Granite Hill. So I guess the demonstration accomplished something."

Livingstone smiled broadly and clapped quietly. "I'll say you did! You got the range to admit their facility was dangerous, and they agreed to make improvements. That's a victory! You didn't get everything you wanted, but you got something. Progress is often made in small steps. Congratulations to you, Taylor, and all the other Roxbridge student-citizens who gave up their weekend to fix a safety and environmental problem. I can't wait to share your good news with Dr. MacKenzie."

31

Curly-Q Asks About Vouchers

"Muchas gracias, Q. Again, thank you for hosting the picnic. It was lovely. My kids had a great time wading in the brook, and the older, Carlito, found an animal's skull in the field."

"Are you keeping it, Raul?"

"We are. Once we've flushed out the mud, it will be part of Carlito's treasure collection. But first, I'll give it a Clorox bath."

"My brothers had collections of odds and ends. Mo was interested in rocks and fossils. Lars had stuff about hunting. He had a collection of spent cartridge casings aligned in a row on a bookshelf. He called it his brass brigade."

"Young boys are instinctive collectors, Q. Girls, too. Almost every Roxbridge child I know has a collection of garnet crystals."

"Did they find them along the dirt roads? I've been told the road crew used gravel from an abandoned garnet mine."

"That's right. The kids all think they've found valuable jewels, but the culls are industrial grade. Before the mine fizzled out, the tailings were ground up and used to make sandpaper."

"You know, Raul, since I've been coming up here, I've found

out a lot about Roxbridge. It always surprises me when I learn how much small-scale industry was in these hills. You'd never know it now with the regrowth of the forests and the spread of residential housing."

"Right. Fortunately Roxbridge has dealt with growth fairly intelligently, cautiously proceeding to be kind to the land. I'm lucky to live here."

"Yes, you are. So was Mo. Hey, the last time we talked about education you filled me in on charter schools.

"Sí, I did."

"And I got the impression that they were not severely impacting public schools. Am I right?"

"It depends on what is meant by severely impacting. Nationwide, I understand only about five percent of schools fall within the so-call charter category. In my opinion, there's nothing wrong with having alternative choices, Q."

"Yes, you mentioned the five percent number last time."

"Sí, I'm sorry, I did. And I also said, private schools have been around a long time. The problem nowadays is that charter schools want a slice of the public school budget without having to deal with the requirements public schools have to meet."

"Like what?"

"Often they don't evaluate students adequately to measure progress. And when they do, they're reluctant to publish results, as if they have something to hide--like their students aren't doing as well as they promised. Additionally, many charter schools, and I'm including church-backed operations, don't have to provide for special needs students or deal with discipline problems. Those children are either denied admission or asked to leave. You know what I mean--kicked out."

"That's not fair."

"You're right. It isn't. Public schools must provide education for everyone regardless of problems. That's the great history of education in America, Q. Schooling isn't limited to the privileged classes, as it once was in Europe."

"I see free public education as one of the essential building blocks of the American experiment. Am I becoming too poetic, Raul?"

"Your poetry's far better than the negativism of those who would like to tear down our schools. Charter schools and public schools are not competing on a level playing field, Q, and the public sector--my sector--is pilloried as a failure if some child doesn't make the grade, gets arrested, or becomes a substance abuser. Charter schools weed out the problems before they take root. Public schools cannot. And don't forget the parents' obligation to cooperate with teachers to make it all work. It's a challenge, especially for parents struggling to make ends meet. Poverty in a school district is almost always associated with borderline schools."

"What about this voucher business, Raul? How does it fit in?"

"Vouchers are another scheme to divert money away from the public sector. If they become law, through either direct government payments or through tax credits, parents would receive or save some amount of money they could apply to private school tuition. Trouble is, any voucher amounts now being considered would fall far short of tuition in most private schools.

It might cover some of the costs of a private primary school, but far less for a private secondary school. Any upper school worth its salt has extensive course offerings and comprehensive activities that include clubs and sports. These things are expensive to provide. Poorer parents, even with voucher support, wouldn't be able to afford them. And what if a family had many children? I think voucher programs are being set up as a boon to the rich--as just another tax benefit."

"How would that affect your family, Raul?"

"In my family's case, if a voucher scheme amounted to a tax credit of $6,000 per child, I would save $12,000 in taxes. Conceivably the money could be applied to private school tuition--$6,000 for Carlito--$6,000 for Belen. But I'd have to come up with $12,000 the first year in addition to the part of the bill not covered by voucher money."

"Wow! That's steep!"

"Absolutely. I make a pretty good salary, Q, but I'd be hard pressed to pay full tuition for my two at Millbury Montessori, where per-child tuition is $10,000 per year. For my family, that's twenty-grand! I wouldn't get any tax assistance until the next tax submission date."

"When you describe it like that, Raul, I can see the shortcomings. I'm guessing you're describing a federal scheme. Will there be any state voucher plan here in Connecticut?"

"I don't know, Q. That's yet to be worked out. But I doubt it. Connecticut's strapped for cash. All-in-all, vouchers don't seem fair to me, Q. Do you agree?"

"Raul, my feeling is that any federal voucher program pushed by Betsy DeVos or a Connecticut voucher plan sold by Constance Van Cortland are two vats of poisonous snake oil. Two rich ladies are furthering their own self-interests and advancing harmful philosophies at the expense of the rest of us."

The Decision

★

The Fourth Folio

"Follow your heart."

Willie MacKay

"Trust your instincts, and make judgements
on what your heart tells you.
The heart will not betray you."

David Gemmell

32

The Bequest

"Won't you regret not owning Rose Gate Cottage? Fiona lived there for fifty years. She willed it to you." Maryann searched her husband's eyes looking for signs of remorse or sadness. Oddly, she detected relief, as if he had just finished struggling with a novel woven with too many plot twists. She knew Rob had spent seventeen years living in the cottage on the southeast shore of Loch Lomond in the wee boating community of Balmaha. It was where he was lovingly raised by his mum and her brother, Willie MacKay.

Fiona's sudden death had been a shock. Rob grieved but took solace learning she hadn't suffered. Her B&B employee, Karen McMaster, daughter of the Balmaha harbor master, Ian McMaster, found Fiona collapsed on the kitchen floor preparing evening soup and scones for a young trekking couple. They were in out of the rain after their second day slutching the muddy trails of the West Highland Way. Authorities attributed Fiona's death to a ruptured cranial aneurysm. Karen later remembered her complaining of a persistent headache.

His mum's passing instantly made Rob the sole heir and executor of her estate. His decision regarding the future of Rose Gate Cottage at first dismayed Maryann. Finally, she admitted his plan fit perfectly with his love of family and reverence of Scotland. His action meshed with his ethic of *do the right thing* and *follow your heart*. These maxims were two of the principles guiding his life. They were part of his primary moral guide, ULAR, a variation of the Golden Rule.

"Nae, my love," said Rob, returning to Maryann's question. "The cottage is rooted in Scotland. It's become a fixture on the West Highland Way. I'm an American citizen now. You and Jake are my life. I have no interest in returning to live permanently in Scotland. Nor do I have any desire in managing a B&B. Of course, when we go I'll be excited being in Scotland again, but my home's here with you in Roxbridge."

Maryann caressed the nape of his neck. "I love you for saying that, Rob. A thousand thank yous for loving me and making Jake a part of your life."

He kissed her hand. "You're welcome, Annie." He hesitated, and a smile eased his wistfulness. "How can I not love the lad? Jake makes me laugh. When I'm feeling out of sorts, all I have to do to feel better is talk with him. The other day I asked him what he was cogitating about, and he said he wasn't Jello. He mistook cogitating for coagulating. He had me in stitches."

"Did you straighten him out?" asked Annie, grinning widely, nodding her understanding of her son's mix-up with words.

"Aye, at least I tried. We had a long conversation about the differences between thinking and the stiffening properties of fluids, like Jello. He caught on quickly. He equated Jello stiffening to blood clotting. That seemed to be hilarious to him. He laughed in his usual crazy-Jake way. For all I know, he may start calling scabs, Jello shots. I never know what he's going to say except, 'cool!'"

Maryann chuckled at another image of Jake that persisted in her memory. At her wedding her son was wound in an over-sized kilt. He was in charge of both the ring and her flowers. Jake had insisted he be titled Gold Bearer and Plant Man in the nuptial bulletin.

A second memory was of the Roxbridge community Seder where Jake asked question after question and commented on everything Rabbi Marx said. Afterwards, Rob had described her son as a wee mensch.

Jake was maturing faster than Maryann wished, but with each passing milestone, more and more of his eclectic personality emerged. What a joy he was!

"At last we're going to visit Rose Gate Cottage!" said Maryann enthusiastically. She laid her hand on Rob's wrist. "It's too bad we didn't go sooner, while Fiona was alive."

"Aye, but we're going to pay reverence. That's a bonny reason."

Following Rob's suggestions, Maryann began planning their trip to Scotland. The visit had two pieces--to participate in the ceremony where Rob bequeathed Rose Gate Cottage to the Countryside Commission and to trek the West Highland Way.

Rob's gift to the nation was generous and his plan well designed. Rose Gate was to remain open for business--rented and operated for a nominal sum by a qualified young couple starting out in the hospitality industry. In turn, the new managers were obligated to run the B&B according to accepted hostel practices, but offer preferential accommodations to trekkers tackling the one hundred miles from Milngavie to Fort William.

Rob stipulated a codicil be added to the new ownership title. It guaranteed Rob and his family free lodging. But, like any other customer, he needed to make advance reservations. The demand for room and meals at Rose Gate was continuous. When Maryann and Rob visited Balmaha for the bequeathing ceremony, the cottage was where they would stay. All that had been arranged.

Maryann could barely contain her excitement anticipating sleeping in the same building in which Rob had been raised. She regretted not bringing Jake along for the trip, but hiking one hundred miles would be too much for him. And he didn't like sightseeing in cities, something she and Rob planned to do in Glasgow. Staying with the Higgins and twins, Peter and Paul, was fine with Jake. He had been assured by Maryann that someday he'd get to visit Scotland.

She and Rob were scheduled to leave New York after school let out. The bequeathing ceremony was during the last week of June. Glasgow's Orangemen's parade stepped off a few days later.

★

"I can hear the drums, Rob. You were right. They don't sound too far away."

Maryann and Rob stood on the sidewalk outside the Argyll Guest House, their accommodations for two days in Glasgow on Sauchiehall Street. Maryann was stuffed from the huge

Scottish breakfast served in the hotel's dining room. Fried eggs, blood pudding, a ramekin of baked beans, a grilled tomato half, mushrooms, sausages, bacon, triangles of toast, tubs of butter, an assortment of jam; it was all too much, yet wonderful at the same time. A chalkboard in the dining room pictured a small oval creature with six legs fleeing a net. It was captioned: "We catch our own haggis!"

The MacKenzies had returned to Glasgow after spending Maryann's dream night sleeping at Rose Gate Cottage. The previous day Rob conveyed the deed to Rose Gate to Scotland's Countryside Commission at a bequeathing ceremony A small crowd turned out for the event held under a marquee on the lawn of the cottage. Fiona's cherished entrance gate was bursting with early summer roses.

At the ceremony, Rob and Maryann were treated like royalty, but she sensed many in attendance were there mainly out of respect for Fiona. Maryann wasn't surprised by how few folks remembered Rob. People had moved on. Most old-timers were in their graves. Rob had lived away from Scotland for thirty years and now was an American citizen. She guessed many thought of him as an oddity. But a few friends recalled the crack piper he had been as a lad before heading west toward a new life.

Ceremony day was bright and cool. Maryann feasted her eyes on Loch Lomond and the surrounding highlands Rob had so eloquently described. The country was more beautiful than she imagined and much grander than depicted in *Rob Roy* and *Braveheart,* her two all-time favorite movies. Five years earlier, the two Scottish films kicked *The Three Stooges* off the top of her short list of favorites.

A highlight of the ceremony was the mounting of a bronze plaque on the whitewashed wall next to the entrance.

★————————————————————————★

Rose Gate Cottage
Fiona MacKay MacKenzie, Owner
Opened to guests, 1970

Generously donated to
The Countryside Commission
30 June 2017
by Robert MacKenzie.
Let weary travellers
Rest today,
Sheltered along the
West Highland Way.

★————————————————————————★

The plaque was beautiful in its simplicity. A short poem by Rob was its coda. The officials and Rob toasted the event with wee pours of scotch whisky. The ceremony concluded with a thunderous "Sláinte!" The roar was the signal for a piper hidden on Conic Hill to play *Auld Lang Syne* followed by *The Flower of Scotland* and *Scotland the Brave*.

The happy throng crowded around Rob shaking his hand and giving him bear hugs. At last, when the scotch bottles were empty, and Maryann was exhausted by the outpouring of emotion, a taxicab appeared and stopped in front of the cottage to take the MacKenzies to the Argyll Guest House in Glasgow.

★

They planned to spend two days in the city, one watching Orange Day festivities, the second visiting places Rob had frequented as a child. Additionally, they needed to purchase a few items for the long walk.

Rob insisted they buy golf umbrellas. Maryann couldn't get him to tell her why, other than the obvious--rain.

"In Scotland, when it pours it pours hard," he teased her. "Then it pours even harder. And just when you think it's letting up, it pours again."

"But we have our Proof-tex rain jackets," she pointed out.

"Aye, those might come in handy. You'll see what I'm talking about on the moors." He spoke as if foretelling the future. "We won't run short of water."

When fully provisioned, in three days they would begin their trek north toward Fort William, returning to Balmaha on day two, again sheltering in Rose Gate as guests.

On the flight to Scotland, Rob had admitted to Maryann he wondered if everything in Glasgow would be the same as he remembered. She told him not to be disappointed if things were different. The world had changed in thirty years.

★

After the ceremony, before they slid into the taxicab for the return trip to the Argyll Street Guest House, Rob called to the new hoteliers. "Good luck, Mr. and Mrs. Scott! You're going to love living here. When Annie and I return next week, I'll show Ewan my favorite fishing hole. And I'll give you old photos Fiona sent me. I brought them to Scotland. They picture how Rose Gate's matured over the years, and what she looks like in the winter under a blanket of snow.

"Lilly, if you want, you can mount the photos in a pictorial montage. There's one of me as a wee lad holding the practice chanter my uncle gave me. I'll also bring you a piece of piping music I composed. Its called *Fiona's Rose Gate Cottage*. I'd be pleased if you frame it, and give it a place of honor on a wall."

"How lovely, Rob!" gushed Lilly. "We'll mount it behind the reception desk."

"Brilliant!" Rob responded, expressing his pleasure by covering his heart with his hand.

Maryann stretched up to Rob's ear. She whispered, "I hope you made copies, dear. I haven't heard you play it."

"Don't fret, Annie," he reassured her. "I made copies. They're home. But I've already learned the tune. I'll give it a wee toot for you when we return to Roxbridge."

He called goodbye to the Scotts. "Cheers for now, folks! See you in a few days!"

The Scotts returned his farewell. "Thank you Rob and Annie. Thank you for giving us the chance to begin our careers here and keep Rose Gate Cottage alive and well."

Fiona's Rose Gate Cottage

Quick March   Composed by Rob MacKenzie

33
Glasgow City, Day One

A short walk along Sauchiehall Street brought the MacKenzies to a staging area for the parade. Maryann saw knots of jawboning uniformed marchers clustered in a barricaded intersection, many smoking cigarettes. Snare drummers had cords and tassels swinging beneath their drums. Stout bass drummers hefted elaborately decorated instruments lettered with the group's name, its founding date, and a painted seal or crest with heraldic symbols.

Ruddy cheeked musicians wore uniforms ranging in color from bright primary reds and blues to more somber earth tones, such as tan and black. Maryann noticed not a kilt was in sight. Band members wore trousers or *trews* as Rob called them. Some bands sported police-style hats with gleaming black patent leather visors, the crowns circled with red and white dicing. Other outfits had oddly shaped Balmorals, strangely molded to not resemble berets. They were unlike the style of tams Maryann had seen worn by pipe bands. Nor did they resemble Glengarry bonnets or Irish caubeens. Having enjoyed U.S. bands on the march and watching the World Pipe Band Championships with Rob on

YouTube, Maryann had become aware of the Scottish national uniform, the kilt and its regalia. The designs of the Orange Day uniforms were alien to her.

Moreover, the band names were amazing: *The Apprentice Boys Flute Band, The Black Skull, The Protestant Boys*. It quickly became clear to Maryann that Protestant-Catholic animosities continued to run deep in Scotland, as well as in Northern Ireland.

"Where are the kilts, Rob? Where are the pipe bands? I don't see or hear any. This is a surprise to me."

"Aye, things are different for the Orangemen's Parade. These bands and marching units represent religious groups, all of them Protestant, all against popery. Pipe bands come from a military tradition," he explained. "Even civilian pipe bands don't march on this day. You'll hear plenty of music, but it will come from wooden flutes, button accordions, and small squeeze boxes or concertinas."

Rob scanned the intersection recalling his youth. The scene was the same but also somehow different. The sheer number of participants had grown. And he was seeing an event now through the eyes of an adult, not a child.

Maryann asked, "Are flute bands like fife bands we see in the U.S.? You remember, the *Ancient Nutmeggers* in Connecticut?"

"Nae, a wee bit different, lass. The fifes in the U.S. are small. The flutes these lads play are larger with more holes than fifes. Many holes are covered with keyed felt pads. But both styles are usually made of blackwood, like the bagpipes."

They wove through the curbside crowd heading farther down Sauchiehall Street. Finally they found a clear viewing spot between a Renault and a Mini. As far as they could see in either direction, the road was lined with police barricades. Mounted Strathclyde Police in day-glo yellow vests patrolled the sidelines.

On either side of the MacKenzies were small knots of young men, some shirtless and tattooed, all well into their day's ration of beer. Other than testosterone induced male posturing and a few *fucks* tossed here and there, for the moment they were behaving themselves. Whether good manners would persist as the day wore on was anyone's guess.

Just minutes before the procession began, Rob told Annie the parade they were about to see was the fourth division of a much larger multi-divisional event. "Thirty years ago the entire parade stepped off from up the street, Annie, at the intersection we crossed. But with Scotland's economy improved and a growing population, many starting points had to be designated. The end result is the convergence of thousands of marchers and spectators at Glasgow Commons. That's where the fun begins. After a day in the sun drinking beer, eating meat pies, and strutting around like bulldog puppies, tempers will be tested."

"Are we going to the commons, Rob?'

"Nae, lassie. I want to keep us intact. We have a long trek ahead of us."

"Here come the blighters!" yelled a youth well into his cups. Maryann saw stares of annoyance directed his way. The faithful were having none of it. A thick-set gentleman in suit and tie pushed his way over to the offender.

"You keep yer yap shut," she heard him growl. "Yer a worthless piece of shite. Keep it up, and I'll tear yer arsehole wide enough to fit me size thirteen brogan." The good Samaritan stared menacingly at the other youths. They backed away. The drunk lad spewed into the gutter.

"Good example of Christian benevolence," Rob mumbled to Maryann, as the parade got underway.

Maryann felt a wave of anticipation sweep up and down the throngs lining the side of Sauchiehall Street. She watched unit after unit stream past with scant belly to butt spacing between organizations. The Black Skull Flute Band led off followed by dozens of Protestant charities, religious lodges, and more bands. Many groups were led by male drum majors flinging batons high overhead hoping to snare them before they landed on the bonnet of a parked vehicle or a bonnet worn on the noggin of an unlucky observer.

Shrill flute music and nasal squeeze box tunes made the parade sound like competing bands in a one-room ceilidh. Wee lads tried to emulate adult drum majors by weaving small batons under their arms and behind their backs. Some bands had children marching in formation. The wee'uns crashed away with cymbals or tapped triangles.

Lodge women were demurely dressed in knee-length straight black skirts and collared white blouses. They reminded Maryann of post-war ladies she had seen in photos from the 1950's. Their male counterparts were snug in dark suit jackets, white shirts and black ties, proud chests crisscrossed with bright orange sashes. Some wore fedoras, but most were hatless. Seeing many receding hairlines, Maryann wondered if male-pattern baldness was a genetic trait in middle-aged Scottish men. She quickly glanced at Rob's head. His hair was still thick.

The color orange was everywhere. Orange streamers flew from the corners of large banners held aloft with poles and guy ropes. Maryann gaped at one she couldn't decipher. "Rob! Look at that banner!" she said, pointing. "What does it mean?"

"It's a reminder of the siege of Derry," he said. "The encounter predates the Battle of the Boyne by a year or so. Irish Protestants in Ulster refused to succumb to a military takeover by Roman Catholic King James II, so he sent units of his army to take over Londonderry. The Protestant citizenry locked themselves in the city and endured a siege that lasted one hundred days.

"Meanwhile, James's troops, the Jacobites, built a wooden boom across the River Foyle to prevent reinforcements and supplies from reaching the entrapped city. Eventually, ships of William of Orange broke through the boom carrying supplies. The Jacobite siege was broken. That's what that banner commemorates."

Rob hesitated a moment to consider how he could explain all the hatreds and animosities that rent Scotland, England, and Ireland for hundreds of years. Even being schooled in Scotland, and having had to endure the convoluted stories heard in history classes, he couldn't keep all the plots and subplots straight. But Annie deserved some sort of explanation.

"Look, honey," he began, "it would be easy to attribute all the Gaelic hatreds to Catholic versus Protestant bigotry. That would be simple. But the reality is, the fabric of Scotland is woven with dozens of competing rivalries. As you know from today, there's the Catholic-Protestant mess, but also Anglicanism against Presbyterianism, clan versus clan, highlanders hating lowlanders, east coast versus west coast, lairds versus lairds, the crown versus the proletariat, the gentry versus the serfs. It goes on and on.

"The pride and emotions you see today at this parade only touch on the underlying resentments that still fester in the U.K. Look at these people. They're exactly the same stock of humanity that wears green in March. Change the color of the sashes, and you wouldn't be able to notice the difference."

He squeezed Maryann on the shoulder. "Too bad nobody parades for the Golden Rule, my love. Things might get better."

He kissed her forehead. "We've been here an hour," he said, after checking his watch. "That's long enough for me. Let's find a basement tea room and have some Earl Grey--maybe some scones, too. It's almost lunch time."

Maryann was happy to move on. "That would be lovely, sweetie. Tea and strawberries with clotted cream. Count me in. I can hardly wait!"

34

Glasgow City, Day Two

"I'm hungry. Can't we do this later?" Maryann studied the arrangement of clothing and supplies Rob had spread out on their bed.

"I'll only be a wee minute more, love. We're going out today for umbrellas, but there might be something else we forgot to bring from the states. We can pick up missing gear in city center."

Maryann sighed in resignation. When Rob was on a mission, he was hard to deter. "I'm not laying out all my stuff," she said. "It's packed and ready to go. But I'll get my checklist and make sure my gear matches up with yours."

"Brilliant! I'm quite sure I have what I need, but you can never be too careful. Uncle Willie liked saying, 'Don't let good dominate perfection.'"

Maryann laughed. "Jeepers! Another silly Willie maxim. How does that fit with what you're doing?"

"He sarcastically meant, 'Forget your gear. Get the hell out of the croft and start moving'. Stupidly, I keep trying for perfection."

"What do you think you'll forget this time?" she asked.

"I'm not sure, Annie, but one thing I'm absolutely certain about. I'll remember to bring you." He kissed her.

Rob's Clothing and Equipment List

rain jacket w/ hood	small Maglite torch
2 pr quik-dri socks	insect repellent
2 quik-dri briefs	sunglasses
1 pr trekking shorts	cap w/ bill
1 pr trews	1 btl Aleve
fleece jacket	water bottle
1 collared shirt	first aid kit
1 Quik-dri trekking shirt	2 bandanas
Tevas	20' parachute cord

Waterproof case (w/ passport, ins cards, driver's lic, health info, map and trail guide, sm notebook, mech pencil), sm. bagpipe practice chanter, iPhone.

1st day wear: long sleeve Quik-dri shirt, under briefs, trekking shorts, nylon belt, socks, water-proof low-cut boots, gaiters.

Envelope w/ photos of Rose Gate; folder w/ *Fiona's Rose Gate Cottage* score.

Maryann looked over Rob's equipment assortment and compared it with her checklist. She felt confident she was prepared. "Are you sure you can repack all that stuff in your rucksack?" she asked. "I don't recall that amount when you first loaded up."

"Aye, it'll all fit in. When I removed the two small folding umbrellas, it made a wee bit more room. The two brollies we get here in Glasgow will be bigger and sturdier. We'll be carrying them in our hands, not loading them in our packs."

"No compass?

He laughed. "None needed, lass. I know much of the route and Scotland's cardinal points of the compass are in my genes. Even when it's not sunny, I know the way."

She smiled. "We'll have to test you on that one. I see you've listed your belt as part of what you plan to wear tomorrow. Was that really necessary?"

"Aye, remember what I said. You can't be too careful. I don't want my shorts falling off, especially if somehow I'm lost on the moors."

The breakfast lounge was half full, early morning conversations hushed, human batteries recharging. Rob and Maryann checked the buffet side-board offerings, poured coffee, then moved to a small table beside a window overlooking the street. The sidewalk was wet. Pedestrians hurried to their jobs protected by umbrellas. The sunny Orangemen's celebration of the previous day had been swallowed by Glasgow mist and gloom.

The MacKenzies returned to the buffet. Maryann passed by the rich Scottish offerings selecting, instead, granola with yogurt. She saw Rob take a slice of cantaloupe, scrambled eggs, and toast. While at the sideboard, he cut a thin wedge of haggis. He was determined to have her at least try a taste. She had agreed, stipulating it be no more than a wee bite. "In the nibble range," she directed. As she returned to her seat, she passed by the cartoonish haggis image still galloping across the chalkboard.

"Okay, love, you agreed to try it," he said, returning to the table. "Scots sometimes brighten the flavor with HP Sauce."

"I prefer my haggis neat," she said, forking a small piece into her mouth. She let it sit on her tongue, chewed a bit, then smiled. "I admit, it's not too bad. It reminds me of liverwurst with oats mixed in--not quite the same--but close."

"Aye, Annie, that's what I've been telling you. Haggis is a grand pudding."

"I wouldn't go that far, sweetie. Like liverwurst, it's still made from an animal's guts."

She remembered a story she heard while in college. "A swimmer friend, Margie Oswald, had a big dog--German Shepherd, as I recall. One day she was helping her mother make liverwurst sandwiches. Naturally, her dog was underfoot. Somehow a slice of meat fell on the floor. Before she could pick it up, the dog was on it."

"Aye, I'm not surprised. Gobbled it down, I'm sure."

"No! To her amazement the dog was rolling on it, trying to smear the meat into his neck ruff. Margie concluded the dog thought it was either decomposing carrion or poop. By contrast, we smarter-than-dogs humans eat it with relish."

Rob laughed silently, shaking his head in wonder.

"Whether shite or bad meat," continued Maryann, "that was the dog's take on liverwurst. I wonder what he would have done with haggis?"

Rob laughed again, "I don't know for sure, but with a big dog,

I think I'd tread carefully. You try to take a delicacy like haggis away from a carnivore, and he might try to take an arm away from you." Rob poured more coffee. They began eating.

A new couple entered the lounge, scanned the available tables, picked one next to the MacKenzies, then marked their spots, she with her purse, he with a red baseball cap. Maryann felt a sudden dread while watching them at the buffet pile their plates high with food.

The missus was heavy-set with doughy skin, double chins, and loose waddle under her arms. She was wearing a floral muumuu and white sneakers. Her mouth was small and round, her eyes thin and mouse-like, her round cheeks rust-red with rouge. A mass of unnatural copper ringlets covered her head.

Her spouse was even larger. He was bald and burdened with a plump nose that bore the ravages of alcohol. He wore a Hawaiian floral shirt, huge baggy Bermuda shorts, and black socks with tan shoes secured by Velcro straps. His shorts were tightly cinched around the equator of his girth. Maryann couldn't remember the last time she had seen two people so ill-prepared for their environment or so unpleasant looking since--she thought--the Republican presidential campaign in 2016! *If they're Democrats*, she thought, *I'll eat more haggis.* It was a vow she knew wouldn't come true.

It took some willpower, but Maryann finally ignored the couple and asked Rob about their impending trip. "Honey, you keep saying tomorrow's destination is Mullguy. But when I looked at the map, our B&B's in a town spelled m-i-l-n-g-a-v-i-e. What gives? The spelling and your pronunciation aren't even close."

Rob swallowed his mouthful, then chuckled. "Aye, lass, it's one of the dozens of Scottish words and places where spelling and pronunciation don't match. Many evolved out of pre-Gaelic ancient languages and have been garbled into a variety of Scottish dialects. I guarantee, Annie, there are Scots who sound like they come from the States, and others who sound like they come from Outer Mongolia. The variety of dialects is astonishing."

Uninvited, the heavy-set male guest at the adjacent table pushed his way into their conversation. Apparently he had been listening in. "I couldn't help hear what you're saying, mister. I've noticed the same thing since we've been here. Damn shame this country can't get its language straightened out. Might solve the anger issues Gert and I saw yesterday at the parade. At least you and your female friend are understandable."

Rob was stunned by both the intrusion into his private conversation with Maryann and the paternalism rudely implied about Scottish speech patterns. "I beg your pardon," he responded, annoyed. "What did you say?"

Manyann saw Rob stiffen. She reached across the table and put her hand on his wrist.

The man continued spouting his nonsense. "In my country we're getting everyone to speak American. Enough with Spanglish and Arabesque. Yellow ching-chong, too. If we're gonna be great again, we all need to speak the same god-damned language. Capiche?"

Rob's eyes narrowed. "I don't know what you think, sir, but I'm an American citizen. I was born in Scotland, but I've lived in America for thirty years. I served in the U.S. Army. How about you?"

"I've lived in America my whole life," he said with a grin, patting his belly. "Born in Dayton. Didn't serve, though. Bunions. Regret it to this day." He scooped up a pile of baked beans with a soup spoon and stuffed his mouth.

Maryann used her eyes urging Rob to back out of the conversation.

But the man didn't let Rob retreat. He wiped his mouth with a napkin and continued with his verbal jingoism. "Yeah, years ago we let anyone in. It was a big mistake. That's why we're in the predicament we're in now. But finally we're making laws to keep aliens out of our country. Too many want to come in and sponge off welfare or take jobs away from real Americans."

Rob stood and faced his fellow citizen. The round man tried but couldn't easily stand. His paunch interfered with his effort. When he saw Rob's height and sinewy build, he thought better of it and stayed seated.

"What kind of work do you do, sir?" asked Rob, leaning on the man's table staring him coldly in the eyes.

"Shut up, Randy!" barked Gert to her husband. "Let this man finish his breakfast."

Rob ignored Gert and persisted. "I asked you, sir, what kind of work do you do?"

Randy sucked at his teeth, then replied. "Good, hard, honest work. I used to make cars for Ford. Hurt my back. Now I'm out on disability. How about you, Scotty? What's your line?"

Maryann was now standing at Rob's side, her hand grasping

his belt from the rear. Even though she recognized the couple as "ugly Americans" and worthy of a tongue lashing, if not more, she wanted her husband to diffuse the situation. "Rob," she pleaded, "there's another table across the room. Let's finish our coffee over there."

Rob straightened up. He put his hands in his pants pockets and answered the man's question. "I'm a scientist and teacher," he said through clenched teeth. "I deal in reason."

"Crap!" spat Rob's tormentor. "You're both an alien and a liberal! Thank God Trump's got things under control! We're getting back to a level of greatness again. Andrew Jackson, Old Hickory--know who he is?--called U.S. domination, Manifest Destiny. God's decided we're the chosen people. Trump's working for God and the American voter. Certainly that's true in Ohio, where we live."

Rob stood silently wondering if this man might be some kind of joke foisted on him by an old friend. He saw the man's untouched blood pudding and fantasized what he could do with it. He felt Maryann's tug at his waist. He decided to end the conversation with a lesson in history. After that he planned to leave the bloody fool to wallow in his trough. "I'm disappointed meeting a fellow American who's so uneducated," Rob said. The man tried to interrupt, but Rob stared him into silence.

"The America you so ardently promote is based on a track record of stealing from native peoples," Rob said slowly. "It grew on the backs of four million enslaved Africans. Capitalist practices were encouraged that bamboozled working stiffs like you for the benefit of men who consider themselves royalty. It's an America that has fought wars on all continents and looted other countries of their resources. It's an America that constantly threatens to take away health insurance from millions of people. Because of its evil and cowardly history, America never was great, isn't great now, and will never be great in the future. No amount of baseball hats will change that."

Rob ended his face off with pieces of advice. "It's raining today, sir. I suggest you stay indoors so you don't melt. Protect that bad back of yours. Or if you get the itch for some exercise, buy umbrellas and go for a walk. In fact, I have two you may have. Looking at you, I suspect some exercise will do you good. But for the sake of St. Andrew, laddie, change your clothes before you go out. You're in bloody Scotland, man, not Hawaii. Aloha."

"Have you given any more thought to the job posting you saw on the website of the American Association for the Advancement of Science? You remember, at the University of Colorado?"

Maryann and Rob sat on the upper level of a red double-decker Hop On-Hop Off bus making its way through Glasgow City Center. If the weather had been fair, they would have taken seats in the rear beyond the protective canopy shielding the first seven rows. But a persistent drizzle forced them under cover. Their destination was Affordable Golf, a store on Hydepark Street, only a few blocks distant from a designated bus stop.

Maryann's question startled Rob back into awareness. He had been thinking about the encounter in the breakfast room with the fat man from Ohio. He regretted he had been lured into the confrontation. He remembered an Uncle Willie saying: "If you argue with a fool, it's difficult to tell who's the fool."

"Aye, Annie, I've thought about it." He looked at his wife, as if apologizing for having done something foolish. "The opportunity's perfect for me. There may never be an opening like it. And I fit all the qualifying requirements like a hand in a kidskin glove."

Maryann entwined their fingers and kissed his cheek. "I think you ought to go for it," she encouraged him. "You're a multi-faceted scientist, too valuable to spend the rest of your career in a small high school." She hesitated seeking the right words. "Don't get me wrong, Rob. Roxbridge kids deserve the best, but your future ought to be helping a broad spectrum of science academics learn to make their discoveries understandable to a wider audience than simply to more fellow academicians. Do it, honey! Apply for the position."

Listed by the AAAS, the opening was to assume the chairmanship of a small, interscience communications department at the University of Colorado in Boulder. The focus of the program was to teach number-crunchers, laboratory researchers, graduate and college upper-class students majoring in the sciences, the art of clear writing as it pertained to progress reports, discovery announcements, data analysis, and manuscripts being submitted to academic journals for publication.

The job was listed at the Associate Professorship tenure-track level. It required teaching two sections and advising students. It was expected that the chair would develop and expand the program, eventually hiring two more instructors as enrollment grew. Internet tutorials were a goal for the future. Salary and benefits were generous and included membership in a local health club.

From the moment weeks ago, when Rob had mentioned the opening, Maryann had urged him to apply. If he was hired, with her knowledge of nuclear waste issues, she was confident she could find employment along Colorado's Front Range where A-Bomb triggering devices had been manufactured at Rocky Flats. Once a toxic Superfund site, the rangeland northwest of Denver persisted in emitting radiation despite being cleaned up. And if a nuclear-waste job wasn't available, advocacy groups concerned about methane pollution from fracked gas wells was another avenue for her to pursue.

Moving to Boulder would mean she'd be farther away from Tippy, her mom in Pennsylvania. But a direct flight to Pittsburgh from DIA took no more time than driving from Connecticut to Mars. Besides, finally she could reunite with her brother Fred, his wife, Lois, and her nieces, Lindsay and Jeannie The idea of having her brother close by was especially sweet.

What else about a move west appealed to her? If it happened, Jake would be at the right age to start middle school in a new location. And for him, there were indoor rock gymnasiums along with the allure of the mountains with unlimited outdoor climbing. Boulder was ringed and crossed with hundreds of miles of bike trails. The city had three recreation centers. Restaurants were abundant. She might be able to jettison a car. Unlike western Connecticut, abundant public transportation was available, buses running into Denver and as far out as the airport.

If pressed, Maryann might also have admitted she was curious to learn about the Flagstaff Star, a huge lighted pentagram draped on the mountainside overlooking Boulder during the winter holiday season. Fred had emailed photos of it to her. It looked magical. She wondered if it had religious roots. As a pentagram, maybe it was satanic . . . probably not, she chuckled to herself. If they were to head to Boulder, before they moved she vowed to research its history. That was part of her nature--dig into the unexplained and challenge the debatable. She wondered what her husband, Mr. ULAR-man, would make of a mountainside star.

They remained on the Hop On-Hop Off bus until it reached a designated stop on Finnieston Street. From there it was a three block walk to the golf store. The sky was darkening, heavier rain threatened. Buying umbrellas now meant they could get on and off at city attractions without getting soaked. Rob knew it was better to test their brollies before heading into the hills.

The skies opened up as they neared the store. A short trot got them inside out of the wet. Had they been avid golfers, the business would have looked like a bonanza. The showroom was a treasure trove of clubs and bags representing all price points and prestigious name brands.

"Where are you hiding your umbrellas?" Rob asked a clerk.

"Over there, sir." He pointed to the rear of the shop. "Are you planning a golfing holiday? We have top of the line clubs on sale, and I can book you a starting time at any number of courses. If you're going to be in Scotland for more than a week, I can even get you a tee time at St. Andrews. Usually, you have to reserve a year in advance. But if you buy new equipment, I can get you in." He winked slyly at Rob indicating commerce opened all doors.

"Don't want to visit St. Andrews," said Rob. "I've been there."

"I can tell from your accent you're a Scot," said the clerk. "How well did you play? Those pot bunkers sink the strongest golfers."

"Didn't play golf," said Rob, hoping to confuse the clerk. "When I was a lad, I piped there for a wedding."

The clerk appeared surprised. "Oh, a piper! I understand. You're not a golfer."

"Nae, I am not!" said Rob with emphasis. He glanced around. "Now, about those umbrellas?"

"Aye, the umbrellas. Is it simply to fend off the rain, then? If it's only that, I suggest, sir, you visit the souvenir store just down the street. They have small foldable models that cost a fraction of ours."

Rob looked at Maryann then back at the clerk. "We don't want light-weight models," he said, "ones that will rip apart at the slightest breeze. We're trekking the West Highland Way. I want two heavy-duty models to keep us dry and stand up to the wind. And when the weather's fair, we'll use them as trekking poles."

The clerk interrupted, "But what about your waterproofs? Surely, you're taking rainproof parkas. It can get cold along the loch."

"Aye, lad, we have jackets. But I've learned if you wear them when it's warm and rainy you get wet. It's the sweat that soaks you, not the rain. Using brollies will keep us dry and let our condensation evaporate."

"It also helps to get the stink blown off," Maryann chipped in.

The clerk laughed. "Aye. The wee lass never said a truer word."

"Our umbrella stock is over by the shoe display. Follow me and I'll fix you up with the perfect trekking poles for your big walk."

★

Equipped with solid golfing umbrellas and full-day passes for the Hop On-Hop Off double-decker, they toured Glasgow stopping at attractions that interested Maryann. She quickly realized she'd be unable to visit every museum and place of significance. Perhaps on another trip to Scotland, she would see more of Glasgow. Rob told her they ought to return in August when the world-famous Military Tattoo took place in Edinburgh.

As the bus followed its route, Rob admitted he didn't recognize much of Twenty-first Century Glasgow. Bob Hardie's piping store was gone from where he thought it should be. Its business was now conducted out of the National Piping Center.

The seventeen storey mid-rise, mixed-use skyscraper, St Andrew House, was still standing, its footprint on the same block of Sauchiehall Street. But the post WWII Tower Blocks were long gone. Hastily erected to fill Glasgow's post-war housing shortage, the architecture was as dismal as Soviet era apartment schemes still littering eastern European cities. No amount of geometric designs garishly painted on concrete block façades could mask the buildings from what they rapidly became--slums.

They spent four hours in the Kelvingrove Art Gallery and Museum. Built in 1901, and refurbished in 2006, the Baroque masterpiece contained more than eighty galleries. It was too much to digest in one visit. Dinosaurs, arms and armour, prehistoric mammals, objects from ancient Egypt, and scores of other rarities reminded Maryann of the collections in the Museum of Natural History in New York.

But other galleries under the same roof contained French Impressionists, Dutch Masters, Salvador Dali's *Christ of St John on the Cross*, and a gallery dedicated to the Scottish architect, Charles Rennie Mackintosh. It featured the so-called *Glasgow Style*, a design movement which was the UK's contribution to art nouveau. Maryann tried to locate any work by Robert Rauschenberg, but she came up cold. She was warmed, however, remembering it was in the Guggenheim she first met her husband. Anyway, the art collection at Kelvingrove prompted her to equate it with the offerings at New York's Metropolitan Museum of Art.

The rain had reverted to a drizzle when they exited the building. That allowed them to stroll along the lawns among the classrooms and laboratories at the University of Glasgow, sited in a park-like setting near the museum. Rob helped Maryann get oriented to where they were by pointing out the Hop On-Hop Off bus had been following a circular route, interrupted with numerous detours and switchbacks. In fact, standing in the middle of the university, they were only a few blocks away from the Argyll Street Guest House, their Glasgow accommodation. The bus stop they used to begin their morning search for umbrellas was down the street from the hotel.

Rob had called their brolly mission, "searching for the Holy

Grail." As if preordained, they had struck pay dirt with two Ping brand golf umbrellas.

"I think these two brollies will bring us good luck," said Rob. "After all, one meaning of the word ping in Chinese is 'peace'."

Maryann then reminded him that ping in Chinese also meant 'apple'.

35

Maryann's Trip Journal

Day 1: Glasgow to Milngavie: 8 miles.

Cloudy & rainy in Scotland. Hot & sunny at Wimbledon. Will Andy Murray be UK hero again? Left Glasgow in soft rain about 8:30 a.m. New umbrellas perfect! Had lovely walk despite being on sidewalks next to busy roads. Reached Milngavie (Mull-guy!) at 11 a.m. Found Drumlin Guest House easily, but no one home. Walked to town center & had light lunch in supermarket coffee shop.

After lunch, skies cleared. Sat on bench in park-like setting. Rob tooted on practice chanter. I read & napped. Returned to B&B in time for Wimbledon. Weather blew clear for beautiful evening & lovely dinner at wine bar. Enjoyed watching rough & tumble kids on playground. Parents stood outside fence unconcerned. Neighbor guests in B&B are German & Dutch. Hiking WHW, too.

Day 2: Milngavie to Drymen: 12 miles.

Sun continues with lovely, clearing breezes. Up & ready to

walk! 12 mile hike was rolling with absolutely dazzling weather. Made good time of close to 3 mi/hr to Drymen. Rob smart having us "train" on Conservation Trust properties. But nice finally carrying useful gear in packs rather than sand bags.

Walked past Mulberry lodge & had to circle back to find reference point: 1800's gate. B&B newly restored & expanded. Cleaned up, rested, then walked to village center for dinner of seafood salad & salmon.

Followed Old Gartmore Road to Clairinch Way. Saw Rob's piping teacher's cottage. (Pipe Major Angus MacKay). Cut across field to Drymen Primary School, Rob's old haunt. Showed me his room through window. How did he fit in those wee chairs?

Returned to village & watched lawn bowling at hotel. Back to B&B. Program on TV re nuclear test site in NM, USA. Radioactive waste now even more a threat. Sad what we've done to our environment.

Soft but comfy twin beds.

Day 3: Drymen to Balmaha: 7 miles.

Overcast & thunderstorms predicted for 7 mi. hike over Conic Hill to Balmaha. Didn't worry--had umbrellas. Lovely forest walk up Conic Hill thru stands of Norway Spruce. Forest replanted after blow-down. Near top, Rob showed me fen that supplied water to Rose Gate 30 yrs. ago. B&B now has well. Top of CH very windy. No thunder, no storm. . . yet! Clouds restricted view of Loch Lomond. CH not cone-shaped--long hogback ridge. Steep descent down rocky trail to Balmaha car park. Arrived at 12:15. Restaurant opened at 12:30.

After lunch Rob got harbormaster, McMaster, to motor us N. to end of lake to see Isle I Vow where a nasty clan killed nuns. Couldn't follow Rob's story. He sounds like Uncle Willie?

Returned to Balmaha at 4:00 & took packs to Rose Gate Cottage. Rob gave Lilly photos & sheet music. He played tune on practice chanter so Mr. & Mrs. could hear. Ewan showed Rob wall of honor for displaying tune.

Hot showers & rested in master bedroom before supper. Lilly invited us to eat with them. Lovely couple. I'm so excited to be sleeping again in cottage where Rob grew up. I love my husband.

Rob relaxed in an armchair in the parlor. He smiled at Annie sitting on the couch, her shoeless feet tucked under her. He laced his fingers behind his head, digesting the lamb, neeps, and tatties Lilly Scott had served for supper. Even though Rose Gate Cottage was officially listed as a B&B, there were always scones and lentil soup ready for the chilled trekker in the winter. But now it was summer. However, as honored guests he and Annie had been invited to sup with the fledgling innkeepers.

"You urged me to go for it," said Rob, "so I did."

"You mean the Colorado job," acknowledged Annie.

"Aye. I emailed Jack Dawson at the National Center of Atmospheric Research to find out more about the opening and what were my chances."

"How do you know Jack?" Annie's curiosity was aroused. Rob's mention of an email meant he was seriously thinking about a Colorado move.

"We studied at UNC together. We've kept in touch."

"What kind of work does he do at NCAR?"

"He and his team are measuring rates of increase in ozone levels along the Front Range, particularly as it's impacted by Denver's population growth."

Maryann didn't see the connection between Jack Dawson and a new program at the University of Colorado. "How does he know about the CU job?" she asked. "Does he have contacts in the science department?"

"Aye, lots of them. Everyone's connected. They all participate in UCAR, University Corporation for Atmospheric Research. Institutions across the country take part. Each contributes research data collected in their sector. As weather patterns change and global warming increases, more and more environmentally aware students are becoming involved in the sciences involved. That means college students, graduate students, graduate assistants, lab technicians, researchers--thousands of young people and established scientists, too, are submitting scores of research papers to journals around the world."

"What did he say about your chances?"

"He said they were good. Apparently, someone with my background is exactly what they want. There aren't too many of us with my array of skills."

Rob leaned forward to make his point known. "All these new scientists need training in how to write clearly and persuasively, Annie. If they want their findings to be believed and accepted, they have to be able to communicate without ambiguity. That's what the new program at CU will do. It's aimed at CU students, but will also be developed into online tutorials."

Annie was amazed by all Rob had learned in just a few days--or had he been mulling it over for longer than she knew? She was excited for him. Then, thinking about how their lives might change, she was excited for herself but became cautious.

"Before we make any decisions to leave Connecticut, Rob, shouldn't we first visit the new place?"

"Aye, if there's time and I apply, I'll have to go to Boulder for interviews. Of course, you and Jake will come with me. I hope it can be arranged."

"As I said on the bus," she urged him, "go for it. It's not if you apply, it's when you apply. As soon as we get back to the States--do it." Annie reverted to mother speak telling him how to live his life. She knew he loved her for her assertiveness.

"I will, sweetie. I'll send off an email to CU saying I'm an applicant and will forward my credentials when I return to the U.S."

He became reflective. "You and I have a habit of jumping into things quickly, Annie, like our marriage, me taking a job at WestConn, and your decision to start your own law practice in Roxbridge. But it always seems to work out. I'd credit our Ping umbrellas for the good luck, but providence preceded them. Sometimes you can mull over things too much. Uncle Willie said, 'Follow . . .'"

Maryann interrupted, ". . . I know, I know. Follow your heart!"

★

Day 4: Balmaha to Rowardennan: 7.2 miles.

Enjoyed meeting couple (Adams?) from Maine at breakfast. Niece graduating from St. Andrew's. They plan to fish on loch today.

After B'fast on WHW again! Sky cleared during walk along Loch Lomond shores & forest to Rowardennan Hotel, which Lilly Scott said was lacking. After Scott's superb service last night & this AM, anything else would look dim.

Umbrella is good for walking stick & twirled like baton. Bats away flies (cleggs). Bugs not as bad as expected--so far!

Spent afternoon on high ferry pier overlooking Loch Lomond with Ben Lomond looming above our right shoulders. Rob & I are propped against steel cable getting drunk in the sun with southerly breezes. A motor boat dragging two inflated tubes with kids passed by. Various fishermen drifted here and there. Maine couple among them?

Day 5: Rowardennan to Inversnaid: 7.3 miles.

Part sun. Have packed lunches. Glorious walk up forestry road overlooking Loch Lomond. Rougher after descent to shoreline. Trail rocky & uneven near loch to hotel, but no complaints. Bracken growing higher.

Arrived at bridge over Arkat Waterfalls about 12:15, just in time to take off boots, air out feet, & eat lunch.

Early afternoon--swam (quickly) in loch as Rob watched & took photos. Enjoyed hot bath afterwards & prepared for tomorrow. Supposed to be harder part of walk coming up.

★

They stretched out on their bed, charging batteries for the next day's slog. Rob broke the quiet. "You were a brave lass gettin' in the loch," he said smiling. "I have some lovely photos of you on my iPhone. Why didn't you take off your t-shirt? You had a sports bra on underneath."

Annie laughed at the memory. "I thought I'd stay warmer with the shirt on, but I was wrong. That water's cold!" She inched closer to him. "I hope you're not gonna post those pictures on Facebook," she said. "I look like a waterlogged puppy."

"Nae, lassie, I'll keep them confidential until you want people to see what you did on your vacation. Besides, I don't want other men gettin' ideas."

"You're not becoming jealous, are you?" She poked him in the ribs.

"Just being smart. You're my bonny lass alone. I don't intend to share you, except with Jake. I love you."

She beamed. "Thank you, dear. Yes, I'm all yours." She threw a leg over Rob's calf.

She asked about Colorado. "It's been convenient for you to use the hotel's internet connection and computer to contact Boulder. Any replies to your messages?"

"Aye, I was planning to tell you." He nodded and turned on his side facing her. Now her leg was straddling his thigh.

"There's good news. It's from CU's Environmental Studies Program. The Director, Dr. Gail Wiseman, let me know they're thrilled I'm considering joining them. She'll hold the position open until we get back to the States when I can formally apply."

"Rob, I'm so happy for you! It reminds me of when you told me about the WestConn appointment. I'm certain you'll be a terrific addition to their faculty."

Annie slid even closer to Rob and kissed him softly on the lips. She thought to herself, *changes are a-coming*! But first, before any changes, she knew it was important to make love on the West Highland Way. Immediate action was part of her nature. It was time to get to the point.

She touched him gently and felt him respond.

★

Day 6: Inversnaid to Inverarnan: 6.5 miles.

Purchased packed lunches. Rumor: Brit Rail may strike (what a surprise!)--doesn't affect walkers. Overcast but dry. Rained early on, but not heavy enough to cause trouble over rocky areas. Crossed streams in boots. Lucky to have boardwalks spanning marshy bogs. Arrived at Drovers Inn B&B shortly before noon under grey skies. Ate packed lunches under cover of old barn to escape midges. Nasty beasties!

This would have been a good day to add another 6 miles. Walked over rickety bridge to A82, past construction. Followed A82 to ancient Inverarnan pub for ale and tea. Sat outside for hour reading while Rob chantered before rains began in earnest. Headed back to covered barnyard area to wait to get into B&B. Nice umbrellas!

Thunder & lightening wiped out electricity, so room couldn't be Hoovered. But it was good to get inside thick walls, regardless of carpet condition.

Mrs. Hepburn, congenial Brit, married to deerslayer of estate. Room pleasant, but amenities such as soap & hot water limited. I've been spoiled.

Day 7: Inverarnan to Crianlarich: 6.5 miles.

Cloudy. Shared breakfast chatter w/ English youngsters. She's about to start teaching. He's a chemistry student working toward PhD. She looked about 18, especially with nose ring.

Skirting clouds broke apart to partly sunny, beautiful day. Picked up more bites from flies, but not as bad as warned. Rolling walk near river before crossing & onto old military road above A82. Wide open views of Crianlarich. Lunched outside pub before walking to Ben Mhor Lodge with long views out our window. Looks like dinner is included in our room charge. Not bad! Nope! Found out later, additional charge for dinner.

Long afternoon, good meal, pleasant chat w/ British couple (David & Janet) who travel non-stop during their 3 yr. marriage. They sleep in camper, eat in B&Bs. B&Bs very flexible. Returned to room to watch, *The Gods Must be Crazy*. Can't escape Coke ads.

Day 8: Crianlarich to Tyndrum: 6.5 miles.

Mostly cloudy but rain held off for another short, easy walk back & forth across A82 on old farm & military road to Tyndrum. Surprised by # of shops & tourists in area. Even has Tourist Info. Office where we booked one night in Fort William. Glengarry B&B removed from town center, out on A82.

Lovely old home & very comfy. Rob downstairs in sitting room chantering. I bought Scottish history book. Time to read.

Glengarry B&B has eclectic art collection that's outstanding. The Mrs. has an eye for bargains & arrangements. Breakfasted with Hendersons who both work in Dumfries.

★

The MacKenzies adjusted their packs and walked away from their B&B. Water bottles were filled. Focused on preparing for another day on the WHW, this was the first time Annie had a chance to update Rob on what had been sent to her iPhone via the cloud.

"Honey, I got a message from the Higgins to email them when we have a chance." Maryann laughed.

Rob was concerned. "Is it about Jake? Is Jake okay? Why are you laughing?"

"Yes, dear. It's Jake news. Nothing to worry about, though. Kitty said he wanted to tell you he's writing and illustrating a comic book. He couldn't wait until we got home to tell you."

"Did Kitty say anything else?"

"Only that his story has Miracle in it."

"You mean the pig?" Rob shook his head in disbelief. "Up to now he's refused to write anything during summer vacation. I wonder what changed his mind?"

"Don't know, love. You'll have to be patient waiting to find out."

★

Day 9: Tyndrum to Bridge of Orchy: 6.75 miles.

Rain on & off but not hard. Good test of umbrella mechanism: up-down, up-down. Saw Janet & David last night with car & camper. His car parked outside Bridge of Orchy Hotel when we arrived for lunch. Couple not around.

Lovely (I keep saying that) walk out of Tyndrum on old dirt road almost whole way. We met up with a Brit. & a Canadian who had been walking with the Dumfries Hendersons last few days. They fell behind since they're only going to Inveran, just 3 mi. farther on. We actually have longer trek w/ 4 mi. to B&B. Look forward to the extra distance this afternoon.

The River Orchy is beautiful with rapids, falls, & rocks. Looks great for kayaking. The one-track paved road made for easy walking, especially since there was little weekday traffic. The hotel sits in the river valley below a huge mtn. caldron that winter ice climbers frequent. Tea & cookies & coffee cake served to fatten us up from the additional 4 miles we walked since lunch. Melon, raspberries, tomatoes & lettuce & quiche for dinner, plus a pitcher of OJ--material for an explosive evening. First firm mattress in the UK for a solid night of sleep. French wife pleases.

In the hotel lounge, Rob logged into Kitty Higgins' email. She reported Jake was titling a comic book, "The Granite Hill Billies." There were three main characters: nasty Pop Ular, Ann Knee, and Jay Cobb. The story had lots of details including "supersoaker" weapons, constant rain, and Trump brand beef jerky. Jay Cobb had a pet piglet named Miracle. Kitty couldn't make sense of his plot. She reported saying Rob would have to sort it all out when he got home.

Jake wanted to know if his mother had seen any haggises. Maryann told Rob to tell Jake so far she had seen only one--in the dining room of the Argyll Street Guest House. "It tasted good," Rob added to her message.

Rob closed by saying they'd be home soon. He asked Kitty to tell Jake to Google, "Rock climbing in Colorado's Flatirons."

★

Day 10: Bridge of Orchy thru Inveroran to Kingshouse: 12 miles.

Overcast w/ forecast of rain. Well, we made our 12 mi. Hike in less than 4 hrs. & actually walked in sun part of the way. In bunkhouse again, we got settled & clean before the rains came.

We first walked along a one lane road out of Bridge of Orchy to Inveroran Hotel. We completely missed the trail that cut the corner away from the road. But, if we had kept to the trail, we would have by-passed the shoreline of Loch Tulla & remains of old forests. We rejoined the Old Military Rd. for our stretch over Black Mount & through Rannoch Moor. This is the way to cross moorland--on a hard packed, dry road. It did seem a bit of a pedestrian highway with large numbers of walkers, at least a few being day hikers. Kingshouse Hotel undergoing renovation but new Kingshouse Bunkhouse open for business. With more & more trekking WHW, many beds needed in Glen Coe.

Room for two ready. Bunk beds. £ 25.00 per bunk per night. Able to get sheets, blanket & pillow from mgmt. Not all walkers have sleeping bags. I'm on top. Mattress hard! Showered in peat tinted water, but clean and hot! Raining again! Turning into blustery & steady downpour, but we're warm & toasty. Met new friends in pub & lounge. Lots of laughs this evening.

Returning to room, we found note from Janet. An x-ray in Ft. Wm. showed she had fractured toe, so she'd have to give up on last day of hike. Too bad, but she & Dave can return & complete it together another time.

Day 11: Kingshouse to Kinlochleven: 9 miles.

Cloudy turning to downpour after pub lunch. What a day! We walked for a while w/ Veronica & Willie until Devil's Staircase. Veronica had to change from treaders to boots. We continued on. Flies were at their worst today. Devil's Staircase was a puffer, but doable. In fact, a team of men was working improving trail on the backside. Long, easy walk at end--two miles down to Kinlochleven past water plant & pipes.

At the Antler Bar we met Alastair Doone. Invited us (& Anne & Adam - PhD mech. engineering students at Leeds) back to his house for coffee. On the way Adam asked if I'd seen that white car before. It was Janet and Dave waiting for us to come off trail. They joined us at Alastair's, too, & are spending the night at his house. Dave wants to hike to Ft. Wm. with us tomorrow.

Earlier, Alastair tagged Rob at bar about piping. He's a brilliant dabbler & ex-social worker who loves the Scot's culture & creating odds & ends from leftovers. He gave us handmade copper coils, a wooden horse carved from privet hedge, & aluminum fish. He's also a storyteller who would have loved having us all stay at his place. His wife's away with daughter who's expecting their 5th grandchild.

When finally we had pounded on Alastair's bass drum & bodhran, & Rob had played the chanter, we left for wet walk to our B&B, *Eden Coille*. Anne & Adam are just a couple of houses away with Sara & Paul, who we caught up with along the way. Our room is lovely.

*Forgot--This AM at about 9:30, Scottish AF jet flew low thru Glen Coe--actually below us--we were on Devil's staircase.

Dined at the Stag's Head Inn w/ Veronica, Willie, & young Irish woman, a forensic expert in Glasgow. It was warm & noisy--fun! Walked home under umbrellas again.

Have met lots of lovely people & have recorded their names when I remember to. Didn't get family names of most. Not sure I'll be able to figure out who was who a year from now.

Day 12: Kinlochleven to Fort William: 14 miles.

On to Ft. Wm. Still raining but tapered off w/ only one shower while hiking. Met up w/ Dave, Janet, & Alastair in center of K town. Dave was trying to get Janet on bus, but she couldn't manage it. She was in rage w/crutches, so stayed at Alastair's.

The three of us took to the hills & had a real British walk thru streams & even a few bogs. Far vistas thru glens, in spite of clouds. Listened to Dave's life story. Yesterday he showed us a porcelain headed doll he bought to add to his collection. Today he told us that his daughter died in an auto accident & he's been buying dolls ever since. Touching story.

Passing those who started ahead of us, we sauntered into Ft.

Wm. about 3 p.m., took obligatory photos, & Rob gave Dave his WestConn cap. Shook hands good-by, headed for B&B. Dave hitched back to Kinlochleven. We ran into Andrew (pianist) & girlfriend who took coach to Ft. Wm.

Our new B&B is only okay. We're on the 3rd floor under the eaves--bathroom is on 1st. We booked new hotel in old town center for tomorrow eve. Presently waiting seafood dinners on dock at harbor. Spoiled hikers.

Walked back thru town center in time to hear local high school pipe band warming up. Stayed to hear performance. Rob said group was first rate. Located a hotel we thought Dumfries Hendersons were staying in. NOT! Back to our own B&B for early bed. Ready for sleep even though still light outside.

Day 13: Fort William: 0 miles.

Blue skies at 6 a.m. turn grey by 7:30. Packed & ready to visit Tourist Info. Office to book rest of trip. Then dropped off bags at new hotel & dirty laundry at *Ruth Sleighter's* Laundromat. Rob asked what I meant by Ruth Sleighter (Ft. Wm. laundromat named Tubs o' Suds). I told him Tippy will know what I mean. Sleighter is an old family joke.

Looked for souvenir shop to buy WHW t-shirts. Found six, considered five, bought two. One with official patch too dull. Silly is better. I picked one. Rob picked other. Will have Jake guess which shirt was picked by which person. The shirt themes prompted Rob to write a poem.

We Slutched
☂ The Wet Highland Way ☂
One hundred miles of Scottish Rain

Milngavie to Fort William

West Highland Way

Rain, Clouds, Rain

The Haggis Happiness Trail

☺ West Highland Way ☺

Clegs, Midges, Wet Feet

All I got was this t-shirt!

West Highland Way

Its price got my parents soaked!

Milngavie - Mull-Guy

Ben Nevis - Clear sky

West Highland Way

★

The Wet Highland Way
By
Rob MacKenzie

The sun's dazzle, celestial drenching,
Which steers the cosmic flow?
Forest and loch, mosses and rock,
Wetscapes we ought to know.

One foot forward, then the other,
Thru bracken and dampened vales.
Memories blinded or darkly reminded,
It's a wet place with secret tales.

Trek it to love it, endure its damp,
Search for a dry place at night.
A soaking walk spurs hopeful talk,
Will skies brighten or rain at next light?

Day 14: Fort William: Chores.

Listening to Ulsterites on telly worry about Brexit doesn't sound promising. Scots just as divided. Welsh an enigma, but leaning toward UK. Brexit has caused big confusion about who should stay in EU & who will remain in UK. Saw somber Orange Day faces in Glasgow. Celts/Gaels lovely people, if they like you. Whole Prot.-Cath. tribe neither forgives nor forgets.

New hotel room is a beautiful rounded corner suite. Worked

on plans for next week. Still think we'll climb Ben Nevis tomorrow. Then day after BN, we take coach to Mallaig for two days--one will be to cruise mailboat around Inner Hebrides: Eigg, Rùm, & Canna.

Banked & then bought Rob an eggplant-color woolen hunting sweater with leather patches on shoulders. Handsome man, but he doesn't hunt. Boat ride out to seal harbor. Rain closed over sunny day. Love our best friends--umbrellas: Ping 1 and Ping 2.

Returned to hotel & napped while Brit. Open at Royal Birkdale was on TV. Jordan Spieth leads by three. We think golfers with Ping equip. have best chance. Learned Roger Federer won Wimbledon. Yea for the elderly! Evening pub meal, walk thru center, & back to B&B for more telly & bed.

Day 15: Climb Ben Nevis & return to Ft. Wm.: 8.5 miles.

Partly sunny/cloudy. Up and ready to try Ben Nevis--4,406 ft. Took tourist route but still rugged. Rocky switchbacks, some we missed. Result: Straighter, rockier climb up into the clouds.

We've never seen so many hikers on a mountain. Many were well equipped but some looked like they were gonna be cold on top. Saw one bearded man in kilt, but wearing deerslayer cap, heavy woolens, thick socks & sturdy boots. He knew what he was doing, the old ghille!

Nearing top, we were practically run over by what seemed to be three bus loads on the way down. Top looked like a mangle of ruined huts with refugees fleeing in streams. We didn't stay long to eat our packed lunches before heading swiftly back down.

Blustery cold and foggy on top with spits of sleet. Why do I persist ordering cream cheese & olive sandwiches? Ugh!

Heading down we found all switchbacks for a more gradual descent--easier on knees. Bypassed snowfield we slushed through on way to pinnacle.

Sunny at lower alt., so we disrobed & enjoyed warming stroll back to town, followed by hot, soothing baths in our glamourous hotel room.

Rob dined on steak & I had burrito filled w/ seafood followed by Mississippi mud pie & ice cream. Another fine Scottish meal. Ha!

Day 16: Coach to Mallaig: 43 miles.

Rained hard all night. Slept until almost 8:30 a.m., ate, packed, bought mid-day food & new pen so I could continue recording trip.

Mallaig: Sat in upstairs cafe drinking coffee & tea & sharing a scone. We overlook the dock & can see our new B&B across East Bay, where our room looks out on water, is clean with own bath & TV. Went back and watched Brit Open. Don't know new batch of young pros. Both napped--it's a vacation, after all! We left for dinner with our two pals, Ping 1 and Ping 2. Windy, wet, & chilling. Great snuggling weather! Reminded Rob what snuggling meant. He said he remembered & tonight would prove his memory was still good. Can't wait!

Day 17: Mailboat trip from Mallaig to Eigg, Rùm, & Canna: appx. 30 miles.

Sun & cloud mix for what appears will be a lovely sail to

islands. Spotted porpoises/dolphins on way out. Passengers disembarked/embarked by way of island motor craft. A hydraulic crane aboard ship transferred supplies. People must love isolation to live, even visit these places. Inevitable rain & cold finally drove us below deck.

Back in Mallaig--ate again! Wonder if my weight's spiked? Shorts & pants still fit around my middle, but they haven't been washed for a while. Should have laundered them in Ft. Wm. Maybe stretched out of size? Returned to B&B for hot showers, TV, & Rob again!

Day 18: Train from Mallaig to Ft. Wm. & coach to Oban: 86 miles.

Sunny and clear for our trip to Oban! That is, assuming we're able to book accommodations. We'll take train to Ft. Wm. & then coach to Oban.

In Mallaig found a book, *From Renfrew to Rùm*, by Elizaberh Renfrew. What a surprise! Renfrew, PA, only 10 miles from my hometown, Mars, PA. Renfrew kids went to Butler HS, but I knew many through sports. Book says Elizabeth was a great, great granddaughter of D.A. Renfrew who had grist and lumber mills in Renfrew & became wealthy when coal-oil was discovered on his property. She eloped with Scottish swain, Colm McCandless, (McCandless a town near Pittsburgh--one coincidence after another!) who was heading to Inner Hebrides to start a vet practice. How many animals can there be out there? Lots of sheep and herding dogs, I guess. Any haggises? Anyway, she's lived most of her life isolated on small island.

I remember boat picking up old lady in Rùm & bringing her to Mallaig. We saw her again this AM before I bought the book. I regret not talking with her while on the boat. Cigarette smoke from passengers below deck (and her?) drove me topside despite rain. Now with book, I wish I had her autograph. Her story is fascinating & quick read.

Later, in Ft. Wm, Rob returned to a store to buy a ceramic piper that we thought was £79, but turned out to be £179--too expensive! We had our sandwiches (no cream cheese & olives for me this time!) & apples on town bench before I bought large ice cream. It was good, but tiny by our standards. Boarded bus to Oban & waited to depart.

Oban--tourist coastal hustle and bustle. Our B&B is a steep climb up from town center. Comfortable enough. Rob found music store for chanter & pipe reeds, plus book of Scottish sing-along tunes & dance music w/ CD.

Walk around Oban included watching glass paper-weight craftsman. A tower built in 1900 to resemble walled fortress overlooks town. Also spent time in art gallery, but we have enough art at home (Rauschenberg prints) to have our own gallery.

After dinner as Rob chantered on pier, we heard a pipe band & followed the music. It was Oban Grade 2 Pipe Band. Terrific sound, in tune, perfect timing. (To think once I hated bagpipes!) Made the evening perfect!

Day 19: Coach from Oban to Glasgow: 97 miles.

Sunny! Packed & walked to Tourist Info. Office to book night in Glasgow. After booking, Rob bought new kilt pin. Found bench on green overlooking West Bay where Rob chantered, I read, & both enjoyed beauty of bay & day. (Hey, Rob, I can rhyme words, too.)

Ate fresh prawn sandwiches on seawall while waiting for Glasgow bus. Returning to Argyll Street Guest House--same place we stayed at beginning of trip. Watched crazy sheep dog catch, drop, & prey on piece of plastic strap. Same routine everyday. Nutty mutt!

Arrived in Glasgow, showered, walked to Tron Theater to purchase tickets for *The Minstrel & the Shirra* (sheriff), a biographical sketch about Sir Walter Scott. At dinner, acted like gluttons with nachos, sour cream & jalopeño peppers, whisky, beer, wine. Huge salads w/ chunks of fresh Italian bread blotted out our desires for dessert. Fortunately, to kill time until the doors opened, we walked lots o' blocks around theater. Good for digestion.

The one man act w/female singer-harpist-accompanist was pleasant way to end vacation & pay tribute to Rob's heritage.

Day 20: Return to America: 3,218 miles.

Overcast & cool start for our sprint to bus station for 7:45 a.m. coach to airport. We have folding friends, Ping 1 & Ping 2 in tow. Alien umbrellas are emigrating to Connecticut to live with us. Hope they don't get snared by ICE in travel ban. We're both ready to go home. Cheers, Scotland!

36
Opportunity Taken

The decision was made. In fact, while in Scotland, Maryann realized a move to Boulder was in their future. Rob was too excited about the chance to teach at the University of Colorado for her to object. She loved him unconditionally. She would never stand in his way to follow a new path.

Moreover, there were troubling conditions arising in Roxbridge that made a new start tempting. The growing power of fundamentalist theology, like the Apple Church, and the spread of charter schools were factors. Maryann knew they couldn't run away from these insidious trends--they were nation-wide. But new surroundings, new opportunities, and new friends could promote intellectual and emotional growth for Rob, her, and especially Jake.

★

The MacKenzies were moving to Colorado. Maryann reflected on the events that had occurred since returning to

Connecticut. Rob was offered a professorship in the Department of Environmental Studies at CU. Not only would he teach and promote the art of science writing, he was tasked with developing a distance learning, online tutorial writing program designed for fledgling scientists, researchers, and data analysts. Enrollees would be welcome from international and American universities and think tanks.

After communicating with department head, Dr. Gail Wiseman, via email and Skype, Rob flew to Boulder to meet his new boss, tour the campus, and inspect his office. He met with two computer savvy students who had applied for an assistant's position as a computer developer in his new program. Dean Wiseman knew Rob would need help setting up his online tutorial within the maze of university websites. Rob was promised he could choose his assistant.

To affirm his appointment he received a formal letter of employment from Dean Wiseman, handwritten congratulations from the Provost, and a contract stipulating salary and benefits. The contract also affirmed that his position was on the track to tenure (decision in three years), his specific teaching responsibilities at the university, and progress mileposts he would be expected to meet in setting up the online tutorial. He was given a modest budget. Finally, he was required to sign an agreement to abide by the university's policies regarding sexual harassment and the reporting of incidents. A second clause warned about plagiarism and the requirement for accurate author attribution when citing research.

The university treated him royally. Maryann followed his

progress via email and saw his accommodations. He was put up in the city's premier historic landmark, the Hotel Boulderado. She learned he had been invited for dinner at Dean Wiseman's home where he met her husband, Dan, an environmental lawyer. Two Wiseman teenagers kept him in stitches with stories about their two competing city high schools: Fairview and Boulder. Fairview dominated in football, Boulder in robotics. Both kids had eyes trained on eastern colleges.

Meetings and tours were scheduled for mornings, so Rob had afternoons to check out housing. He met with a real estate agent who showed him houses new to the market. If he saw a desirable contender, the agent advised him to jump on it quickly, make an offer. The housing market was hot. Boulder business start-ups and a huge new Google office were enticing young professionals to Colorado's Front Range and particularly to Boulder.

Maryann was disappointed she and Jake hadn't made the initial trip to Boulder. Decisions had happened so fast. But Rob kept her in the loop with a constant stream of emails and daily phone calls.

Finding a potential home on his second search, Rob phoned Maryann with the details. He told her she could see the property via thirty computer photos on the agency's website. The structure was a stand alone building on a small lot, but backed up to soccer and lacrosse fields adjacent to the East Boulder Recreation Center. The center itself had top-notch exercise equipment, a lap pool, a climbing wall, tennis courts, and offered dozens of vigorous classes. Via a bike path, the house on Rim Rock Circle was less than a quarter mile away from the school Jake would likely attend, the Manhattan Middle School of Arts and Academics.

"I love the architectural style, lass," phoned Rob. "It's modern prairie Bauhaus with shed roofs and big windows. Facades are painted with geometric shapes of grey, white, and cream, with black accent trim. It has a tan brick foundation. It's very handsome. And Rim Rock is a name associated with geology. What could be better?"

"How far away from your work is it?"

"Only three miles. And bike paths go almost door to door. A shopping center's half a mile away. There's public bus service. I'll bet one of our cars will be spending a lot of time in the garage."

After finding the property listing on line, Maryann said, "The photos certainly make it look large, and the kitchen's nicely laid out--plenty of counter space."

"Aye. Also, there's more total square feet than we presently have in our colonial. You're right. The kitchen's grand. All the built-ins are staying, with the exception of the fridge. The seller's taking it."

"The bedrooms appear to be spacious," Maryann said brightly, her enthusiasm building. "Which one do you think would be best for Jake?"

"Look at photos sixteen and seventeen. The room's on the southwest corner. It has fantastic views of the mountains to the south and the Flatirons to the west. I think he'll love it. Our room would be down the hall away from his. Photos nineteen and twenty show it has an easterly view overlooking meadows."

Maryann was excited and itched for more information. "The

listing says there are three and a half bathrooms. That's more than we have here. Are they up-to-date? You know how important bathrooms are to women."

"Aye, all are lovely. The colors and tiling are first-rate. I think you can get an idea as you scroll through the photos. And the loos, sinks, and showers have water saving devices. No more well water, love. Rim Rock uses city water."

"Rob, it looks perfect!"

"Aye, lass, that's what I thought. But I'm hesitant to do anything without you here."

"I love the house, Rob," Maryann gushed. "The views of the Flatirons are magical. I've never seen the Rockies up close. The farthest west I've been is to Pittsburgh and Lake Erie when I was a kid." She thought for a second, then added, "And a soccer field behind the house? Jake will be in heaven. I trust your judgement, laddie."

"Have you told him yet, Annie? I hope we're not blindsiding him. I don't think he understood why I had to go to Boulder so soon after returning from Scotland."

"Not yet, Rob. I'll tell him tonight. He's been so wrapped up with his comic book project he hasn't thought about much else. Also, I didn't want to bring up the matter until your job was certain. But now that I have photos to show him, I think that will help."

"My professorship is a signed and sealed deal, love. Good luck telling Jake."

"Rob, make an offer on the house. Give your agent a deposit check. We have the savings. Go for it. But whether we wind up on

Rim Rock Circle or some other place, I'll immediately have our Roxbridge property listed on the market. From what you've shown me, it ought to be a fairly even trade price-wise. The market's hot here, too. Make Rim Rock Circle our new home. You can do it. I love you!"

"Aye, lass, I'll get cracking. I'll phone you tomorrow at the same time or email if something happens sooner. See you in a few days. I love you, too."

"You have the two West Highland Way t-shirts Rob and I brought home. We wondered if you could tell who picked which." Maryann eased back into the couch with her feet on the coffee table. An iPad was on her lap. Jake was next to her with comic book drawings ready to be explained. "That's easy, Mom. You picked the red one, Rob chose the green."

"That's correct. But what about the slogans. Didn't they give you a clue?"

"Not really. Both were pretty lame. Colors gave you away."

"Really? You said I picked red. That's right, I did. How did you know?

"I once heard Rob call you a red-hot lassie."

Maryann chuckled. "You heard that, huh? Do you think that's true?" She looked at her son with interest. She wondered, *Is this the time for the birds and bees speech?*

"You're pretty cool, Mom. I don't know about the hot stuff, but you look good wearing red."

"Thank you for the compliment, honey. What about Rob?

Wait a minute, I think I know. He picked green because he's an environmentalist."

"Sorta, Mom. Also he has a green car."

"That's right! It's so obvious. I should have known."

Maryann, laughed, then asked about Jake's comic book. "Okay, honey, come clean. Mrs. Higgins emailed us in Scotland that you were illustrating and writing a comic book."

Since her return to the states from Europe, Jake had mostly been invisible preferring to spend hours alone in his room wrestling with his comic book creation. Maryann had to urge him to go outside on the nicer days, suggesting that he work on the project in the tree-house now roofed over and embraced by fat limbs of the white oak at the edge of their property. Darling Rob had guided and helped Jake complete the hide-away. After settling the West Highland Way t-shirt issue, Maryann asked Jake how he was progressing with his literary endeavor.

"I'm almost done, Mom," he said, a pencil wedged behind his ear. "I got the idea when Rob and I found the dead pig in the mine."

"Dr. Shea was there, too," she reminded him.

"Yeah, I know. Did I tell you he's got a cool knife? He cut that pig open like it was a watermelon."

"Yes, honey, you told me. But what about your story? Is it about finding the dead pig and saving one of her babies?" Maryann folded her arms hoping she'd be able to follow Jake's logic and details.

"Pigs are part of the story, Mom, but not all of it. Rob's religion is part, your knees are mentioned, and the hero is Jay

Cobb, a super farm boy who suddenly appears from a cornfield when troubles threaten the town."

"What's the town's name?"

"Granite Rim. It's like Roxbridge, except it's balanced on the edge of a quarry."

Maryann was startled when Jake said the name of his imaginary town. It was eerily similar to the street which featured the house that Rob was suggesting. Had Jake been listening to her conversation with Rob? No, she realized, that hadn't happened. He was in the tree house at the time. But what an amazing coincidence, she admitted to herself.

"Wait a minute," she continued, referring back to the details of Jake's story. "How is Rob's religion part of your story?"

"The villain's name is Pop Ular. Get it? ULAR!"

Maryann laughed and shook her head. "Yep, I get it. But what about my knees?" She stretched forward and rubbed them.

"It's simple, Mom. Pop Ular's wife is Ann Knee." He giggled. "Everytime I say it, I laugh." He giggled harder to prove his point.

"It sounds like you enjoy your own writing. That's good, Jake. Have confidence in what you're doing."

"Yeah, I'm becoming a good writer. Rob helps me. And I'm Jay Cobb," he added, "the hidden warrior dedicated to fight Pop Ular and his scheme to own all the corn."

"I see," said Maryann. "Many years ago two wealthy brothers from Texas tried to buy up all the world's silver."

"Why did they do that?"

"I'm not sure. Maybe so the Lone Ranger would have to use lead bullets." She managed to keep a straight face.

"Like what happened at the New Milford gun range," affirmed Jake. "That's stupid, if you ask me."

"I agree. Now, getting back to your story, you said Pop Ular is evil. Are you referencing Rob?" She frowned, feigning concern.

"No, Mom. Rob's not Pop Ular. Pop Ular's a person I made up. He lives a life fattening pigs with corn, then killing them. Rob spends his life teaching kids, and I don't mean goats. It's not the same thing."

Maryann guessed there might be some coherence to her son's story, but her guess was only a hunch. She remained confused, although amused. "So let me see if I've got this straight. Pop Ular is not Rob. Pop Ular spends his time controlling the corn markets and killing pigs. Is this happening at Granite Rim?"

Jake grinned and nodded his head affirmatively. "Yes, Granite Rim is part of Granite Hill, and Pop Ular lives in one of the tunnels."

"But honey, if Granite Rim is on the edge of a quarry, how can there be a hill?"

"Duh, Mom! The people who live in the quarry think Granite Rim is the hill. It's so obvious. The tunnels are in the walls of the quarry."

"Hmm, I should have seen that. Okay, Ular lives in a tunnel and hunts pigs . . ."

"No, Mom! He doesn't hunt pigs. He kills them."

"Wait a minute! You mean there are so many pigs that hunting isn't necessary?"

"That's right, Mom. All Pop Ular has to do is step out of his tunnel then--blam! He has sausage for breakfast."

Maryann felt herself sliding into one of her laughing jags. With each question posed, the story became more and more intricate and convoluted. Yet it came from the perfect imagination of a young boy's mind. She couldn't resist exploring what else might be lurking in Jake's head. She asked, "Any eggs with Pop Ular's sausage breakfast?"

"C'mon, Mom, be reasonable," counseled Jake. "Eggs are from chickens, not pigs."

"Yes, I know," she admitted sheepishly. "Only wondering."

Jake continued. "Anyway, Ann Knee is the cook, so she fries up a batch of sausages. They eat them, then they go to bed."

"But it's morning. Why are they going to bed?"

"They're tired, Mom. Don't you understand?"

"I'm trying to understand, honey. But I'm an adult, and you should know by now that adults can be dense. Perhaps when you've finished your comic book, I'll learn how it all fits together."

"I don't know, Mom. Your brain is becoming too rigid to understand the mind of a comic book kid."

"You're probably right."

"When you see my book after it's finished, you'll be amazed and exculpated."

"I'll be found not guilty huh? I can't wait."

Maryann removed her feet from the coffee table and turned to look directly at Jake. She had her iPad ready for support. "Let's talk about the comic book later, Jake. There's something else I want to discuss with you now. It's important."

"Am I in trouble? I behaved myself like you said I should when I was at the Higgins's."

"No, you're not in trouble."

Maryann considered how to broach the Colorado news to her son. Should she detail the facts up front, or lead him to the conclusion through a series of questions? She chose the second approach. "Honey, have you wondered where Rob went?"

Jake shrugged. "Not really."

"Not really?" She frowned. "Aren't you curious what he's been up to?"

"I know what he's been up to, Mom. He went to Colorado."

Maryann was amazed. "How do you know that? We haven't mentioned anything."

"Mom! You've gotten better about telling me things. You don't say, 'I'll tell you later,' as much. But you often speak in codes with Rob, so I have to keep my ears open to find out what's going on. I know Rob went to Colorado about a job."

Maryann was nonplussed. At this moment, if she asked the wrong questions, she was frightened by what Jake's answers might be.

"Rob's been offered an important job at the University of Colorado, Jake."

"Cool!" he chirped, beaming. "When do we leave?"

"You're not upset, my son?"

"No, why should I be? When I heard Boulder, I looked it up on the computer. Mom! It's fantastic! They have a race where 50,000 runners compete! There's 300 miles of paved trails! I'll be able to jog fifty miles a day and not worry about getting hit by a car! And they have flat irons, Mom. I'm not sure what they are, but you can rock climb on them. It's better than Disneyland."

"But you'll be leaving your friends."

"I left friends in New York when we moved to Roxbridge. I'll make new friends in Boulder. Is that the town we'll live in?"

Maryann began to weep. She wrapped her arms around Jake holding him tightly. "Yes, dear, I think we're moving to Boulder."

"Ease up, Mom, you're crushing me. Why are you crying?"

"I'm crying because I'm so proud of you, honey. You're so flexible and agreeable. Most kids would put up a big stink over a move like this. But you're enthusiastic."

"I stretch in the morning, Mom, that's how I stay flexible. Do they allow dogs in Boulder? I wonder what our new house will look like? Will I have my own room. Will I be able to play soccer? Can I learn how to ski? Will I need a new bike? Will you and Rob get bikes? Can I see a college football game? Are there any rivers for swimming? Where will I go to school? Do they have Mexican food?"

Maryann laughed and slowed him down. "After dinner I'll try to answer all your questions, sweetie. I'm not putting you off, I'm through with that. I hope by then I'll have heard from Rob and will know more. In the meanwhile, Google *Boulder Recreation*. See what they have to offer. Also, check out the Boulder Open Space Mountain Parks website. The trails are awesome."

She went on. "Rob's been looking at houses. As soon as he knows something, he'll let us know. Until then, I don't want to show you any places that might not come true. I don't want you to get your hopes up before something happens. When it does, together we can look at photos of our new home."

Maryann wiped her nose. She remembered an additional

piece of information she had planned to use, if Jake had been resistant to the move. "I forgot to mention something else, love. We'll be close to Uncle Fred, Aunt Lois, and your cousins. Aunt Lois has a slew of nieces and nephews on her side of the family. We'll be exploding from a small family of three to a large clan. What do you think of that?"

Jake grinned broadly and expressed his pleasure with two thumbs up. "I love it, Mom, and Rob will be happy to be in a clan again. He'll say, 'Hoots, mon!' Hey, Mom, what the heck does that mean?"

After a dinner omelet filled with sausage and veggies, the home phone rang. It was 7:10 EDT, 5:10 MDT. From the caller ID, Maryann knew it was Rob. She felt her pulse quicken, took a deep breath, then answered. "It's me, love. I've been on pins and needles waiting for your call. What's happened?"

"We own a Boulder house, lass. We still haven't paid for it, but the seller and I reached an agreement. He came down five thou, I moved up five thou. Our realtor has the deposit check."

"Is it the Rim Rock house?"

"Aye, it is"

"Sweet, honey! Hold on a moment. I'll get Jake on the other line. It may take a minute, he's out in the tree house. Ask him about Granite Rim."

"What? Did you mention Rim Rock Circle?'

"No. It's about his comic book." She started laughing. "Wait until he hears his new address. Hold on. We'll be right back."

Maryann hustled across the field calling for Jake. She pictured Rob sitting in his hotel room wondering what was happening at the homestead. Did Rob twiddle his thumbs? Jake slid down the rope, and the two of them raced back to the house. Maryann picked up in the study, Jake in the guest bedroom. Maryann went first. "Phew, we just got our evening workout. Honey, are you still there?"

"Aye, that I am. Is Jake there?"

"I'm here, Rob."

"Do you know where I'm calling from, lad?"

"Sure, Boulder, Colorado."

"Did your mother tell you?"

"No, I figured it out myself."

"You're a smart jocko, laddie. Aye, I'm in the Centennial State. I have a new job at the University of Colorado. The thing is, I don't want to live alone out here. I want you and your mum to join me. What do you think? Are you willing to leave Roxbridge?"

"Sure! When can we come?"

"Soon, lad. Annie, are you still game?"

"Aye, love. Your wife's started to think about packing."

"Then it's a deal. The important news is we have a Boulder home. It's the one on Rim Rock Circle. There are plenty of photos on the agent's website. You two loves can scroll through them when we finish talking. And Jake. Google Manhattan Middle School of Art and Academics to see where you'll be studying. Also check out the Boulder Recreation Centers. One's a stone's throw from our front door."

"Hey Rob, wait a minute," interrupted Jake. "My school's

called Manhattan? You aren't sending me back to New York, are you?"

"Nae, lad. I don't know why it's called that, except it's on Manhattan Drive. You can research it when you're out here."

"And Rob," continued Jake, "guess what my comic book town is called."

"Balmaha?"

"No, that's stupid. I call it Granite Rim."

"You chose that name before learning your new house is on Rim Rock Circle?"

Listening to the conversation, Maryann could picture Rob's eyebrows arching in surprise.

"Yeah, I did. Pretty spooky, huh? Maybe it was because of *tele-transportalizing.*"

Maryann could hear Rob chuckling. "Aye, lad," he said. "Maybe it was that or just a coinkydink."

"Rob," she interrupted, "Roxbridge--Boulder--Rim Rock Circle. And Jake's Granite Rim. Jeepers! You'd think we were groupies following the Rolling Stones."

Late summer and early autumn were hectic times for the MacKenzies. Maryann kept a record of their completed responsibilities and accomplishments. Later, looking back, she was amazed by how three lives had been so quickly uprooted and replanted. A new life for them was blossoming in Boulder.

Maryann continually added to their lists of new experiences, written records for each of them. She easily secured an associate's position at a Pine Street law firm. The group specialized in litigation concerning the carbon extraction industries. Now that she was in Colorado, she was back in the game of championing environmental preservation. With her career as an adversary of radioactive waste generators and municipal experience as Roxbridge's town attorney, she was hired during her first job interview. An online record of her cases and arguments was the glue that sealed the deal. Moreover, she passed the Colorado bar examination at the end of August.

To celebrate her employment, the partners entertained her at the Hotel Boulderado for a sumptuous dinner. At last she saw the landmark where Rob had stayed earlier in the summer.

For his part, Rob was an immediate success in his new job. His two university classes filled to the maximum. CU students began mentioning how great a teacher he was, as had students at WestConn and Roxbridge Regional High School.

He received permission to hire both program assistant candidates. Rob convinced them to job share, thereby proving their willingness to work as a team. If they were successful, he promised they would be rewarded with strong job recommendations. He noticed in the first week that Josh and Samantha were hitting it off just fine.

Conferring with his department chair, she and Rob agreed that at the beginning, his online tutorial would not be offered for university credit. Rather, upon successful completion, enrollees would earn Continuing Education Credits (CEU's) and certificates of achievement. Both documents would be helpful in promoting the careers of young scientists.

It became clear to Rob that it was not physically possible for him to personally communicate with each on-line enrollee. Instead, he set about developing writing paradigms, models of excellent scientific prose. Supplementing each paradigm were rubrics illustrating a range of quality writing, from the unintelligible to layman's clarity.

His first cohort of enrollees included three young meteorologists from NCAR (National Center for Atmospheric Research) and four statisticians from NOAA, the National Oceanic and Atmospheric Administration. During the semester he was able to visit each facility and introduce himself to his enrollees. He wanted them to know that behind the paradigms and rubrics was a caring teacher.

Where Maryann and Rob had focused on their new careers with laser-like intensity, Jake found himself in a smorgasbord of opportunities. Maryann watched him taste everything, but by mid-September he had not settled on a main course. She and Rob encouraged him to keep nibbling. They told him he was too young to become a specialist.

Maryann received a note from Jake's homeroom teacher. She was told her son was thriving at the Manhattan Middle School of Art and Academics. He easily made new friends, she was assured, no doubt spurred by the fact that he was the new kid from Connecticut.

His quirky, infectious personality served him well. He joined the camera club. Then he volunteered at the school's newspaper as a guest cartoonist and began producing a series of one-cell images. He called his creation, "Nutmeg Nuggets." referencing

Connecticut's nickname. His second cartoon depicted a stick figure rock climber, scaling a large walnut. The caption read: "I'm nuts over climbing!"

Surprisingly, Jake found pre-algebra much easier and understandable than expected. Spanish classes resulted in him naming everything at home using index cards with Spanish words. In language arts, when assigned the task of composing an essay, he wrote about renewable energy and referenced the hundreds of wind turbines he had seen in Iowa on the relocation drive from Roxbridge to Boulder. He also described the five new turbines standing in the ocean off shore from Rhode Island's Block Island. His writing was filled with fact backed opinions.

The East Boulder Recreation Center became a hangout. He was either in the gym shooting baskets, straining to heft dumbbells in the weight room, or out back watching canines tear around the enclosed dog park. Some reminded him of Talcum, a loyal dog that lived in Roxbridge. He enjoyed seeing Hispanic men playing handball and tried understanding their cries and calls with his limited Spanish. Swimming laps became a chore, especially since he couldn't gossip with his head under water. So he used the pool to cool down during hot spells. He hadn't kept count of the days of clear weather since his arrival in Boulder, but he believed the claim that there were three hundred sunny days a year along the Front Range.

The rec center had a small climbing wall with moveable hand holds. It was similar to the wall at Dalton, his former New York City school. Hanging and climbing on artificial holds was fun, but his goal was to feel real stone. His appetite for granite had been whetted.

Early one Saturday morning, Rob drove Jake to Chautauqua Park, part of Boulder's Open Space and Mountain Park system. Maryann stayed behind and walked to the rec center's tennis courts, where instruction for women was being offered. At Chautauqua, Rob and Jake picked up the Mesa Trail and headed south. Each had rucksacks filled with water bottles, granola bars, hats, extra sunscreen, sunglasses, and maps. The trail ascended gradually with intermittent steep ups and downs. Soon, the forest around the trail thinned. On their right emerged a huge rock wall. To Jake it appeared as if it had sprouted like a flat fungus out of beds of moss at its base. Jake craned his neck up but couldn't locate the top. Rob said he thought it might be the Second Flatiron, but he wasn't certain. He added that he didn't know the wall's height but did point out it was pitched about 55° westward. He guessed it was part of the foundation for Green Mountain, 8,000' high and a 2,500' elevation gain from where they stood. Somewhere above them they could hear the clinks of climbing hardware and the laughter and calls of a climbing party.

When Jake returned home that evening, he told his mother the whole story of the hike, including seeing three mule deer in a draw by a creek. Judging by his reaction to the day's adventure, Annie knew that in Jake's imagination he had been roped up and belayed. He did three sets of push-ups before climbing into bed.

★

Daylight dwindled as autumn advanced. The beautiful late October weather spurred the MacKenzies to climb the trail hidden between the First and Second Flatirons. The air was clear and crisp, no trapped Front Range pollution making it difficult to breath. In fact, since moving to Colorado, all three had become acclimated to Boulder's altitude of 5,400 feet.

On the ascent they were enchanted with sun-lit copses of glittering golden aspen, made even more brilliant tucked into stands of dark green spruce. At the top they were rewarded with expansive views of the Colorado plains to the east and the majestic Continental Divide thirty mile to the west. Thirteen thousand foot mountain peaks were already covered with snow.

A chill wind sent them hustling back down the trail and into the Chautauqua Dining Hall. As the sun disappeared behind the Flatirons, the air temperature dropped ten degrees. Having reservations, they were able to claim a table near a fireplace in the old fashioned dining room. They chowed down on thick bison burgers, sweet potato fries, and for Maryann, roasted brussel sprouts. They marveled at the fact that they had experienced three climate zones within five miles of their new home.

They talked about the Boulder Star. Maryann told what she had learned from her brother, Fred. Rob confirmed the sketchy details he knew with their waitress.

"Yes," affirmed their server, Pam. "I've worked here three years, and I've seen it lighted. It's beautiful. It's on the mountainside off

Flagstaff Road. They fire it up for the holiday season starting Veterans Day evening."

"I heard that families go up there to see it," said Rob. "Is that possible?"

"Yep, it's true. A parking lot near the Flagstaff House Restaurant is the starting point. The trail is steep so bring flashlights. If you guys were able to climb to the top of the First Flatiron today, the walk to the Boulder Star should be a piece of cake and doable. Give it a try. Oh, by the way," added Pam, "speaking of cake, tonight our dessert special is chocolate lava cake with vanilla ice cream. I can tell from your smiles you're interested. One? Two? Three?"

Maryann signaled one.

"Okay, I'll bring out one with three spoons."

When Rob first learned of the Boulder Star, he hatched a plan to visit it. In his imagination he, Maryann, and Jake would stand below the star superstructure at the lighting ceremony. He couldn't think of a more symbolic way to celebrate a new home, new jobs, and new schools. As Veterans Day approached on November 11, he made preparations to spring a surprise at the event. He told Jake his plan and how Jake could help. He asked for Jake's pledge of secrecy. Jake smiled and vigorously nodded his head in approval at the plan. He swore a vow of silence.

Meanwhile, after agreeing they ought to attend the ceremony, Maryann devised a plan of her own. When it was confirmed the three of them would make the pilgrimage to the star, she set her scheme in motion. She told Jake what she planned and asked for his secrecy. He agreed with a wide grin and vigorous head nodding. Again, he pledged silence.

Aware that his parents were planning surprises for each other, Jake conjured up his own surprise. For two days he wrestled with ideas about what he might do. Finally, with the keen eye of a gemologist, he planned a meaningful tribute to them, the adults he loved and admired. He began preparing for the star ceremony, accumulating the needed bits and pieces. He hid them in his room.

Veterans Day was one more of the three hundred sunny days predicted for the Front Range. It dawned clear and bright. But the MacKenzies had learned as soon as the sun slipped behind the Flatirons, the evening would became cold. All Saturday the MacKenzies fiddled with their surprises making sure everything was in place for the lighting ceremony, scheduled for 4:30. Each was edgy and anxious for their adventure to begin.

At 3:15, Rob drove them to the designated parking area and found a spot. Each shouldered their rucksacks and set off on the climb to the star, maintaining a slow, steady pace. The pink, gold, and mauve tones of the descending nightfall captivated them. They stopped to enjoy the lights sparkling below as Boulder City began twinkling in the gloaming. Turning on their flashlights at 4:15 enabled them to navigate the last few yards to the star clearing without being tripped by root toe-grabbers.

At last they entered the open space. It was laced with spider-like strings of unlit bulbs suspended on a framework of ten-foot tall poles held rigid by guy wires. The three made their way to what appeared to be the star's center. Small family clusters had also made the climb and were scattered around the clearing. Everyone was waiting.

Suddenly, magic happened! A huge star exploded above their heads with astral magnitude.

At first the light was blinding, the same effect as four-hundred flashbulbs exploding in unison. Gradually their vision adjusted, and they stood spellbound, as if watching a supernova explode, billions of light years away. Hushed murmurs of family awe and surprise drifted across the clearing. The moment was surreal, emotional, and sublime.

When her eyes had adjusted, Maryann got to work. She removed her rucksack and took out a small box. She stood in front of Rob, tip-toed high to kiss him, then began to speak. Jake stood at the side knowing what was coming next.

"Rob, my husband, I love you. When we were married, I thought our ceremony was perfect. And it was, except for one thing. You gave me this wedding ring," she showed him her band, "but there wasn't a ring for you. Tonight I'm correcting that oversight. Here is my gift to you, my love. Please wear it knowing

my deep admiration for you and for the joy you have given me."
She smiled and handed Rob her gift.

Rob opened the lid and grinned. Inside was a gold band.
There was enough star light to see it was engraved with thistle
flowers. It was pure Scottish jewelry.

Annie removed the ring from its slot and slid it on his left ring
finger. At first it refused to slide over his knuckle, but a gentle
twist eased it to where it belonged. He shook his head in wonder,
kissed it, then encompassed Annie in his arms. He kissed her
forehead ignoring the stares of other star watchers.

"Thank you, my wife," he gulped. "Truthfully, I sensed I was
missing something. This ring was it. It's perfect! I'll wear and
cherish it the rest of my life. I love you." He held his hand aloft
and watched starlight sparkle off the gold.

Jake moved closer. "Hey Rob, Mom fooled you! Let me see
your ring. Cool, dude! I like it. Will you have to take it off when
we go rock climbing?"

"No, lad, it's staying on. Besides, I don't know if I can get it
back over my knuckle."

"Use some goose grease, Rob. It always works for me." All
three laughed at Jake's joke.

"Now it's my time for a surprise," said Jake. "I have a gift for
both of you. It was all I could come up with. I have no money."
Jake fished out two envelopes from his pack and gave one to each
adult.

Maryann and Rob were surprised by his gesture. Jake had
not let on that he was planning anything. Simultaneously,

they tore open their envelopes. Inside each was a dark red garnet.

"They're from Roxbridge," Jake explained. "I discovered them along the sides of the dirt roads. These are the best two I found. I thought you'd like to have souvenirs from Roxbridge."

Maryann and Rob pulled Jake between them and hugged him tightly. It was what they had done at the conclusion of their wedding ceremony and was just as appropriate now. What a caring child! But he was changing. Both noticed he had grown taller.

"Oh, honey," bubbled Maryann. "These are perfect, and you found stones that have such flat sides." She held hers up toward a star bulb. "Look Rob, you can see the blood red color glowing inside!"

"Aye, Annie," Rob agreed. "They're brilliant!" He turned toward Jake. "Thank you for thinking of us, lad. Did you know your mother was giving me a gift?"

"Yeah, I did. But Mom didn't know what I had planned."

"Good going, Jake. Now it's my turn for surprises. You know what I planned, Jake, please help me set it up."

Maryann was puzzled as she watched her boys remove a small, portable cassette player from Rob's rucksack. He took a paper from his parka's breast pocket and unfolded it. He gave a signal to Jake, and the boy pressed the play key.

A familiar melody began drifting across the clearing helped along by a cold breeze. Other visitors turned to the sound. They watched as Rob sang a love song to his wife in soft baritone. Jake heard a child excitedly say to her mother, "Mommy, I know that song! It's about a bug and a puppet!"

When we visit Boulder's star
Seen by dreamers from afar
My love pours out enough to fill
The holy grail.

Here on Boulder's mountainside
My love for you does not hide
I love you, Annie, you're my life
My dreams come true.

When we trekked West Highland Way
On that trip and to this day
I share my life with you my love
Come what may.

Annie, Jake, and I are three
Family fusion, three makes we
Underneath the star at night
Our love sets sail.

Will our hopes and dreams converge?
Will our lives completely merge?
If we pledge our hearts for life
We can not fail.

When Rob finished singing, Jake turned off the recorder. Maryann was weeping. Bystanders applauded. Someone across the clearing yelled, "Well done, man!" Then, slowly, people drifted away. The MacKenzies packed up for the trek back to their car. They headed down the trail.

"Och, Rob!" called Jake. "Now that ye have a wee ring, can I call you, Daddy?"

"Cool, Jacko. But if you call me Daddy, I get to call you, Sonny."

"Aye, that be fair enough."

"Okay, Jacko. Like we're cool with it, dude."

"Hey, my two sweet nitwits. Let's get a move on," Maryann urged. "It's cold, and I'm hungry. It's time to get home and put a meal on the table."

"What's for dinner, Mom? Haggis?"

"Something better than that. I hope everyone likes Spam, but you'll see soon enough."

"Hey Mom, now that we're a real family, can we get a dog?"

37

Mo's Curtain Call

Sweet scene, huh? Love under the star? Annie and Robbie MacKenzie. What a lovely and loving couple! And their papoose, Jake? He's a free spirit, if ever I've seen one. I should know. I'm a spirit now.

I'm certain their story continues, but I can't tell you what happens. I'm not hiding anything, I just don't have the answers. I'm now a real spirit, not spirited like Jake, and my time here is almost at an end. I'm about to disappear forever. I won't get to see what happens to Rob and Annie as they settle into their new lives in Boulder. I won't learn if Jake thrives at the University of Colorado. Remember? A while ago I said he was interested in the fracking industry. That's what Maryann told me in a letter I received before I expired. So, if you're interested in following the MacKenzie saga, it will be up to you to search for their story.

What about me? Are you surprised I've returned to bring this tale to an end? I admit it's an amazing piece of legerdemain. But if candidates concentrate hard enough at exactly the right moment before they expire, they can hang around a bit longer. They get to see what happens to their bodies. They can see how friends react to their deaths.

You might wonder why I refer to death as expiring rather than passing, kicking the bucket, going to a final reward, or any of the other trite metaphors we use to label our demise. To me expiring is the perfect description. Our last breath eases out our lungs. Someone once said you die twice. The first time is when you exhale your last breath. The second is when your name is mentioned the last time. Anyway, I like the word expire. It's my choice how I define my end.

I won't describe what happened to my cadaver. It's too gruesome to report. It didn't hurt. I didn't feel anything. But the visual image is a bit unnerving.

I was one of the few allowed to defer my spiritual disappearance. Not everyone is so lucky. As my ethereal persona, I've chosen the concept of spirit. To me, it has an uplifting sense about it, like good Scotch single malt whisky. I think MacKenzie would agree.

Since my expiration, in addition to keeping tabs on Maryann and Rob, I wanted to make sure Ruggles was pampered. No need to worry there. Lars and Curly-Q are caring people. Ruggles is in good hands. Someday when I'm touring eternity, I'll see him again. Everyone knows a dog's spirit lives forever.

My brother and sister are hale and healthy. The good news is, following the lead of Rob MacKenzie bequesting Rose Gate Cottage to Scotland, my siblings have drawn up papers to donate my house and land to Roxbridge's Conservation Trust. That makes me very happy.

Although I don't know how life will play out for the

MacKenzies, I have some final insights on how history might unfold for you. My ideas are, of course, only opinions, so I expect many of you will disagree with me. That's fine. Discourse and debate are healthy. Put away your guns, though. Debate with facts and informed opinions. Don't debate with lead. Disagreement is fine and can be enlightening without the need to turn to anger and killing.

Becka might have been uncomfortable with my final thoughts. She was less confrontational than I was. She urged me to think and say nice things about people. But for me, that was hard to do. It was hard to ignore insane leaders, lying politicians, and the degradation of our environment by looting industrialists.

Becka's not here. Since this is my last chance to pop off before I disappear, I'm going to end my existence with observations, warnings, and predictions. I hope the predictions don't come true. I hope you and the MacKenzies lead full, productive stress-free lives. Predictions are like fragile Danish pastries, braided together with marzipan opinions and spun-sugar guesses. So, with that caveat, here goes.

It's impossible to miss how humans have ruined parts of our planet. The destruction continues. There's no need for me to detail how it happened. Open up your science books. A brief list illustrates what I'm saying:

- The disappearance of the Aral Sea.
- Rain forest destruction.
- The Dust Bowl.
- Chernobyl, Fukushima, Three Mile Island.
- Alberta tar sands.

- Global warming, climate change.
- Freshwater depletion.
- Spreading desertification.
- Pollution of air, land, and water.
- The accumulation of nuclear waste.

That's ten. Ten's enough to make my point. You can add to the number, if you wish. It's not hard to do. But if you do, don't forget to add war to the list.

The causative factors creating this list can be narrowed to two: human arrogance and uncontrolled population growth. First, human arrogance. Humans think our planet is theirs to plunder and poison. They believe resources are infinite. Humans claim dominion over all. Sadly, religious teachings support this belief. That's why Rob MacKenzie and I were so harsh with our indictments of religion. We saw faith for what it is, unrepentant superstition. If the human species is to survive, logic, reason, and good will toward others must prevail.

Second, uncontrolled population growth. Reducing humanity's impact on the Earth is a harder problem to solve. It will require a gradual reduction in human numbers and a mechanism to maintain a steady state. As numbers increase, the quality of life deteriorates. Today, people demand more than a subsistence living. As a result, the Earth's natural wealth is being depleted at an astonishing rate, and human detritus is fouling the air and oceans. For example, environmentalists recently determined that millions of square miles of ocean are contaminated with plastic.

I don't know how you're going to solve these problems. But a first step might be electing people to office who are troubled by these trends and determined to fix them. Thank goodness Trump and his band of criminals have been swept away. What a sad chapter that was in our history!

I wish your new president good luck. She's going to need it to form governing coalitions, now that there are three major political parties.

Republicans are beginning to accept their past actions as harmful to a large segment of America. They're beginning to signal they realize that country is more important than party.

Democrats are starting to field candidates who have ideas and vision. Their candidates have expressed a desire to compromise. It's no longer sufficient for them to build an agenda that's only anti-Republican.

Surprisingly, the Renewal Party is growing in strength and promoting exciting new ideas. It's been heartening to see the wealth of talent they've recruited. Maybe, if the three parties work together, America might become great for the first time.

That's it for me. Goodbye. My stay has come to an end. It's time for me to vanish. I hope some of you will help spread my story by saying my name. That will forestall my complete disappearance.

In case you forget, my name's Mo--Mo Klein. Please remember me.

Epilogue

Klein - Miller Preserve
Dedicated 1-1-2020

Becka Building
Permanent Headquarters
Roxbridge Conservation Trust
Dedicated 10-10-2020

This building and land were bequeathed to the
Roxbridge Conservation Trust
through the will of the late
Morrison Klein, a Roxbridge resident
for fifty-two years.
In accordance with Mo's request,
the building is named in memory of
Rebecca Lynn Klein,
Mo's wife of fifty years.
The shed behind the house is
Ruggle's Roost,
named in honor of Mo's dog.

Printed in the United States
By Bookmasters